Praise for Ellen Hart and her Sophie Greenway mysteries

DIAL M FOR MEAT LOAF

"This is a hearty, satisfying meal of a mystery, with chunks of good characters and more than a dash of wit."

—*Alfred Hitchcock Mystery Magazine*

SLICE AND DICE

"The pace quickly bubbles from simmer to boil. . . . The complexity of Hart's novel is admirable."

—*Publishers Weekly*

THIS LITTLE PIGGY WENT TO MURDER

"Strong characters and a rich Lake Superior setting make this solidly constructed mystery hard to put down. Another winner for Ellen Hart!"

—M. D. LAKE

FOR EVERY EVIL

"Another splendid specimen of the classical mystery story, nicely updated and full of interesting and believable characters."

—*The Purloined Letter*

Please turn the page for more reviews . . .

Praise for Ellen Hart
and her Jane Lawless series

HALLOWED MURDER

"Hart's crisp, elegant writing and atmosphere [are] reminiscent of the British detective style, but she has a nicer sense of character, confrontation, and sparsely utilized violence. . . . *Hallowed Murder* is as valuable for its mainstream influences as for its sexual politics."

—*Mystery Scene*

VITAL LIES

"This compelling whodunit has the psychological maze of a Barbara Vine mystery and the feel of Agatha Christie. . . . Hart keeps even the most seasoned mystery buff baffled until the end."

—*Publishers Weekly*

STAGE FRIGHT

"Hart deftly turns the spotlight on the dusty secrets and shadowy souls of a prominent theater family. The resulting mystery is worthy of a standing ovation."

—*Alfred Hitchcock Mystery Magazine*

By Ellen Hart
Published by The Random House Publishing Group:

The Jane Lawless mysteries:
HALLOWED MURDER
VITAL LIES
STAGE FRIGHT
A KILLING CURE
A SMALL SACRIFICE
FAINT PRAISE
ROBBER'S WINE

The Sophie Greenway mysteries:
THIS LITTLE PIGGY WENT TO MURDER
FOR EVERY EVIL
THE OLDEST SIN
MURDER IN THE AIR
SLICE AND DICE
DIAL M FOR MEAT LOAF
DEATH ON A SILVER PLATTER

DEATH ON A
SILVER PLATTER

ELLEN HART

THE RANDOM HOUSE PUBLISHING GROUP • NEW YORK

A Fawcett Book
Published by The Random House Publishing Group
Copyright © 2003 by Ellen Hart

Death on a Silver Platter is a work of fiction. Names, places, and incidents are a product of the author's imagination or are used fictitiously.

www.ballantinebooks.com

ISBN 0-449-00731-6

Manufactured in the United States of America

First Edition: September 2003

OPM 10 9 8 7 6 5 4 3 2

To my buddies in the Minnesota Crime Wave: Carl Brookins, Deborah Woodworth, and William Kent Krueger. Thanks for your constant friendship and all the ridiculous good fun.

"Grub first, then ethics."
—BERTOLT BRECHT

"You first parents of the human race . . . who ruined yourself for an apple, what might you not have done for a truffled turkey?"
—ANTHELME BRILLAT-SAVARIN

CAST OF CHARACTERS

BRAM BALDRIC: Radio talk-show host at WTWN in St. Paul; Margie's father; Sophie's husband.

MARGIE BALDRIC: Bram's daughter.

NATHAN BUCKRIDGE: Chef; owner of Chez Sophie.

MICK FRYE: Tracy's boyfriend.

SOPHIE GREENWAY: Owner of the Maxfield Plaza in St. Paul; restaurant reviewer for the *Minneapolis Times Register*; Bram's wife.

DR. WALTER HOLLAND: Retired doctor; old friend of the Veelunds.

ROMAN MARCHAND: President of KitchenVisions.

HENRY TAHTINEN: Sophie's father; original owner of the Maxfield Plaza.

PEARL TAHTINEN: Sophie's mother; original owner of the Maxfield Plaza.

ALEXANDER (ALEX) VEELUND: President and CEO of Veelund Industries; Danny and Elaine's brother; Millie's son.

CARL VEELUND: Founder of Veelund Log Lodges; Millie's husband; Elaine, Danny, and Alex's father.

DANIEL REED VEELUND: Writer; Millie and Carl's son; Ruth's husband; Elaine and Alex's brother.

ELAINE VEELUND: CEO of Veelund Log Lodges; Tracy's mother; Danny and Alex's sister; Millie's daughter.

MILLIE VEELUND: The Veelund family matriarch; owner and chairman of the board of Veelund Industries; Elaine, Danny, and Alex's mother.

RUTH VEELUND: Danny's wife.

TRACY VEELUND-WILLARD: Elaine's daughter.

GALEN ZANDER: Millie Veelund's personal assistant.

Pearl's Notebook
March 29, 1972

I couldn't write a single word after it happened. That was two weeks ago. Even now, my hand is shaking. God forgive me, I should have seen the disaster coming, should have acted to prevent it, but I didn't put all the clues together until it was too late. It's not my fault. But if it's not, why do I feel so guilty?

I arrived at the party all decked out in my new blue evening gown, my husband and daughter by my side. I came for Carl's sake, to honor a man I'd loved and admired since I was sixteen years old. I thought we'd all have a good time. Instead, the celebration became a turning point, one of those rare moments in a life when a small action might have changed everything, spun the world in a different direction. But I was afraid—afraid of my feelings, of putting my needs above others. I wasn't raised like that—to put feelings before my responsibilities—so I kept my thoughts to myself, tucked my emotions deep inside, and, like watching a ball roll out of my open hand, let the tragedy occur.

It all started so innocently. Henry, Sophie, and I had

been invited to a housewarming party at Carl and Millie Veelund's new home. This wasn't just any old house, but a mansion, one that Carl's company had built to his exact specifications. Carl had inherited the family lumber company when he was twenty-six, but he'd made his fortune in construction, as a builder of log homes. Veelund Log Lodges had become one of the hottest new names in the industry. In just six short years, his fortune had grown into the millions. This house was to be his masterpiece.

The celebration that night was my first opportunity to see the place firsthand. Carl had told me all about it, how it would combine traditional concepts with the latest technology. Western red cedar logs. Three stories high with twenty-five rooms. He called the house Prairie Lodge. It was a gift to his children, whom he adored beyond all reason, and his wife, for whom his feelings were more complex.

That evening I danced with Henry, then with Carl, and finally with Carl's handsome eighteen-year-old son, Alexander, the one everyone calls Alex. I laughed at all their jokes, all the while sensing that something was terribly wrong. Carl should have been on top of the world. This was the culmination of years of hard work. But instead of euphoria, I sensed a deep anxiety in him. He seemed distracted, distant, worried. I didn't understand.

Carl's wife, Millie, was in her usual high spirits, presiding over the affair like the belle of the ball. Millie was born on the Iron Range in Northern Minnesota, just like me. She'd grown up in a small miner's house, wearing hand-me-downs, just as I had. But unlike me, Millie had serious pretensions. She'd gotten lucky when she married

Carl Veelund. Her life was lived now on a silver platter. It was apparent to me that Carl had left the interior decoration to Millie. Carl's tastes were far more simple. Millie, on the other hand, had social and cultural "aspirations." Her bedrock conservatism was always at war with her need to be considered "modern." She was a difficult woman with a prickly nature. She always rubbed me the wrong way. But then, that was to be expected, I guess. I don't claim to be a saint.

Almost as soon as I'd walked in the door, Millie dragged me aside and confessed that she'd hired two housekeepers—two!—and was thinking of hiring a full-time gardener. This revelation was accompanied by world-weary sighs and shrugs of despair. Behind the act, it wasn't hard to see the sparkle in her eyes, the pride, the dream of a dirt-poor little girl finally coming true. Oh, and Millie had also hired a cook, a man who'd worked at the Pillsburys for many years. She dropped the name as if she had dinner with them every Friday night. Construction on the tennis court would start in July, and Carl was dickering with several companies over installing a swimming pool—for the kids, of course. As long as it was for the kids, Carl would agree to anything.

Millie feels superior to Henry and me because she knows we bought an old clunker of a hotel in downtown St. Paul a few years ago and are still struggling to make a go of it. She never fails to ask me how business is. She allowed herself an amused smile when I lied and said that it was good.

The truth is, almost everything we earn is put back into the hotel's restoration, so things are pretty tight right now. But I knew they would be, and that's okay by me. Henry was incensed that the city fathers would even think of tearing down the historic Maxfield Plaza. The art deco architecture alone should have kept it standing. When I tried to explain all this to Millie she sighed and patted my hand, commenting that men were men, and women were their unfortunate pawns. It never occurred to her that I might share my husband's dream—the desire to one day see an artistic and historic landmark returned to its former glory.

I'd never been a stranger to hard times. But more important, I knew the real score between Carl and Millie. Millie could feign happiness all she wanted, she could pretend to be the Queen of England for all I cared. I knew her marriage to Carl had been a disaster from day one.

As the night wore on, I noticed that Carl was drinking more than usual. His face had taken on a rosy glow as he walked his youngest son, Danny, around the room, introducing him to business associates and potential clients. My daughter, Sophie, and Carl's middle child, Elaine, have been friends since they were nine, so I assumed their absence meant that they were off somewhere in the nether reaches of the log mansion trying on Millie's makeup or plotting to overthrow the government. At fifteen, both of them seem to swing wildly between attacks of hormones and attacks of intellect.

It was just after ten when I noticed a waiter, one who had been hired for the evening, enter the living room and walk over to Carl. He carried a silver tray. On top of it was an envelope. Carl picked it up and dismissed him. He looked around for a couple of seconds until he spotted his wife—she was talking to several men by the fieldstone hearth—then he tucked the letter inside the jacket of his tux and left the room.

*I know I had no business following him, but I did.
Something was up and I wanted to know what it was. Carl
cut swiftly into a back hallway that led to a room at the
far end of the house. During the home-tour part of the
evening I'd learned that this was "Mr. Veelund's" study.
Carl closed the door, but it didn't shut all the way. Standing as quietly as I could outside the room, I watched him
sit down behind his desk, switch on a reading lamp, then
rip open the envelope.*

*"Damn you," he said after a couple of seconds. His
face blanched. "Damn you!" he said again, dropping the
note. He picked up a crystal paperweight and hurled it
across the room.*

*I wanted to go to him, wanted to read the note, have
him explain to me why he was so upset. But his anger
frightened me. Carl was a powerful man, with powerful
friends and enemies. He'd been "my Carl" once upon a
time, my love and my lover, but that was a long time ago.
He was a different man now. I was a different woman. To
intrude at this moment seemed far too intimate an act,
filled with its own dangers.*

*I stayed by the door and watched him crush the letter
in his fist and plunge it into the trash by his desk. He
looked like a man in agony. I had to talk to him, but I hesitated. And it was during that moment of hesitation that
he got up. Fearing that he'd find me, I twisted backward
and ducked into another room just as he burst into the
hallway. I waited until his heavy footsteps had died away,
then entered the study and retrieved the letter from the
trash. I felt brazen and guilty, intruding on his privacy
like that, but I couldn't stop myself.*

I smoothed the piece of cheap stationery against the

desktop and read the message. I read it again and again, shaking my head, trying to make sense of it.

Finally, realizing that I'd never know what it meant if I didn't talk to Carl, I folded the paper back up and slipped it into my evening bag. Finding my courage at last, I left the room.

1

"We're comin' home!" announced Henry Tahtinen, a crackle of noise on his end of the line.

Sophie stood behind a beat-up metal desk in a small room in the subbasement of the Maxfield Plaza, the voices of her maintenance men shouting all around her. A badly rusted pipe had burst a few minutes ago, sending water gushing into a storage area. Already, her shoes were soaked. She had a vision of the water filling the storage room, rushing out the open door into the office where she was standing, covering her feet, then her knees, rising to her waist, and finally her neck. The only way out was a narrow stairway, which would be blocked by floating debris. She would die an ignominious death in the subbasement trying to swim her way up through thousands of rolls of wet toilet paper.

Sophie had an avid imagination. It was one of her more endearing qualities. "Where are you now?" she asked, watching two men carry a heavy trunk to safety.

"Bangkok. The Regent Hotel. We've spent the last two months in India and Nepal. Your mother's become a Buddhist."

Sophie could hear her mother in the background,

protesting the comment. The last time Sophie had heard from her parents, they'd been in Tasmania.

"I had a hell of a time dragging her out of Katmandu," continued her father. "She couldn't get enough of the temples. She even learned to meditate. Me, I spent my time studying the vistas. 'Ah, another vista,' I'd say. Those Himalayas are hard to beat. While your mom soaked up the culture and lost her religion, I spent my time hiking. I'm in pretty good shape for an old geezer."

"Dad, you're not a geezer."

"Of course I am. My hair's about three shades grayer than it was when we left two years ago. God, has it been that long since I've seen you? How's everything at the hotel?"

"Fine," said Sophie, finding no reason to tell him about the pipe.

Before her parents had left on their world tour, they'd formally retired and handed the reins—or more accurately, *sold* the Maxfield Plaza for one dollar—to Sophie and her husband, Bram. Henry wanted to keep the hotel in the family. Rescuing the historic art deco landmark from the wrecking ball and restoring it to its former status as *the* premier hotel in downtown St. Paul had been his life's work, his claim to fame in the Twin Cities. Sophie loved the hotel almost as much as he did.

What she hadn't been thrilled about was the daunting task of taking over a family business that she knew very little about. She'd lived at the Maxfield when she was a teenager, worked the front desk before she left for college, but that didn't mean she had any real, hands-on experience running a major metropolitan hostelry. Her father insisted that his staff, primarily his general manager, Hildegard O'Malley, could teach her everything she needed to know.

The first year was a crash course. Sophie was constantly terrified that she'd screw up, so she worked like a madwoman, which could have put her marriage in jeopardy. Thankfully, Bram was a patient man. He was already well established in his own career as a talk-show host for a local radio station, so he gave her the time she needed with a minimum of grousing. From the beginning, he made it abundantly clear that he had no interest in running the hotel. He said her parents were kind to include him in the deal, but the Maxfield was *her* inheritance. She would have to run it.

After Sophie's parents had taken off for points unknown, Sophie and Bram sold their home in Minneapolis and settled into a beautiful apartment on the top floor of the hotel's north tower. They quickly discovered that they adored living at the Maxfield, loved all the amenities a hotel could provide. The change in their lives had brought new stresses and strains, but new opportunities as well.

By the second year, Sophie felt much more confident in her position, so confident that she took on the job of restaurant critic for the *Minneapolis Times Register*. This caused another round of grumbling from Bram. He insisted that he needed to make a date just to catch a glimpse of her. The truth was a little less dramatic, but still, all life, including married life, was a negotiation. When he learned that Rudy, Sophie's son, would be taking over the majority of the duties at the paper and that Sophie's involvement would have limits, the grousing turned to manageable murmurings.

Bram understood something fundamental about Sophie, and for that she was grateful. Food would always be one of her prime passions. Since she'd done reviews for the paper in the past, the job offer hadn't come completely out of left field. In a few more years she hoped to bow out gracefully and let her son take over as senior restaurant critic—as long as he promised to allow her an occasional guest review.

"Your mother wants to talk to you," shouted Henry. The connection was growing worse. "I'll say good-bye."

"Bye, Dad," said Sophie, noticing one of her maintenance men rush past the open door. He was soaking wet from head to toe.

"Hi, honey," said Pearl, Sophie's mother. "How's Bram feeling?"

"Much better," said Sophie. "He's lost almost twenty-five pounds since the surgery."

"Good for him. Give him my love."

"I will," said Sophie.

Bram had undergone double bypass surgery last November. That was ten months ago. He was doing much better now, almost back to his normal self. Except, his illness had caused repercussions that Sophie hadn't entirely expected. Bram had always been so full of zest and self-confidence. He made no bones about loving the good life—champagne and chocolate cake at midnight when he was in the mood, dancing on the balcony with Sophie in the middle of a snowstorm. He had wit and unpredictability, and Cary Grant good-looks. And yet, lately, he'd turned into Mr. Fitness Center. Mr. Sprouts and fresh greens with low-fat dressing.

Sophie understood his motivation: He didn't want to die. He was fifty-two years old, several years older than Sophie, with a family history of heart problems. His father had suffered a heart attack when he was fifty-two, and his uncle on his father's side had died of heart problems at the same age. Bram would be fifty-three soon, so he'd beaten the family curse, but he was still scared. And that fear was on the verge of turning him into a different person.

"We're heading up to Shanghai tomorrow," continued Sophie's mother. "Then on to Tokyo. We should be home soon. We'll call later and give you all the particulars—the flight number and arrival time."

"Great," said Sophie, hearing a crash in the next room.

"Is something wrong? You sound kind of funny."

"I feel like I'm standing on the deck of the *Titanic*."

"What?" said Pearl. "This connection isn't very good. Sounded like you said you were standing on the deck of the *Titanic*." She giggled.

"I'm fine, Mom. We'll all be so glad to finally have you home again."

"Honey, your father just walked out of the bathroom. He's signaling that he wants to talk to you again."

Henry came on the line. "Soph, here's the skinny. I want you to call that friend of yours, Elaine . . . whatever her last name is now."

"She's gone back to her maiden name," said Sophie. "Veelund."

"Whatever. Tell her that when we get back, Pearlie and I are gonna look for some land up on Pokegama Lake. I want that company of hers to build us a log house. We're done with our jet-setting lifestyle for a while, so I want to have a spot where we can go when we feel like getting out of the city. A place where I can fish, and where your mom can meditate on her new Buddhist leanings." He laughed, calling, "Pearlie, stop it. I'm an old man. I can't take that kind of excitement."

Sophie could only imagine what her mother was doing to him.

"See if you can get me some hard details, Soph. I know they have packages, standard plans, that sort of thing. Find out what you can, okay? I want to move on this right away when I get back."

"Sure, Dad. I'll call Elaine tonight."

"You're still buddies with her, right?"

"We're still great friends."

"Good. Maybe she'll give us a deal. Never hurts to ask."

Sophie smiled. "I'll see what I can do."

"It's tomorrow here, you know. Where you are is yesterday."

"Excuse me?"

"It's Saturday. Where you are is Friday. And it's seven A.M. What time is it in St. Paul?"

"Four. In the afternoon."

"Your mom's telling me to hang up. Since I *always* do what your mom says, I better get off the line. Talk to you soon, sweetheart. Over and out from sunny Bangkok."

The line clicked.

To say her parents were a tad eccentric was an understatement, thought Sophie. Fifty years of marriage and they were still going strong, still having fun together. They were the happiest couple she knew. She wondered what their secret was. Sometimes they acted more like kids playing in the backyard than like an old married couple. She couldn't help but think of her marriage to Bram, of what their future would hold.

A maintenance man sailed by the office door with a dolly loaded with drenched boxes.

Sophie called after him, "Did you get the water stopped?"

"Yeah," he hollered back. "But it's a mess in there. The pipe's got to be replaced."

She spent a few minutes surveying the damage, then headed up the narrow stairs to the basement, and from there took the elevator to the lobby. Her shoes squeaked on the marble floors as she made her way as quickly as possible to her office. Several people stared at her feet, but she ignored them, adopting a look of what she hoped was quiet dignity.

Once behind closed doors, she dumped her shoes in the trash. They smelled like sewer gas. She doubted she could ever get the reek of decaying pipe out of them. It was a warm September afternoon, so she wasn't going to catch pneumonia in bare feet. She took off her nylons and cleaned up in her office bathroom, then sat down behind her desk, not sure what to do next. She had dinner reservations at Chez Sophia at eight. It would be a working dinner, a review for the paper. Rudy was supposed to go with her, but he'd backed out at the last minute. If she didn't come up with another dinner companion fast, she'd be eating alone.

That's when an idea struck her. She checked her Rolodex, then picked up the phone and tapped in Elaine's number. She waited through a couple of rings until a woman's voice answered, "Veelund Industries."

"I'd like to speak with Elaine Veelund," said Sophie.

"May I ask who's calling?"

"Sophie Greenway."

"Just a moment."

Sophie drummed her nails on the desktop for a few seconds. Finally, Elaine's voice came on the line. "Hey, girlfriend. What's up?"

"Dinner. Tonight. It's on me."

"Where?"

"That new restaurant just outside of Stillwater. Chez Sophia."

"You doing a review?"

"Yes, so technically, I guess, the dinner would be on the paper."

"Sounds great to me. Are you planning to bring along that handsome husband of yours? Flaunt your good luck while I drool?"

After a nasty separation, Elaine had divorced her third husband last spring. "He's playing racquetball with a buddy."

"Too bad, but I guess his loss is my gain. We need some time to catch up. Woman to woman. What's it been? Two months?"

"At least. Can I meet you at the restaurant?" Sophie told her the time and gave her the directions.

"It's a date. And Sophie . . . thanks. This hasn't been the best week of my life. We'll talk more tonight."

Sophie worked in her office for the next couple of hours. Now that her parents were on their way home, she felt a double impetus to make sure everything at the hotel was running smoothly. She was engrossed in the financial figures for August when there was a knock on the door. Glancing at her watch, she saw that it was going on six. She had to get a move on if she was going to make it to the restaurant on time.

Sophie always wore disguises when she visited restaurants for review. Her face was well known by restaurateurs in the Twin Cities, so camouflage was the only way she could get a sense of what the average diner would encounter. Tonight's disguise would have to be better than usual because the owner and executive chef at Chez Sophia was, to put it politely, an old and intimate friend.

"Come in," she called, switching off the computer and standing up.

Ben Greenberg, her maintenance foreman, entered carrying a box. As he stepped closer, she saw that it was made of metal, maybe eight inches wide by a foot long, and a good six inches deep. He set it down on her desk, then removed his cap.

"What's this?" she asked, fingering a rusted padlock that hung from the front.

"One of the plumbers found it in the storage room in the subbasement. It's got a name stamped on the side there. Eli Salmela. And the date, 1923." He pointed. "It was on the floor, pushed as far back as it could go under one of the shelves. It looks watertight, but it's old. I thought you might want to take a look at it—whatever it is."

"Eli Salmela," she whispered, touching the top of the box. Eli Salmela was her mother's uncle. He'd been dead for over forty years. What on earth was a box belonging to him doing in the subbasement of the Maxfield Plaza? "How's the repair coming on the pipe?"

"We're still working on it. I'm afraid we lost a lot of paper products. Actually, I need to get back down there."

"Thanks, Ben. I'll take care of the box."

"No problem."

If she'd had more time, she would have pried off the lock to see what was inside, but she had to hustle upstairs to her apartment and don her disguise. A restaurant critic's job was a dirty one, etcetera, etcetera.

The box would have to wait.

2

In a specially made Lords of London suit and vest, Sophie stood next to the reception desk at Chez Sophia, waiting for the maître d' to find the table assignment. Because she was a shrimp—a little over five feet tall—she liked to wear three-inch heels when she dressed as herself. When she was disguised as a man, as she was tonight, her lift shoes—cordovan leather wing tips—gave her added height. A dark brown wig covered her short strawberry blond hair. The addition of a beard lent her male persona a bit of class. Sophie felt she made a rather attractive man, albeit a short one. With an equally short female date on her arm, she might have pulled off the ruse, but standing next to the tall, elegant Elaine Veelund, Sophie felt like a dumpy fraud. Not the best way to start the evening.

"If you'll follow me?" said the maître d'. He'd been stealing glances at Sophie ever since she and Elaine had walked in. He probably figured Lords of London didn't do size eight.

Sophie had a round, suitably curvaceous figure, one that tended to overweight, but with a little help from some special undergarments and a good tailor, she hid it all under the jacket. The beard covered her smooth facial skin. It was her hands that were the dead giveaway. At times like this, she tended to keep them in her pockets. She felt the stance was both casual and sophisticated. Except Elaine wasn't buying it any more than the maître d' was. Both of them had amused little Mona Lisa smiles on their faces as they walked across the crowded room to the table.

Chez Sophia, the creation of the eminent chef Nathan Buckridge, hadn't been reviewed since it opened in June. Sophie had been putting it off, which wasn't very professional of her. She could have made sure the restaurant was covered in a more timely fashion by passing the review on—if not to her son then to a guest reviewer. But that seemed like cowardice and Sophie wasn't a coward. The truth was, she dreaded the dinner at Chez Sophia, but she was also curious. Just because Nathan Buckridge wanted her to divorce her husband and marry *him* didn't seem like a good enough reason to ignore his new establishment. But it also complicated her job. If her experience at the restaurant wasn't entirely positive, and if the review reflected it, would he take it personally? Or, if the review was glowing, would he perceive it as a meaningless gift, a whitewash, and not a true critique of his skills?

Nathan Buckridge had been Sophie's high school sweetheart. They'd met when she was sixteen and he was eighteen. It wasn't love at first sight. It took a couple extra glances before Cupid launched his arrow, but launch it he did. If Sophie hadn't ended up at that fundamentalist Bible college in California, hadn't given herself heart and soul to the teachings of the egomaniacal minister Howell A. Purdis, she might very well have married Nathan and lived happily ever after.

In his despair at losing Sophie, Nathan had entered the

University of Minnesota to study anthropology. He eventually chucked it all and fled to Europe, where, after a personal epiphany while eating tripe Niçoise at a small French restaurant in Lyon, he earned a degree from the famous Cordon Bleu culinary school in Paris and spent the next fifteen years cooking his way across Europe. A chance reunion a year and a half ago had brought them back together.

Sophie was drawn into his life again because of certain family problems. For a time, Sophie thought Nathan's mother might be involved in the death of a local restaurant critic. Sophie quickly found herself in way over her head—with both the murder investigation and with Nathan. She loved her husband, that was never in doubt, but she couldn't ignore her attraction to her old boyfriend. Nathan was like a pink elephant standing in the corner of a room. You might not look at it every second, but you could hardly forget that it was there.

Equally compelling to Sophie was the enigma of just who Nathan Buckridge really was. Great parts of him had always been a mystery to her, and she loved a mystery. Maybe she was the only middle-aged woman on earth who'd ever indulged herself with a fantasy of an old boyfriend returning to her life and still being wildly attracted to her. For Sophie, that fantasy had come true. And it had turned into a nightmare. The guilt she felt after their brief sexual encounter was almost crushing. The question of who Nathan was had turned into the question of who *she* was. If she could cheat on her husband, what kind of person had she become? It was a mystery she was still trying to solve.

After Bram's heart attack, Nathan had finally backed off. He wasn't an insensitive man—anything but. While

Bram was in the hospital, Sophie had committed herself to him with her whole heart, and she meant it. Nathan was out of her life for good. That's the way it had to be. She knew she might cross paths with him every now and then, but she felt they both realized that the past was past. Bram was her present and her future. Nathan would have to find his own.

After they were seated at the table, Elaine ordered a Scotch on the rocks and Sophie a dry martini. While they sipped their drinks, they examined the menu. Elaine had come along on Sophie's review nights several times in the past year, but Sophie repeated the drill, just to refresh her memory. They would order several appetizers, soups, salads, entrées, and desserts. Sophie would inspect the wine menu to see if it was balanced and offered anything of particular interest. She would also need to taste every dish that arrived at the table.

The first order of business was to choose a wine. Sophie ordered a Borgo Scopeto 1999 Borgonero. It was a Tuscan wine, one she'd heard good things about. For appetizers, they selected a pan-fired soft-shelled crab with asparagus risotto and a lemon beurre blanc; a veal sausage wrapped in phyllo and topped with fresh watercress and artichoke cream; and a shrimp dish called Scampi Sophia that was served on toasted sourdough tips and drizzled with a buttery wine and garlic sauce. All three were spectacular.

Next came the soup. Sophie ordered the house specialty, a French white bean purée garnished with prosciutto and a fresh arugula pesto, and Elaine tried a lovely cold potato leek. Both were superior, rich but light, all the flavors in perfect balance.

For the pasta course, Elaine settled on the Fusilli alla

Puttanesca—fusilli with garlic, anchovies, black olives, capers, parsley, and grated Pecorino cheese. Sophie ordered the Perciatelli with Tomato and Guanciale. The guanciale, a cured pork cheek bacon, was a surprising change from prosciutto, and far more traditionally Italian. Two more bull's-eyes. Sophie was in heaven. Nathan's food was glorious. In her estimation, a man who could cook like this was worthy of worship.

Three main courses arrived next. First was an applewood roasted quail with chevre and sage sausage stuffing served on crispy polenta and accompanied by a fresh fig relish. Next was a pan-roasted duck breast in a cherry Merlot jus, with goat cheese mashed potatoes and garnished with a fava bean ragout. And finally, a pork tenderloin with Gorgonzola cheese and hazelnut stuffing, whipped sweet potatoes, and braised red cabbage with an orange port glaze. Everything was amazing, from the beautiful way the food was plated, to the harmony of flavor and texture. This review would write itself.

Sophie had learned long ago that, when it came to reviewing, she didn't need to clean her plate. She tasted a little of this and a little of that and then made notes on a small notebook she kept hidden in her lap. So far, this experience had been perfection. Fine restaurants today were every bit as much about theater as they were about food, so the stage set was a vital piece of the puzzle. The interior of Chez Sophia, an old Cistersian monastery with rough-hewn beams and high vaulted ceilings, was atmospheric without seeming cold. The colors—greens and golds, with just a hint of soft peach—were muted yet alluring. The lighting could almost be called reverent. Nathan had created, in Sophie's opinion, the finest restaurant experience in the metro area. It was located in the rolling hills just outside Stillwater, an added plus for Twin Citians looking for a chance to get out of the city. But . . . did she dare write such a paean to Chez Sophia? There were people in town who knew about Sophie's former relationship with Nathan. Would it look fishy? Did Sophie care?

During dinner, Sophie and Elaine brought each other up to speed on their respective lives. In Elaine's case, she was recovering well from divorce number three. Her track record with men was truly abysmal, but she was already on the lookout for number four. Her quick gray eyes roamed the dining room, lingering on a particularly attractive man. Sophie loved Elaine, as one loved an old, deeply flawed friend who had a constant need for romantic drama in her life. Over the years, Sophie had sat through many tear-filled, late-night phone calls. Elaine's last husband had gambled away a fortune—his fortune. When he started on hers, she called it quits.

"How's your mother?" asked Sophie, tapping a napkin to her lips. She was hoping for a neutral subject, not that there was one when it came to Elaine's family.

"The same. God, it's been an awful week."

"How come?"

"Did you know Mom turned seventy-five last Tuesday? She needs to slow down. But she still micromanages the company. Dad always intended for his children to take over the business, but Mom just can't let go. Between you and me, I think she's an untreated bipolar control freak with delusions of grandeur."

"Don't stifle your opinions, Elaine. It's not good for you."

"She thinks she knows *everything*. There's not much Alex can do except wait—and hope for debilitating infirmity."

Sophie picked up her wineglass. "That's kind of cold. But no colder than the untreated bipolar control freak thing."

Elaine shrugged. "You remember what we used to call her?"

"Mad-dog Millie. Who came up with that?"

"Alex. She's diabetic and asthmatic, but she's just like a Timex watch. She keeps on ticking."

"But Alex is the CEO."

"As CEO, would *you* like to run everything past Mommy? She's still chairman of the board of directors and the board does what Millie Veelund wants."

Sophie shook her head. She'd heard the refrain before.

"With the recession, business hasn't been all that great, except for the Log Lodges."

"Your division."

"It's made us rich. It's still in the black, but the rest of the company is pulling it down."

"You mean the wood-flooring company Alex bought a while back."

"That and the kitchen company he bought two years ago."

"Kitchen Visions."

"He did some pretty fast tap dancing and convinced Mom it was a smart financial move. As part of the deal, we retained the owner to run the division. Alex even put him on the board of directors, against my wishes I might add. KitchenVisions has been a drag on our bottom line ever since. But Mom, in her infinite wisdom, thinks owning a kitchen company is a 'seemly' thing for a woman to do."

"What's being a woman got to do with it?"

Elaine drew her wineglass in front of her. "You know

Mom. She's a political fascist and a religious crackpot. There's nothing more frustrating *and* confusing than a fundamentalist Lutheran."

Sophie laughed. She remembered now that Millie was Missouri Synod. While that didn't make her a fundamentalist in the classic sense, it did make her deeply conservative. Sophie also knew that Millie brought her own ideas to the table, some that certainly wouldn't be sanctioned by the church.

"Mom believes that men should run the business world. Women's sphere is the home, femininity, beauty, nurturing the children, baking cookies."

"Your mother is the *least* nurturing person I've ever met."

"Tell me about it."

"She doesn't see any irony in that?"

"Her case is always a special circumstance. Her husband died in the middle of his career. Her children were young and she had to think of their future. She had no choice. She didn't trust anyone not to swindle her, so she had to take over the business herself."

"But she has a choice now."

"Yes, but there's still the matter of trust."

"She doesn't trust her children?"

"Well, I'm a woman, so I'm automatically out of the running. And you know Danny. He's never shown the slightest interest in running the family business. Besides, Mom doesn't like his wife. That eliminates him right there."

"You're kidding."

"Haven't I told you about that?"

"Not that I recall."

"Well, remind me and I will. Another time. But back

to my point: When it comes right down to it, Mom doesn't trust anyone but herself. She grew up poor, so the power of the purse strings means everything to her. She may talk like God ordained men to run the world, but she's not about to let one run hers."

Sophie waited for the waiter to pour more coffee. "You said the Log Lodges were still selling well?"

"This was a banner year. Next year may be even better. That division of the company is *mine*, Sophie. It's fine with me if Alex wants to be CEO of Veelund Industries. He can have his office and his Mercedes and his status. He does a lot of charity work—that's where his heart really is. He's a good brother, a kind man, but as hard as he tries, he's not a *business*man." She gazed down into her wineglass. "If they would just cut my division loose, let me take it over completely. I'm the one who developed Veelund Lodges into what it is today. I built it on the foundation my father gave me. I've been in charge of R and D from the day I left engineering school. I've put sweat and tears into every aspect of that division. By all rights it should be mine."

"Maybe you should quit. Start your own company."

"Don't think I haven't given it some serious thought. But I don't have the money to start from the ground up, and besides, I'd be competing against myself, against what I created. When it comes right down to it, I've spent twenty years developing the Veelund name, creating new products, new technology. I shouldn't have to start all over from scratch. I loved my father, Sophie. I want this connection to him. Damn it, I've *earned* it. But Mom's using my division to finance the failure of Alex's acquisitions. Short of a bullet to the head—*her* head—I don't know what to do."

Sophie grimaced.

"Don't get excited. I not saying I've bought the gun."

"You don't need to. Your father's gun cabinet is still in the basement rec room."

"Perhaps this isn't a good moment for you to remind me of that, Soph."

"If it wasn't for your mom, do you think Alex would let you have that part of the company?"

She shrugged. "Maybe. I don't know. We haven't talked about it."

When Sophie looked up, she saw that Nathan had entered the dining room. He was welcoming customers, stopping at various tables, making his way slowly through the room. He looked incredibly handsome in his white chef's coat and checked pants.

Elaine took hold of Sophie's hand. "Don't look so worried. I'm not going to murder my mother."

It took an effort of will for Sophie to return her eyes to Elaine. "What?"

"I said, 'Don't look so worried.' Unless you're worried about something else. What's wrong, Sophie?"

"What could be wrong?" She glanced back at Nathan.

Elaine followed her gaze. "Hey, isn't that Nathan Buckridge? Your old boyfriend? I read he was back in town."

"Chez Sophia is his restaurant."

"Right. He looks pretty much the same . . . except he's filled out, grown into a man. A very attractive man, I might add. I wonder if he's married."

"He's single," said Sophie. "Look, if he comes over here, you do the talking. It's possible the waiter tipped him off that we were ordering a lot of food. He may smell a reviewer. Deny it, okay? And remember, I'm your date."

"Like hell you are. I'd never date someone who looked like you."

"Gee thanks."

"He won't recognize you in that disguise. You look like a miniature version of Mike Myers impersonating a British lord. Then again, I suppose your voice might give you away." She tapped her finger against the side of her wineglass. "I wonder if he'd remember me."

"Here he comes," said Sophie. "Just act natural."

"I always act natural," said Elaine, smiling seductively. "Elaine 'Au Natural' Veelund, haven't you heard?" She turned her smile on Nathan as he stepped up to the table.

3

"Evening," said Nathan, smiling at Elaine. "You look familiar. Have we met?"

"Elaine Veelund." She offered her hand. "I knew you in high school. We have a mutual friend—Sophie Greenway?"

"Of course," he said, folding his arms over his chest.

Sophie could see the wheels turning inside his mind. He looked like he hadn't shaved in several days, which she knew was trendy. It also accentuated the rugged angles in his face.

"This is my friend, Tom . . . Jones," continued Elaine. "We've been enjoying your food. Tom tells me you own the restaurant."

Nathan gave Sophie a nod. "I do. So, what's it been, Elaine?"

"Too long. I don't like to talk years. It makes me feel old."

"You don't look old," he said, his smile turning to a flirtatious grin.

"You're still quite the charmer."

"That's what they tell me. What did you order?"

"I think it's more a question of what we didn't order."

He laughed. "And you liked it?"

"Everything was wonderful."

"Then, in honor of old times, the meal is on the house."

Her smiled clicked into high-beam. "In that case, you'll have to let me return the favor. I don't cook as well as you do, but I've been known to grill a great steak and baked potato combo."

"Really. Is that a dinner invitation? I should warn you: I never turn down a home-cooked meal."

Sophie was hemorrhaging internally. Couldn't he see that Elaine's teeth were really fangs, that her blond hair had dark roots! Did he want to be number four in Elaine Veelund's marital march toward an even dozen?

Before they could swap phone numbers, Elaine's cell phone rang.

"Sorry, but I have to take this."

"Call me at the restaurant," said Nathan, handing her his card. "We'll firm up a date and time. It's great to see you again." As an afterthought, he said, "Nice meeting you, Tom. I hope you stop by again."

Elaine grinned like a predatory wolf as he walked off. Glancing at the caller ID on her cell phone, she pressed a button and said, "This better be good. I'm having dinner with a friend." She listened. "What? When?" Her expression turned serious. "Then break the goddamned door down!" She pulled off an earring and switched the phone to her other ear. "This isn't what I'm paying you for, Mick." Listening another moment, she said, "Okay. Tell her I'll be home as fast as I can make it. If anything happens to her, I hold you personally responsible. You got that?" As she clicked the phone off, her lips pressed together tightly.

"Is everything all right?" asked Sophie.

"It's my daughter. She's . . . not feeling well. Long story. Look, Soph, I have to go. I'm sorry to cut our dinner short, but this is, well, sort of an emergency."

"Is your daughter okay?"

Rising from the table, Elaine said, "She's fine. It's just . . . she's going through a bad time. Like I said, long story." She returned the cell phone to her purse. "This was fun. Really. Let's not wait so long to do it again."

"Actually," said Sophie, rising and placing her napkin on the table next to her empty plate, "I'll probably call you tomorrow. My parents are out of the country right now, but they phoned this afternoon. Dad asked me to talk to you about log homes. He wants me to get all the specs, the different choices, an idea of price."

"He wants to build one?"

"That's the idea."

"Where?"

"Up on Pokegama Lake."

"I'd love to work with your family," said Elaine, hooking her purse over her shoulder. "I promise, I'll make it happen. We'll talk more tomorrow, okay, but right now I've got to run. Wish me luck." She squeezed Sophie's arm, then hurried out of the dining room.

Elaine was a mother with a problem daughter. If ever a child had been born with a silver spoon in her mouth it was Tracy Veelund-Willard. She was the child of Elaine's second marriage, spoiled by both her father and her mother. Every toy she'd ever wanted was hers just for the asking. As she grew, the toys just got bigger.

Elaine often referred to Tracy as having "moods." She was a high-strung and emotional little girl who had grown into a sullen and strangely passive young woman. Elaine adored her daughter, although they always seemed to be at war over something, often concerning Tracy's appearance.

With straight brown hair, heavy, dark eyebrows, a large nose, and a rail-thin body, Tracy hadn't been terribly attractive in high school. Then again, with the right clothes and makeup, she could have been a model. She had one of those looks that could have gone either way. Much to her mother's dismay, Tracy had little interest in maximizing her strengths. She refused to wear makeup and hated dresses. Appearance had always been very important to Elaine, especially in the business world, but Tracy just blew off all of her mother's makeover suggestions.

When Tracy started college, she gained quite a bit of weight. Every time Sophie saw her, she was on a new diet. She looked uncomfortable in her new, heavier body, as if something had happened to her that she didn't understand and didn't much like. She tried to hide herself in large shirts and baggy pants, but the weight had only made her look more attractive, almost voluptuous, not that Tracy saw it that way. She had flawless skin and perfect teeth, and when she smiled, Sophie thought she was quite beautiful, in an odd sort of way. Or perhaps she was odd, in a striking sort of way.

As Sophie resumed her seat, a waiter came over and offered her the dessert menu. Now that Elaine had fled, it would look truly suspicious to order three desserts. Sophie studied the menu, noting five she wanted to taste. Deep in thought, she calculated which two would be the most interesting for her review. As she looked up to wave for the waiter, Nathan slipped into the chair next to her.

"Now that Elaine's gone," he said, folding his hands on the table, "I thought we might talk for a couple of minutes."

She was startled. Had he seen through her disguise?

"My waiter tells me that you've been taking notes on the food." He leaned forward and looked into her lap, nodding at the notebook. "Are you a reviewer?"

She tried to deepen her voice. "Well, ah—"

"I don't mean to put you on the spot, but if you are, I'd love to show you around. I'm very proud of Chez Sophia."

"As well you should be."

"You liked the food, then?"

She nodded. "Very much."

"From what I understand, you haven't had dessert. I'd like to recommend the Torta Milano. It's one of my favorites. We have an outstanding pastry chef here, Donna Randall, but this was an adaptation of a recipe I created many years ago. A fruited pastry cream between layers of sponge cake soaked in rum and maraschino cherry syrup, covered in whipped cream with an apricot and raspberry garnish."

"It . . . sounds wonderful." Her mouth watered.

Nathan snapped his fingers and a waiter appeared. He ordered the dessert.

"This is very kind of you, but I really can't stay," said Sophie, glancing at her watch. It was really Bram's watch. Her own would have given away the game.

"Oh, but you have to at least *taste* it," said Nathan. "I insist."

"Really, this isn't the way I do my reviews," she said, pushing away from the table and standing up.

"Don't go, Sophie," said Nathan, pressing his fingers gently around her arm. "Not yet. I haven't seen you for so long. Not that . . . I'm actually seeing you."

"You rat! You stinking rat! You knew all along."

"What took you so long to get here? We should have been reviewed months ago."

She wondered if he really *was* upset. Not that the lack of a review seemed to have hurt business. "I, ah—"

"It's okay. I know it gets complicated when your ex-girlfriend is the reviewer. And the restaurant just happens to be named after her."

She was caught. She sat down.

"How's Bram feeling?"

Sophie wasn't sure if getting into a personal discussion was a good idea. "He's great," she said.

"The operation was a compete success then?"

"Thankfully, yes. He says he's back to his old 'fighting weight.' "

Nathan looked confused. "He was a boxer?"

She tittered. "Hardly. It's just his way of saying he's feeling fit."

"Good. That's good. And how about you?"

"I'm fine. As always."

"A woman of many disguises."

She looked down. "All of which you can see through."

"I wish. This one was easy. It's the ones you wear every day that I have trouble with."

"Do you honestly think that?"

"I've always wished I understood you better. Once upon a time I thought I had a lifetime to spend figuring you out. There's only one part of you that I've always seen with total clarity."

"And that is?"

"That you love me."

"Nathan—"

"And that hasn't changed, no matter how much you want it to." He covered her hand with his. "I've missed you, Sophie. I've reached for the phone dozens of times wanting to call you, wanting you to come to the restaurant and let me show you what I've done. I'm so proud of this place. Do you remember the first time I showed you the monastery—the grounds, the buildings? Do you remember that picnic we had out by the river, how it started to rain and we got soaked to the skin running like lunatics for cover? We ended up sitting in front of that fireplace right over there while a tornado blew its way across the St. Croix valley. I thought . . . I'd finally come home."

"Nathan—"

"I know. I'll stop. It's just, seeing you here tonight after wishing you here so many times"—he sat back in his chair—"Okay. Tell me you'll give me a decent review."

"Can't. Wouldn't be ethical." Changing the subject, she asked, "Where are you living now?"

"I took over one of the brothers' rooms in the residence hall. It's just a bed and a closet and a window, but I like it. It suits me . . . for now. I spend most of my days here at the restaurant, so why do I need a big place to live?" He picked up one of the napkins and began refolding it. "I bought myself a kayak last spring. I've spent some time on the river this summer. The St. Croix is incredibly beautiful, especially just before sunset. I'm thinking that I might get myself a cabin cruiser, moor it over in Hudson. I figure it will make me feel a little less like a monk. I mean, right now, my life consists of work, sleep, and the little time I steal from the restaurant to spend on the water."

He was so different from Bram. Bram's idea of spending time outdoors was sitting in a soft chair on a veranda, sipping a cool drink. Where Bram was the type to haunt jazz bars, attend the theater and the opera, Nathan was rough, direct, a hunter and a fisherman.

"I planted an herb garden this summer," continued Nathan, "out by the vineyard the brothers started. Next year I'll enlarge it. The idea of being able to step outside and, depending on what's fresh, what's seasonal, combine it with my own herbs really appeals to me. I love this life, Sophie. Every part of it but one."

She looked away, not sure what to say.

"I'm lonely. No matter how much I fill my life with work, it isn't enough."

"Is that why you accepted Elaine's invitation?"

He narrowed his eyes. "Does that bother you?"

"No. Of course not. It's just . . . you should know that Elaine was recently divorced."

"Ah. And I should be careful because she's on the rebound."

"Something like that."

"Something like that, but not *exactly*."

She looked up. "What do you want from me, Nathan?"

"Nothing. And everything. I'm glad Bram's recovered."

"Why?"

"Because I couldn't compete with a sick man."

"There *is* no competition. I'm married. I love my husband. End of story."

"But I loved you long before you met him. We were supposed to get married. We'd be married now if it hadn't been for your detour into religious insanity. You can't deny that, Sophie."

"I get it now. You staked your claim first. I might as well be a piece of property."

"I didn't say that."

"I think you did."

Out of frustration, he tossed the napkin on the table, then raised his palms in a gesture of surrender. "I take it all back. It's obvious that you and Bram were fated to be together. I mean, how many times does a guy have to get shot down before he sees the light?"

"I think you just mixed a metaphor."

"Call the cops."

Sophie's wig pressed hotly against her head. Her brain felt like it was about to boil.

"I won't bother you anymore, Sophie. I mean it this time."

She could tell by the firmness in his voice that he was telling the truth.

As if to soften the statement, he added, "If you can sit in my restaurant, eat my food, and *not* fall into my arms, I've done all I can do." He looked around the room. "Maybe it's time to stop living like a monk. Which brings us back to Elaine. You're her friend. What's she like?"

"Oh, no. I'm not touching that topic with a ten-foot pole."

"I'm just asking."

"What's that old saying? 'Don't worry if you miss the bus. Another one will come along any minute.' "

He shook his head. "You're deliberately misreading my intent. I'm moving on. That should make you happy."

"It does." She straightened her tie.

"Great. Then what are we arguing about?"

"We're not arguing."

"Could have fooled me."

"Don't play with me, Nathan. Dating Elaine won't make me jealous. I only told you about her divorce because I care about you. I don't want to see you get hurt."

He laughed, folding his arms over his chest. "You

know, after I lost you all those years ago, I used to think of myself as bulletproof. In some ways, I think I still am. Don't worry about me, Soph. I'm a big boy. Elaine will be my Zen way of moving back into the dating world. Besides, there are never any guarantees in this life, right?"

"Right," she said, knowing full well the irony of what she'd just agreed to. "No guarantees."

4

A yellow ball of lamplight glowed inside the living room as Elaine hurried up the walk to her front door. This far away from the city, the stars seemed so much brighter, the dark so much darker. She felt a shiver of dread, not knowing what she'd find once she went inside.

The brilliant coldness of the night sky confirmed what Elaine already knew. She was adrift in an indifferent universe. Utterly alone. It seemed amazing to her that, as a child, she'd gazed up at the same sky and felt comforted—by a God who lived in the heavens and loved her, by the feel of her father's hand as it curled protectively around hers, and by the limitless possibility of her own life. How could such a promising fairy tale have gone so wrong?

Pressing her key into the lock, Elaine wondered if her daughter's behavior was simply manipulative and thoughtless, as it had been so many times before, or if this was the crisis, the one her daughter's therapist had warned might be coming.

Tracy was a young woman who was hungry to be loved, and yet, at the same time, she managed to push everyone away. Between temper tantrums, she was either sulky, blaming and easily angered, or flip, unwilling to take anything seriously. Even her grandmother, who had always been able to get through to her, seemed at a loss. Tracy's therapist explained that this behavior was typical, a symptom of the trauma Tracy had been through. Elaine was willing to believe that this long-ago trauma had formed a great part of who her daughter was, but she refused to sit idly by and watch her sink deeper and deeper into passivity and despair.

Entering the house, Elaine found the front room empty. Upstairs she could hear a TV, so she followed the sound. Mick, eating a pizza, was sitting in the den, his boot-clad feet propped up on the coffee table. He was wearing his usual T-shirt and jeans. The T-shirt changed periodically, the jeans never did. Even the food stains remained in the same place, suggesting he had one pair and he never washed them.

"I thought you said this was an emergency," said Elaine, shoving his feet off the table. "Where's Tracy?"

"Jesus, chill, okay? She's still in the bathroom."

"Why didn't you kick the door down like I told you to? You said she was crying hysterically."

"Look, Mrs. Veelund, she calmed down, okay? When I came back from getting her a glass of water, she'd locked herself in. She wasn't crying anymore. She said she just needed some time alone. I get that, even if you don't. We talked through the door while she ran a bath. I told her I might order a pizza and she said to go ahead. You may not believe this, but I care about your daughter. I don't like to see her hurting any more than you do."

"Right."

"It's true," he said, wiping a napkin across his mouth. "I don't care what you think of me."

Mick Frye was twenty-eight, two years older than

Tracy. He worked part-time selling hot dogs and beer at the Metrodome in downtown Minneapolis. He lived with his parents, but from what Tracy had said, he'd been spending more and more time at her apartment near the U. He had a degree in business administration but seemed disinclined to find a regular job. He kept talking about going on for his M.B.A., but so far he hadn't applied to grad school. His weekends at the Metrodome seemed to provide him with enough money to live on—that and the money Elaine gave him to be a companion to her daughter. Beyond that, he seemed to have no visible aspirations.

Tracy and Mick had been "dating" for almost a year. Before Mick had entered the picture, Tracy had lived like a recluse, refusing to have anything to do with the opposite sex. At the same time, she seemed immensely jealous of her friends' relationships, so jealous that, over time, she'd cut them all out of her life. Elaine saw it as a clear indication of how deeply Tracy yearned for what she didn't have.

Before Elaine hired Mick, she made sure that he understood the ground rules. There would be no sex—period—on penalty of losing his sweet financial gig with Elaine. Tracy's therapist explained that Tracy was deeply uncomfortable around men, and terrified of being pressured sexually. She needed time to heal, to talk things through in a safe setting. A friendship bond with a guy her age might be therapeutic, but since Tracy never went out socially, and had stopped taking classes at the U, it wasn't likely she'd find someone to form that kind of bond with. That's when Elaine got the idea to provide her with what she needed—a "safe" relationship.

For a time, Elaine felt it was working. Mick had taken things slowly at first, making a nonthreatening impression on Tracy. During the last few months, however, the two of them had grown quite close. Mick maintained that their relationship wasn't physical. Taken all in all, he wasn't a bad young man, just unkempt by Elaine's standards, and lazy. He had a good heart and seemed to genuinely like Tracy, which was more than Elaine could say for herself at the moment. Intuitively, he seemed to know when to back off and when to stick close.

Mick Frye was actually quite a hunk, which was why he first caught Elaine's eye. Upon closer examination, the crew cut and the tattoos didn't appeal. With his puppy dog eyes, his penchant for obscure German poetry, and his genuine interest in Eastern philosophy, he wasn't the norm, and Elaine knew that would appeal to her daughter. He could carry on a decent conversation, sometimes displaying knowledge of the most arcane topics, and he seemed to have a lively intelligence, one he directed at everything except earning a living. He was also quite clever. It was this part of his nature that Elaine didn't entirely trust.

"Go see for yourself," he said, pointing a pizza slice at the hallway. "She's fine. I mean, I just talked to her a few minutes ago, after the pizza came. She said she didn't want any. I'm saving her a couple pieces anyway, just in case she changes her mind."

Elaine was disgusted. She'd cut her dinner short for nothing but another one of her daughter's tantrums. Charging down the hall, she rapped her knuckles on the bathroom door.

"Tracy, is everything all right? Mick called and said you'd been crying."

She waited.

When there was no response, she said, "Look, I understand that you want some time alone, but I need to know you're okay."

Mick ambled into the hallway and stood behind her, his hands stuffed into the front pockets of his jeans. "Come on, Trace. Let her off the hook."

Still no response.

"Maybe she fell asleep," said Mick, scratching the side of his neck.

Elaine knocked harder this time. "Tracy? It's your mom. I'm not playing this game. Answer me!"

Nothing.

"Tracy. Answer me now. If you don't, we'll break the door down."

"It's a pretty heavy door," whispered Mick. "I'm not sure I can do that."

"Tracy!" Elaine was shouting now. Her heart was hammering inside her chest. "Answer me, damn it!"

She turned to Mick. "Use your shoulder. Break it down. Something's wrong, I can feel it."

Mick stepped closer. "This is really silly, Trace. Just say you're all right." When no response came, he bent down and threw himself against the door—once, twice, three times. It didn't budge. He glanced at the hinges. "Get me a hammer and a crow bar."

Elaine kicked off her high heels and raced down the stairs to the kitchen. She found a hammer in the bottom cupboard drawer. Rushing outside, she flipped the light on in the garage and found the crowbar hanging from a rusted nail. When she returned to the second floor, Mick was talking to Tracy, still trying to get her to answer him. Elaine handed him the tools.

Mick wedged the crowbar into the tiny space between the door and the jamb and pushed and pulled with all his might. He was sweating, cursing. The look on his face told Elaine that he understood the seriousness of the situation. He stripped away the wood, chunk by chunk, leveraging his way in until the lock finally gave. Pulling the door free, he stepped back and allowed her to enter first.

Tracy was lying in the bathtub fully clothed, the water surrounding her stained a sickening red. Her eyes were closed.

"She cut her wrists," said Elaine, her brain switching to autopilot. She plunged into the tub, lifting her daughter up and back until her chin was no longer perilously close to the water. "Wake up, honey. Wake up." She slapped her daughter's cheeks, trying to get a rise out of her. "Come on, baby. Just open your eyes." She felt for a pulse at her neck. "Jesus. It's so weak." Twisting around she cried, "Call nine-one-one!"

"Is she still alive?"

"Yes. Get out of here! Make the call!"

Mick backed away.

Elaine climbed out of the tub and scoured the medicine chest for bandages, but everything she found was too small. The blood was still pumping out of the cuts. Soaking wet, her knit dress hanging around her ankles, she ran back down to the kitchen and grabbed some duct tape from under the sink. There was very little left, but it would be enough. It had to be.

On the way back up the stairs, she peeled off two long strips. After drying Tracy's wrists, she pressed a towel hard against them, trying to stanch the flow of blood, but it was no use. Holding her breath and willing the blood to stop, she slapped the duct tape around the cuts, winding the silver strips as tight as she could. It seemed to work for a moment, but then the blood began to well up from around the edges of the tape. She held Tracy's hands above her head, thinking that might help, but the blood just ran down her arms. She remembered something about tourniquets, but she didn't have one, and wouldn't know how to use it if she did.

"Damn," she shouted, looking around wildly.

Spotting a single-edged razor on the floor by the tub, she grabbed it and hurled it at the tiled wall. It bounced back and hit her face, nicking her just below the eye.

"Stupid stupid stupid!" she screamed, whirling around and nearly slipping on the wet floor. She couldn't do anything right.

"Tell them to hurry!" she yelled, jumping back into the tub and cradling her daughter in her arms. "It's going to be all right," she whispered, squeezing her hand around one wrist, then the other. "Mama's here, honey. Mama's here."

5

On the way back to the Maxfield, Sophie had some time to ponder her evening at Chez Sophia. Seeing Nathan again had left her feeling oddly empty.

Sophie wasn't an unhappy woman. Far from it. She adored her husband, her son, her life, her career. And yet the ruins of that long-ago love for Nathan Buckridge remained fixed in the deepest part of her being, a spidery silhouette of what once existed but could never be again. Perhaps that feeling, related as it was to both defeat and resignation, would never go away. Revisiting the past, however, attempting to make it live again, was a fool's journey. And Sophie wasn't a fool.

She hoped.

On her way through the lobby of the hotel, she hoisted up Ethel, the black mutt who had shared Bram's and her life for almost a decade. Ethel had become the de facto hotel mascot. She sat on a large paisley pillow in the downstairs lobby eyeing the guests with disdainful ennui. Because she moved more slowly than any other living being and was therefore no threat to anyone, because she had great tolerance—not to be confused with affection—for all life forms, and finally, because she could lie comfortably for hours at a time with only an occasional twitch to prove she wasn't dead, she was perfectly suited for the job. The hotel staff took turns taking her for walks so she could perform her daily ablutions. All in all, Sophie figured it was a pretty good life for a dog.

When the elevators opened, Sophie stepped off and set Ethel down on the hallway carpet. Ethel was putting on weight in her old age. She liked to be cuddled and carried, but Sophie was tired, stuffed with food, and in no mood for weight lifting. Unlocking the door to her apartment, she waited for Ethel to amble inside. It was going on ten. Sophie had assumed that Bram would be home by now, but since Ethel was in the lobby, it meant he was still out. That was fine with Sophie. She needed a little time to relax and unwind. She would take a shower, then make herself a Campari and soda, and spend a few more minutes forgetting about Nathan.

Walking into the living room and tossing her purse on the couch, Sophie saw that Bram's checkbook was lying open on the coffee table. That was odd. She picked it up, thinking that he'd forgotten to put it away. She was about to open the top drawer of his desk when she saw that the inside door to the balcony was open. She could hear Bram's voice talking softly, but because all the lights were off outside, she couldn't see the person he was talking to. The smell of cigarette smoke wafted in through the screen. Out of curiosity, Sophie glanced at the receipt from the last check Bram had written. It was to his daughter, Margie, for ten thousand dollars.

Sophie pushed through the screen door out onto the patio.

"The Prodigal finally returns," said Bram, standing up to greet her. He kissed her lightly, then nodded to his daughter who was leaning against the iron railing. The lights of downtown St. Paul spread out behind her.

"This is a surprise," said Sophie, giving Margie a welcoming hug.

For the past few years, Margie Baldric had lived in Austin, Texas. Prior to that, she'd gone to college at St. Cloud University in central Minnesota, where she received her B.A. in computer science. She'd lived with Bram and Sophie early in their marriage, when they had a house in the Tangletown area of south Minneapolis. Margie didn't enter college until a couple of years after high school. Bram didn't want to push her. He felt it would be better if she found her own way. During her first three years at St. Cloud, she'd lived with her boyfriend, Lance, but had dumped him her senior year in favor of a new boyfriend, Kurt Melling. Kurt was also getting his degree in computer science. After graduation, they'd moved to Austin, his hometown.

Margie wrote occasionally. She called a couple of times a year. But her favorite form of communication was e-mail. That's how she and her father kept in touch. Margie was a fiercely independent young woman, with an abundance of spunk, strongly voiced opinions, and intolerances. Sophie found her somewhat arrogant and hard to read, but still, she admired her determination.

Early in their relationship, Sophie had come to the conclusion that Margie didn't like her because she thought Sophie was attempting to replace her mother. In her more honest moments, Sophie had to admit that Margie was probably right—she was trying too hard. Since her first husband had been awarded custody of their son, Rudy, Sophie's confidence when it came to kids was already on the floor. She tried to make things right, to make it clear in every way possible that no one could ever replace Margie's mother, who had died when Margie was twelve. Still, the waters of discontent never seemed to abate.

During the last few years, Sophie had been forced to conclude that she and Margie simply didn't like each other. They got along, for Bram's sake, but they would never be close.

Margie had the same vivid green eyes and chocolate brown hair as her dad, although on her, the elements came together to create a far different impression. Her face wasn't as square as Bram's, it was more of a classic oval, like her mother's. Her makeup was usually tasteful, although she tended to like heavy, dark-colored lipstick—mahogany, deep purple, dark black-red—which Sophie found a bit cadaverous. The nose ring had been added in the last few years, as had the tattoo that ringed her upper right arm. She cultivated a calm, "soul of reason" exterior, one that belied an intense, sometimes anxious, and always judgmental interior. Tonight she was dressed in a white cotton sweater and tight black leather pants. On her well-muscled, slim body, the clothes looked terrific.

In three months, Margie Baldric would turn twenty-eight. Sophie wondered if she'd changed any, if she was as tightly wound and volatile as she used to be.

"What brings you to Minnesota?" asked Sophie, sitting down on one of the lounge chairs. She assumed it had something to do with the ten thousand dollars.

"I'm coming home," she said, smiling at her father.

Bram added, "She's starting a business with a friend of hers."

"What kind of business?" asked Sophie. "A friend from school?"

"Carrie Sontag," replied Margie, flicking some cigarette ash over the edge of the rail. "I met her in Austin. Remember I told you I was working for a wedding planner? She was the right hand to the guy who owned the place. I did the computer stuff in the back room and she worked with clients, coordinating services like catering, flowers, wedding cakes, hall rentals, all the details that go into making a really memorable event. We saw how much money he was making every month, and how little he was paying us, and we thought, hell, why do we need *him*?" She laughed, then held the cigarette to her mouth and took a deep drag.

Thus, the ten thousand dollars, thought Sophie.

"But here's the deal," said Bram, turning to his wife. "Margie flew in just a few hours ago. Came straight here from the airport. She doesn't have a place to live yet, so I thought—"

"Of course," said Sophie. "She should stay at the Maxfield until she gets settled. I'll call down and arrange a room."

"No," he said, elongating the word. "I was thinking more along the lines of something else. See, Margie's worried about me—about my health, which is apparently the main reason she decided to come home. I've told her over and over again that I'm fine, better than ever. But she says she wants to spend more time with her old dad, and of course, that's an offer I can hardly turn down. So I checked, and one of our apartments is vacant right now. I thought, wouldn't it be nice to have Margie live here with us permanently? In her own apartment?"

"I wouldn't want to get in your way," said Margie, tucking her hair behind her ears. "But I'd love living here. This place is awesome."

"What do you say?" asked Bram.

He looked so expectant, so eager, Sophie could hardly say no. "Sure, that's a great idea."

He cleared his throat. "She can't afford the rent until she gets on her feet, so I'll take care of it."

Sophie knew what he wanted. He wanted her to say it was fine to waive the rent. And of course, it was. Margie was family. The hotel was Bram's as much as it was Sophie's, so discussing it with her, asking her permission, was just a formality. Still, Sophie had the distinct sense of being railroaded. She felt as if the whole situation had been manipulated *by* Margie *for* Margie, that it had nothing to do with spending more time with her father. On the other hand, Sophie couldn't think of a good reason to say no.

"You're family, honey," said Sophie. "You stay here as long as you want. When you get your business up and running, we can talk about rent then. The apartment will have to be cleaned and painted before you move in. Actually, I think maintenance was scheduled to start on it next week."

"Could I pick out the paint colors?" she asked, drawing one last time on the cigarette, then flipping it over the rail.

"Sure you can," said Bram. "Anything you want."

"Fabulous! Oh, Dad, thank you *so* much."

"Thank Sophie, too."

"Thanks to *both* of you. Really. This is totally amazing. Wait until Carrie sees this place. It'll blow her away."

"Where is she staying?" asked Sophie.

"With her boyfriend, Kevin. He drove up last week and rented them a town house out by Southdale. Kevin's in banking. He's already got a job up here—at Wells Fargo.

I'm boyfriendless at the moment." She shrugged. "Which is fine with me."

Bram reached over and took hold of Sophie's hand. He looked almost as happy as his daughter. Sophie felt guilty now for entertaining negative thoughts about Margie. For good or ill, she was home to stay. Sophie hoped that, in time, she and Margie could become family not just in name but in fact.

6

For some deeply complicated, possibly even masochistic reason, Danny Veelund planned to board a jet tomorrow morning and fly back to Minnesota. His home was in Manhattan, a three-level brownstone on the Upper East Side, where he'd lived with his wife, Ruth, and his two daughters, Zoe and Abbie, for the past sixteen years. Abbie was in film school now in California, and Zoe had just started her junior year at Brown, so Danny and Ruth were empty nesters, which had its good and bad points.

The good was that Danny's writing day was no longer interrupted by teenage angst of one form or another, though for the last few years the interruptions didn't matter because he hadn't written anything but dreck. The bad points all revolved around missing his kids. He might be accused of favoritism, but his two girls were the brightest, most beautiful, funniest, and kindest young women he'd ever met. If Danny's father had taught him anything, it was to love your children. Perhaps that's why, more than anything else, he had to return to Minnesota, to the family home where his mother still lived.

Daniel Reed Veelund was a moderately well known literary novelist who had written a series of books in the mid-1980s that had catapulted him to a modicum of literary fame and fortune. The fortune was pretty well gone now, though people continued to read the books. He'd struggled to write two more books in the nineties, but neither had been as successful as he or his publisher had wished. Still, because he was a colorful character in his own Midwestern sort of way, he was often invited to speak at colleges and universities, trotted out for the odd commencement ceremony, the occasional TV show. He always accepted because these public appearances made him feel alive in a way his writing rarely did anymore.

Danny knew he should be doing a dozen different things right now in order to prepare for his trip, but instead he sat before the computer in his study, leaning back in his chair, feet thrust out in front of him, hands bunched into fists inside the pockets of his corduroy pants, staring at a list of infinitely dispiriting stock prices. He adjusted his glasses, blinked a couple of times, but the numbers remained the same. His wife probably thought he was working on his new book, the one he had under contract with Random House, but the numbers wouldn't release him from their grip.

Danny's editor was a patient man, perhaps too patient, and had given Danny yet another extension on his newest novel, *The Fool's Gift*, a book that was to be the crowning glory of his literary career. No one but Danny knew that after two years of hard work, all the manuscript consisted of was an assortment of character impressions, jumbled descriptions, and a few lengthy ruminations on justice, fairness, prejudice, modern medicine, the stock market, family ethics, and life in general in these United States in the second millennium. When Danny had the energy, which he often didn't, he alternated between bouts of anger and depression. The only solution he could find was to return to the home of his youth and put things right.

As he sat staring at the screen, his wife breezed into the room.

"I've got you all packed," she said, shutting the window Danny had opened just before sitting down at his desk. The room had grown chilly while his attention had been elsewhere. He hadn't noticed. "Two sweaters, three pairs of slacks, several dress shirts, jeans, two ties— the red one and the blue one—and your new dark blue suit. You'll have to decide on shoes. Oh, and your shaving kit—"

"I'll take care of that," said Danny, clicking off the screen before she could see what he'd been looking at.

Ruth studied him for a moment, threading the fingers of her right hand through the side of her short, black hair. Stepping behind his chair, she put her arms around his shoulders and kissed the top of his head. "I wish you weren't going."

"I know. But I have to."

"We just visited your mother two months ago."

"I told you. I've got some unfinished business I need to take care of."

"But you won't tell me what it is."

He smiled. "It's a deep dark secret."

"I thought we weren't supposed to keep things from each other."

Doing his best Jack Nicholson impersonation, he said, "You want the truth? You can't *handle* the truth." He grabbed her arm and pulled her down into his lap.

"Danny, stop it."

He kissed her properly, passionately, tenderly. At this moment, he loved her more than he'd ever loved another living soul. She was the rock on which he'd built his life. When he was off in the stratosphere somewhere doing his work, he knew she would be waiting for him when he landed. Ruth and the girls were the best part of his world. He'd always had such grandiose notions of who he was and what he would leave behind him after he was gone. It had taken him every minute of his forty-four years to learn that his true legacy would be far less visible, and yet infinitely more meaningful than anything he'd ever written.

"What's wrong?" said Ruth, pulling back, but only just a little.

He could see the effect his touch had on her, and it warmed him. "I don't want to go any more than you want me to."

"Then don't."

"It's not that simple."

She ran her hand over his beard, caressed his cheek. "You frighten me sometimes, Danny."

"Look, Ruth. It's simple. A writer spends his waking hours working with conflict. Conflict is the soul of character. Character is the soul of drama. And drama is the soul of life. You're not afraid of life, are you?"

"Yes, sometimes." She hesitated. "Tell me why you have to go back there. Why I can't come with you."

She could be so exasperating, and yet he found himself smiling. "Because."

This time she pulled farther away. "Because *why*?"

"You're beautiful."

"Don't change the subject."

"My beautiful Ruth Louise Goldfarb."

She cocked her head. "Why did you call me that? I haven't been Ruth Goldfarb in over twenty years."

"I can still see you the way you looked the first time I met you."

"You thought I was a classic Jewish American Princess. Spoiled rotten."

"I *never* thought of you that way."

"Oh, right. You saw me as a butterfly, then. A delicate flower. For your information, buster, you were the only blind date I ever went on. My girlfriend told me you were something special, so I dressed for the Ritz and you took me to a deli for pastrami on rye. What a comedown."

"I like pastrami on rye." He couldn't help but grin. "You were just being a good girl, wearing your best duds."

"And you had on a leather jacket and ripped jeans. Mr. Grunge."

"We were both trying to impress each other in different ways."

She kissed his nose. "Lucky for you that you clean up pretty good. Speaking of fashion, I won't see you the first time you wear your new suit. You'll go out to dinner with your mother, no doubt someplace fancy. You'll look so handsome that all the homegrown Minnesota floozies will slip you their phone numbers."

"I beg your pardon. We don't grow floozies in Minnesota. Just corn."

"And *I'll* be back in New York, teaching and worrying." Ruth taught several classes at Columbia, including a new one on international media and communications. Given her schedule, she hardly had time to breathe.

"You're the only woman I've ever wanted." He touched his fingers to the hollow in her neck. "Do you think I should get a haircut in the morning before I leave?"

"I like your hair longer, a little shaggy. It's the right look for a distinguished author."

He grunted. "Whatever *that* is. I'm starting to gray, you know—or white."

"It just makes your blond hair look even lighter."

He hugged her tight. "I wish I saw the world through your eyes. I think it would be a far more beautiful place. I won't be gone long, Ruthie. Maybe a week. Hopefully less."

"I'll put a candle in the window."

"You do that." He kissed her again, then whispered, "It will help me find my way home."

The plane landed at Twin Cities International shortly after one, central daylight time. It took a little over an hour for Danny to round up his luggage and arrange for a rental car. By two-thirty, he was driving southwest on Highway 59. The Veelund property was located in Ahern County, an hour's drive from St. Paul. In the late sixties, Danny's dad, Carl Veelund, had purchased eleven hundred acres of less than prime prairie from a farmer. It was a section of land that was full of rocks and gently rolling hills, but not much else. Danny's dad wanted a place out of the city where he could build his dream home. He had died suddenly the night of the housewarming party, leaving Danny's mother to run his growing business.

Danny had been twelve at the time. Alex, his older brother, was eighteen, and Elaine, his sister, fifteen. Alex was the first to leave for college and the first one to return home to help their mother run the company. Elaine left next, following her boyfriend to Stanford, where she found she had a knack for engineering. She lost interest in the boyfriend almost immediately, but her studies consumed her, so much so that she graduated near the top of her class. After graduation she'd received a number of job offers, some of them quite tempting, but her mind was made up. She returned home and eventually took over the log house division. By then the company had become Veelund Industries, making not only log houses but also pool tables and log furniture. In the end, only Danny had left and never come back.

Business interested Danny about as much as dentistry or bricklaying. He did his duty and sat on the board of directors. That meant he had to return to Minnesota occasionally for meetings. He always voted the way his sister told him to. He trusted Elaine more than he trusted Alex, and vastly more than he trusted his mother. Veelund Industries was his father's power and glory. Danny respected that and wanted to do his bit, albeit small, to help it continue. Every human being needed a passion. Once upon a time, writing had been Danny's. But no more.

Turning onto Polk Road, Danny sailed along in his rented Firebird, using his last few minutes alone to ready himself for battle. His reasons for returning like this, taking his family by surprise, were born of both indignation and fear. His hands were steady, but inside he was a mess. "That's the spirit," he said out loud, his voice edged with sarcasm. He didn't like to talk about his relationship with his mother, but the fact was, he'd always been scared to death of her. Not her physical presence or her intelligence, both of which he considered meager, but afraid of her judgment and disdain.

The only conclusion Danny could come to was that this reaction was hard-wired into his brain. From all outward appearances, Daniel Reed Veelund was a man of great accomplishment, one who had defied his mother at every turn, flipped her the bird with sweet disregard. But what no one seemed to realize was that his defiance hadn't been deliberate. He'd fallen into it like an innocent lamb falling into a deep, dark ditch. This time, however, the defiance would be intentional. Clark Kent was about to take off his business suit and leap tall buildings. The logic box in Danny's head might still cause his innards to quake, but it didn't touch his resolve.

Turning onto Stimpson, the afternoon sun momentarily blinded him. He reached to lower the visor and only then stepped out of his thoughts long enough to notice how the sunlight had burned the autumn prairie a deep orange gold. Telephone poles with drooping wires rolled past him, marking time to the rhythm of the bumps in the road. High above, a hawk rode the thermals over the warm land. Danny understood again why his father had fallen in love with this vast, rolling earth. A landscape as spare and austere as the northern prairie was like a tonic to the mind. Here, the world was more elemental. A camera could never capture the power, or the inherent eeriness, of the Minnesota prairie. Danny felt the same tug toward this place that his father had. It was a good place to live. And, perhaps, a good place to die.

The main house, called Prairie Lodge, was located on a rise above Dog Tail Creek. The winding stream was visible from the tall, cathedral-like windows in the living room. About ten years ago, Elaine had ordered three smaller log houses built on the property to use as selling tools to show potential clients. She chose three of the most popular models—Morningstar House, Wisteria Cottage, and The Ranch House—though, for the right price, the design staff could create almost any project a client had in mind.

Turning finally onto the property, Danny could see the houses in the distance. None were more than half a mile apart. As he approached the main house, he was surprised to find so many cars in the driveway. He eased the Firebird into an empty spot along the rear of the four-car garage, parked and got out, stretching for a few moments, smelling the sweetness of the air. He wasn't in New York anymore. His lungs wouldn't know what to do without all the car exhaust to wheeze along on.

Leaving his luggage in the trunk, he crossed the yard and trotted up the steps to the front porch. The screen door was unlocked, so he walked in without knocking. In the back of the house he could hear voices. The TV was on in the living room, but nobody was watching it. As he stood in the entryway, Galen Zander, his mother's personal assistant, hurried down the central stairs.

"Daniel," he said, looking both harassed and confused. "Your mother didn't tell me you were coming."

Zander had begun working for Danny's mother shortly after Danny's father had died. At the time, she needed someone to assist her with the upkeep of the house while she was away at the office. Zander supervised the gardeners and the housekeeper. He saw to it that Danny and Elaine were ferried to school and back and taken to other activities. He even did some of the cooking. Over time, he'd made himself indispensable, becoming Millie Veelund's personal factotum.

Zander was in his early sixties now. A small, trim man with Brooks Brothers tastes. Salt-and-pepper hair always clipped short. Clean shaven. Rigid posture. Equally rigid personality. His aura of precision and impeccable personal hygiene made Danny, and everyone else who got within ten feet of his onrushing cologne, feel like a slob.

"That's okay, Zander. She didn't know about the trip."

"Will you be staying long?"

"A few days."

"I'll see to it that your room is made up. Your luggage?"

"It's out in the car."

"I'll take care of it."

"Don't bother. I've only got one bag. Say, why are there so many cars outside?"

Zander stiffened his already ramrod-straight back. "Your niece . . . had an accident last night. She'll be staying here with us for a few days."

"An accident?"

"I think you should talk to your sister."

"Is Elaine here?"

"She's out on the patio with Tracy and Mick. And Tracy's therapist."

"Her *therapist*?"

Zander looked around, then gave a knowing nod.

His manner was so odd that Danny wasn't sure what to think. Out of loyalty to his employer, Zander tended to be very closed-mouthed about family matters—that is, unless he'd been drinking, which was his only obvious flaw. Getting Zander smashed used to be a favorite family game with Danny, Elaine, and Alex. He was a hoot after a few too many Manhattans. He liked to disco dance, tell off-color jokes, and occasionally a bit of gossip would leak out. Alex figured he was gay and said he thought that was revolting, but every now and then Zander would talk about one of his sexual exploits in fairly vivid detail. It was always a woman. He was either lying, or they'd misjudged him.

"Where's my mother?" asked Danny.

"She's in her study."

Zander seemed to be in such a rush to get somewhere, that Danny let him go. Instead of heading out to the patio to talk to his sister, he decided to announce his visit to his mother. She was, after all, his main reason for coming.

Danny found her standing at the window, looking out at an immense oak tree, one his father had planted on the east side of the house. She was frowning, deep in thought. Last summer, her hair had been white. Now it was blue. Tomorrow it would be red, or brown, or gray. His mother was always changing the way she looked, as if she was never satisfied with her appearance. She'd been an attractive, even exotic-looking young woman who had aged into a heavyset, thick-lipped, sour old woman. Danny still remembered the sweet times he'd spent with her as a child. She'd been diabetic and asthmatic for many years, and it had changed her. Or maybe something else had, but the sweetness he knew had faded long ago. Her children referred to her now as The Judging Machine.

Simply put, Millie Veelund was a bigot. She preceded most of her pronouncements with "I'm not prejudiced, but—" African Americans were all lazy and deserved to live in the projects. Jews might try to fool you, but they were only out for money—a stab at Ruth, Danny's wife, who was Jewish. American society was going to hell because of drugs and homosexuals, oh, and intellectuals. One must never forget the evil influence of intellectualism—a stab at Danny *and* his wife. Public education was a disaster and should be abolished—another stab at Ruth. The American Civil Liberties Union was a pack of communists. All left-handed people were suspect. Right was right, and left was wrong. His mother always laughed at that one. The spirit of Joe McCarthy was alive and well and living in Minnesota. Margaret Thatcher was her political hero, as was Ronald Reagan, except that he was involved far too much with the Jews over there in the Middle East. Then again, he'd taken on the labor unions and won. He had a good heart.

Millie Veelund was Archie Bunker without the twinkle. She used religion and politics like a flamethrower. She was human Agent Orange. Danny hated her. And he loved her. And that was the problem.

"Hi, Mom," he said, his voice breaking awkwardly into the silence.

She turned to him and her face lit up. Taking a few steps toward him, she said, "Daniel, I'm so glad you came. Did Elaine call you?"

"Elaine? No."

"Then . . . how did you find out about Tracy?"

"I just learned about it from Zander. He said she'd had an accident, but he didn't elaborate." He shut the door. "What's going on?"

"It's just . . . heartbreaking. I mean, we all knew she was depressed. She has been for years, but her problems started to come to a head last summer. You must have noticed it."

Danny hadn't. He didn't even know she'd been talking to a therapist.

After giving Danny a kiss, she sat down on the sofa, folding her hands in her lap. She looked defeated. Exhausted. Danny noticed that her ankles seemed unusually swollen. Her health wasn't good, but then, neither was Danny's. For years he'd felt that they'd been in a race to see who would kick off first. Except he'd recovered. Four years ago, the doctors had pronounced him cancer-free. Nobody recovered from old age.

Nodding for him to take a chair opposite the sofa, Millie continued, "It happened last night. Tracy and that boyfriend of hers stopped by Elaine's house, supposedly just to talk, but Elaine wasn't home. I guess Tracy had been crying about something, which isn't unusual. They sat and watched TV for a while, then Tracy said she wanted to take a bath."

"And?" prompted Danny, seeing that this was difficult for his mother.

"She locked herself in the bathroom and slit her wrists."

He was stunned. "Why didn't Mick try to stop her?"

"He didn't know what was happening. But apparently he got concerned so he called Elaine. She came home and they broke the door down. Tracy was unconscious by then. She spent the night at the hospital getting blood transfusions. This morning her therapist suggested that Elaine check her into a facility. You know . . . a—"

"Facility."

"Right." She touched the back of her hair. "She said Tracy shouldn't be alone, but Tracy wouldn't have any of it. Elaine finally talked her into staying here for a while, not that she didn't resist that, too."

"Why doesn't she stay with Elaine?"

"Because . . . that's where the suicide attempt happened. The therapist didn't think it was a good idea for her to go back there. Besides, I can provide her with round-the-clock supervision."

"God," said Danny, shaking his head. "Elaine must be devastated."

"She is."

"Why is Tracy in therapy?"

"I wish I knew. Tracy insists that it's her life and that it remain private."

Danny just looked at his mother. He didn't know what to say. "And what does the therapist think about what just happened?"

"She's out on the back patio talking to Tracy right now. As far as I'm concerned, all those people are a load of bunk. Useless. Tracy might as well talk to a witch doctor. She was better off before she went to that woman."

"What's her name?"

"Jhawar. Dr. Durva Jhawar. That's not American, is it? It's foreign. I thought she might be Spanish, but she's too brown to be from Spain. Not the sort of person I'd ever hire. I hold her, at the very least, partially responsible for Tracy's current condition. But," she sighed, "Elaine doesn't agree with me, *as usual*. I'm just her mother and what does a mother know?"

Danny could feel a rant coming on. He tried to distract her. "Does Alex know about the suicide attempt?"

"I called him first thing this morning. Elaine asked me to." His mother looked at him hard, then cocked her head as if something had just occurred to her. "If you didn't come home because of Tracy, why are you here?"

"I needed a break from my book." He lied with such ease he amazed himself. Had he always been such a good liar?

"Is Ruth with you?"

"No."

She seemed to brighten at that. "I'm planning a family dinner tonight. I think we need to be together. Seven o'clock. Alex will be here, too. And Roman. Alex has an announcement he wants to make. I told him that tonight might not be such a good time, but he insisted it couldn't wait. I'm so happy you're here, Daniel. Elaine and Tracy will be, too." She seemed genuinely glad to see him. And that made his reason for coming all the more difficult. He hated fighting, hated the churning stomach that raw, angry words always caused, but this time, he would demand closure. He had to know where his mother stood.

"I think I'll get settled in my room," he said, rising from his chair. "Maybe take a nap. It's been a long day."

"Good idea. I asked Tracy to come see me when the therapist left." She glanced at her watch. "She should be here anytime."

Danny moved over to the sofa and kissed her on the forehead. Her skin was paper thin. He was bewildered by how much her physical presence still tugged at him.

She took his hand. "You can stay for a while, can't you?"

"I'm not sure how long I'll be here. That's something I need to talk to you about."

She studied his face.

"We'll talk later, okay?"

"You'll stay for a few days though, won't you?"

"Sure. A few days."

"Tracy's suicide attempt has taught me something, Daniel. Whatever time we've got left on this earth, we have to make it count."

"Yes," he said, gazing down at her. "My thoughts exactly."

7

Sophie sat on the window seat in her parents' apartment, looking out at the Mississippi River. It was nearly seven in the evening and the sun had almost set. Only a few minutes earlier the city beyond the river had been bathed in a warm peach light. But that was all gone now, replaced by a velvety violet blue.

Sophie still had the cell phone in her hand. After talking to Elaine and hearing what had happened to her daughter, she couldn't seem to move. Just the thought of a loved one attempting suicide was like lead in her heart. It seemed pretty obvious that this wasn't just a cry for help. Tracy truly meant to end her life. Apparently, in the hospital, she'd said it was all a mistake. She'd been drinking. She was depressed and couldn't shake it off. She wouldn't do it again. She promised, over and over. But how could you ever believe it? thought Sophie. How could you ever live another moment of your life without wondering where your daughter was, what she was doing, what she was feeling?

Under the circumstances, Elaine seemed to be doing remarkably well. She believed her daughter, said she felt it was a onetime event and that it wouldn't happen again. Tracy would be staying at Prairie Lodge with Elaine's mother for a while, until she was stronger. Elaine was up-beat about her daughter's mental health, and yet, in her voice, Sophie could hear the strain. She tried to back away from the request she'd made last night. Her father could easily get the specs on the log houses when he returned from the Far East. But Elaine wouldn't hear of it. She invited Sophie out for lunch. Tomorrow. She said to come to the main house at noon. Tracy's therapist gave orders that Tracy not be treated as if she were an invalid—or crazy. But how *did* you treat a young woman who'd just tried to kill herself? Surely some alteration in behavior was to be expected. Life might go on, but it would be anything but normal.

Sophie glanced up at the sound of a knock on the door. Bram's daughter, Margie, opened it a crack. "Can I come in?" she asked.

Sophie saw that she was holding the paint sampler, the one maintenance had given her just this morning. She looked flushed with excitement, impatient to talk about the colors for her new apartment. Sophie would have preferred to discuss it another time. Her hesitance had less to do with Tracy than it did with her misgivings about Margie. Since last night, Sophie had spent some time thinking about Margie's move to the Maxfield. She felt uneasy about it. At the same time, she felt guilty for feeling that way.

"Sure, come on in," said Sophie, forcing a smile. "I was just checking out my parents' place, seeing what needs to be done before they get back."

"God, I love this apartment," said Margie, looking around. "I remember now. I was here the night your dad announced his retirement, the night he gave the Maxfield to my dad and you." Still looking around, she added, "If I lived in a place like this, I'm not sure I'd ever leave it."

"Your apartment downstairs is a lot like this one."

"But without the view, the formal dining room, and the balcony. And it's much smaller. Actually, it's a little cramped."

She wasn't even paying for the place and she was already complaining. Stop it, thought Sophie. Cut her some slack. She was probably as uncomfortable in Sophie's presence as Sophie was in hers. "But you don't have any furniture."

"Sure I do. Well, maybe not tons, but what there is, is arriving next week. Dad said he was going to take me out tomorrow morning and buy me a new couch, one that folds into a bed. But it's going to be a trick to figure out which wall to put it on. The living room's got kind of a dumb design. Not like this apartment."

"Well, when you own the hotel, I guess you get the best place to live." Sophie wondered if the gleam in Margie's eyes had anything to do with the notion that, one day, she might own the Maxfield. She'd probably conveniently forgotten about Sophie's son.

"Dad and you own the hotel now, but your apartment isn't this nice," said Margie, examining a starburst molding at the top of the living room arch. "I love all this deco stuff."

"You think I should kick my parents out?"

Margie laughed. "Nah. That wouldn't be cool."

"Hey," said Bram, standing in the open doorway. "What are my two favorite women up to?"

"Colors," said Margie, holding up the paint samples. "For my new apartment."

Bram, carrying a gym bag, was wearing a pair of green

jogging shorts, white running shoes, and a gray T-shirt. He wasn't on his way to the office.

Sophie had a hard time believing that such a vital, fit-looking man had been in the hospital less than a year ago, fighting for his life. "You on your way downstairs?" she asked, getting up. She walked over to where he was standing, pressed a finger to the cleft in his chin and gave him a kiss. The hotel exercise center used to be the last place she'd ever find her husband. Now, he hit the machines daily. So much for what a large dose of terror could do to jump-start a fitness program.

"I thought I'd get in a workout before dinner. Anybody want to join me?"

Margie shrugged. "Sure, why not."

"Sophie?" Bram grinned. "Come on. It will be fun."

Sophie's idea of fun didn't include sweating. But then, if Bram could turn over a new leaf, so could she. Her figure had always been on the round side, even though her face, especially her eyes, reminded people of a waif in a Dickens novel. "I'll meet you in a few minutes."

On the way out, Margie paused next to a trestle table in the foyer. "What's that?" she asked, nodding to the rusted metal box.

"One of my workmen found it in the subbasement yesterday. It belonged to my great-uncle on my mother's side. Eli Salmela. See?" she said, picking it up. "His name's on the back. I brought it up here because I thought Mom might like to see it when she gets back."

"Looks old," said Bram, fingering the padlock on the front.

"It is. Uncle Eli died forty years ago."

"What's a box that belonged to your great-uncle doing in the subbasement?" asked Bram.

"I've been thinking about that. I figure it must belong to my mom."

"Then why wasn't it in your parents' storage locker?"

"Beats me," said Sophie. She'd wondered about that herself.

Bram studied it a moment, then said, "Well, maybe I'm way off base here, but it seems pretty obvious to me. Your mother was trying to hide it. Most likely, from Henry."

"Why would she do that?" asked Margie.

"Simple. She's got a secret."

"My mother doesn't have secrets," said Sophie indignantly. "She's . . . my *mother*."

Bram cringed. "Careful, Soph. You're playing with universal karma. As soon as you say something like that, it's almost a statistical certainty that you'll learn some deep, dark, dastardly secret about your mom. Like maybe Pearl was a bank robber in her youth. Or, hey, what if she had a secret love affair with J.F.K.? Or what about—"

"You are *so* off base."

"Maybe. But I'll bet you money that there's something juicy hidden inside that box."

"Those locks are easy to pick," said Margie, bending over to get a better look.

"I am *not* a lock picker," said Sophie. If she'd had time last night, she might have opened it. But she'd changed her mind this morning. The lock was there for a reason. She had no business messing with her mother's private life.

"It doesn't look very sturdy," said Bram, giving it a yank.

To everyone's surprise, it came off in his hand.

"Oops," he said, looking guilty.

"Maybe we can glue it back together," said Sophie, grabbing it away from him.

"But, I mean, it almost *fell* off," said Bram, assuming a soul-of-innocence expression. He started to raise the lid.

Sophie slammed it shut. "It still doesn't give us the right to look at something that was obviously meant to be private."

"I am suitably ashamed of myself," said Bram with an undisguised smirk.

They all looked at one another, then watched Sophie place the box back on the table.

"Time to hit the walking machines," said Sophie, snapping off the overhead light.

"But you *are* going to open it," said Bram. It wasn't a question. "Maybe not now, but before your mom gets home."

"No," said Sophie, her tone resolute.

"Betcha will," he said, grinning.

"Stop looking so superior."

"I can read you like a book."

"Not always."

"Come on, Margie," said Bram, slipping his arm around his daughter's shoulder and walking her out the door. "Let's us *morally reprehensible* chickens leave the *righteous hen* to her ethical dilemma."

"I'm right behind you," said Sophie, closing and locking the door. She refused to entertain the idea that she would look inside.

And that was the end of that.

Pearl's Notebook
March 29, 1972

I remember the next few hours with a vividness that will never leave me. My regrets will follow me as well, because, as I said, I could have stopped what happened. I could have prevented a tragedy. But the cost, oh how terrible it would have been—for me and my husband, for Carl's children, and for my dear daughter, Sophie. How could I betray them all?

With the note Carl had received safely tucked into my evening purse, I scanned the crowded living room to find Henry, not that I needed to worry about him. Henry is in his element at a party, the louder the better. He was seated on one of the sofas, talking to several people I'd never met. I waved at him and he waved back, but he went on talking. That was good. I was free to find Carl.

I waded into the crowd and finally located him standing next to the bar, the one that his staff had set up in the conservatory off the living room. He was facing away from me, so I couldn't see his expression. He held a drink in his hand, but didn't seem to be talking to anyone. With one quick movement, he tipped his head back and finished the drink, then held the glass out for another. When he turned around, the look in his eyes made me shiver. The rage I'd seen a few moments ago was still there, but it was masked now, covered by an odd kind of blankness. Maybe others couldn't see behind the mask, but I could.

After downing a third drink, Carl made straight for the front door. I followed, not knowing where he was going or what he was about to do. The only thought in my mind was that I had to talk to him. He was so clearly in trouble. I berated myself with every step I took. I'd never been able to let go of him, not completely. That was my problem. My problem and his. We stayed friends when we should have turned our backs on each other and lived totally separate lives. But the finality of that seemed too terrible. We simply couldn't do it. Our connection was too deep, our history too important. And then our daughters became friends. Carl's oldest son took a summer job at the Maxfield, waiting on tables in the Zephyr Club. Our lives seemed to intertwine no matter how we tried to keep the past in a separate box.

When I stepped outside, I found that the wind had picked up. It was one of those treacherous March nights when a light rain could easily turn to sleet or snow. I'd left my wrap inside, but it hardly seemed important. One of the parking attendants had brought around Carl's Cadillac and as I made my way down the steps from the porch, I saw him slide into the front seat. I knew he was in no shape to drive, so I rushed around the side of the car and banged on the window. My wedding ring hit the glass and that's what finally got his attention. He squinted up at me and rolled down the window.

"Pearl," he said. His eyes looked glassy. "What are you doing out here? Go back inside."

I opened the door. "Move over."

"What? Why?"

"Just do it." I wasn't going to take no for an answer.

"I need to be alone," he said.

I reached in and turned off the motor, removing his car keys.

"Hey."

"Move over, Carl," I said. "I mean it. You're in no shape to drive."

He scowled at me, but finally relented.

Once he'd moved to the passenger's seat, I got in and started the engine. "You can be alone with me driving. I won't bother you. Consider me your chauffeur." Before he could object further, I put the car in gear and we were off.

Once we were away from the bright lights of the house, I felt as if we'd entered a dark tunnel. The rain rushed at our headlights, making it seem like we were going faster than we really were. I switched on the windshield wipers, but realized immediately that it wasn't just the rain that was the problem. Fog had started to form in the ditches and creep across the road. There were a couple moments when I wasn't sure where the road ended and the field began. But I kept going. We drove like that for a while, listening to the wipers slap back and forth, lulled, I think, by the rhythm. Carl kept his eyes fixed firmly in front of him, but I could tell that his mind was miles away.

Finally, we saw a dim light up ahead that heralded the intersection of Polk Road and Highway 59. Carl said there was a wide patch of grass next to the four-way-stop and that I should pull over. I did, but I didn't stop the engine. It had finally warmed inside the car and for that I was grateful. I wasn't shaking from the cold anymore, but I was still shaking.

We sat for a long time in silence. It might have been half an hour. It might have been more. I didn't think to look at the clock. All I knew was that Carl was sitting next to me and that his stillness came from pain. I wanted to help him, but I didn't know how. So I waited. We were in our own little cocoon and the world had grown hushed around us. The soft green lights from the dash illuminated our faces. As I turned off the windshield wipers, I glanced at myself in the rearview mirror. I wasn't a young woman anymore. I don't know why that came as such a shock. Maybe because, with Carl, I always felt young. The same young woman who'd fallen in love with him all those years ago. I tipped my head back slightly and watched the rain beat against the windshield. I assumed he'd let me know when he wanted to go back.

When he finally did speak, it was as if his voice came from a distance. I looked over and realized for the first time that he'd been crying. His head was bent, tears streaming down his cheeks, his straight blond hair falling over his forehead, his big beautiful hands resting in his lap. I closed my eyes and turned away because the sight of him was breaking my heart.

"When I was a child," he began, "I wasn't afraid of anything. As I got older, I saw that life could hurt me. No matter how strong I was, how hard I fought, I might not always win. But losing is a far cry from total ruin, Pearl. A very far cry."

Surely it wasn't that bad, I thought. Surely something could be done to set matters right.

He continued: "In a strange sort of way, there's a certain solace in finally knowing the worst life can throw at you."

I was torn. Should I tell him I'd seen the note he'd been sent? Ask him who sent it? Ask him to explain what it meant? Would he think I was prying into his personal affairs? At this moment, did it matter? Without thinking,

I reached over and touched his arm. I wanted to comfort him.

He put his hand over mine and I felt the tenderness in the gesture.

Carl said: "They say that touch is our first language. And that it's the last sense to leave us."

He held my eyes. I couldn't look away.

"I've never stopped loving you. If only I'd married you instead of Millie—" He drew his hand away. "No," he said, shaking his head. "I didn't mean that. It sounds like I'm blaming you for my problems. I'm not, Pearl. I'd never do that."

I asked him what was wrong, pleaded with him to tell me.

He wouldn't answer. Instead, he sat back, his eyes following the rivulets of rain as they trickled down the glass.

After a few more minutes of silence, I simply couldn't take it any longer. I said, "I saw the note, Carl. The one the waiter gave you. I followed you to your office. I knew something was wrong. Something's been wrong all evening."

"You were watching me?"

I told him I was concerned.

"Oh, God," he said, pressing his hands to his face. "I could have dropped dead in front of Millie and she wouldn't have noticed."

"You were waiting for that envelope, weren't you. That's why you seemed so nervous. After you left, I went in your office and took the note out of the trash. I looked at it, Carl. It was a letter, a symbol. But I don't understand." I couldn't read his expression. "Are you angry? Say something."

"Pearl, let's keep driving. We'll go back to the Cities.

Get on a plane and head south to the Keys, or west to Aspen. Anywhere, just to get away from this god-awful place. Let's do it now. No bags. Just the clothes on our backs. Screw caution. Screw responsibility. For once, let's live just for us."

"Are you asking me to leave my husband?"

"Why not? You love me. Tell me that isn't true and I'll stop."

I couldn't deny what he already knew.

"We'll build a new life together. I'll love you so hard and so strong you'll never have a moment's regret. I'm a millionaire, Pearl. Anything's possible. We could buy a yacht and sail around the world. Live like nomads. No ties. No pressure. Just sun and sea breezes. Just pleasure, Pearl. A dream life."

"But your children," I said. "And Sophie? How could we leave them?"

"God." That's when he broke down, started to cry. After a moment, he said, "We'll bring them with us."

"Tonight?"

"No, no," he said, pulling a handkerchief out of his pocket and wiping his eyes. "I'll hire someone to get them, bring them to us. We'll be a family of nomads."

"You can't just steal children. It's not legal."

"Do you think I care about legalities?"

"But Carl," I said, searching his eyes. "What about Henry?"

"What about him?"

"He's my husband."

"But you love me more."

How could I tell him that wasn't true? I loved them both, but for different reasons. "You're not thinking clearly."

"You figure I'm drunk. That's the only reason I'm talking like this."

"You are drunk, Carl. And you're also married to Millie."

His eyes closed. "It always comes back to her, doesn't it. God, but I loathe that woman. She was the single worst mistake I ever made in my life. You know what, Pearl? If it's the last thing I do, I'm going to make her pay."

His anger was white-hot and it frightened me.

"Drive back to the house," he said.

"Why? What are you going to do?"

"Turn the car around. Now."

When I switched on the windshield wipers, I saw that the rain had finally changed to sleet. The longer we waited the more slippery the roads would become. I worried that Henry was back at the party searching for me, wanting to leave. I was frightened by Carl, and I was frightened for him.

With trembling hands, I put the car in gear.

8

Danny retrieved his bag from the rental car and carried it upstairs to his bedroom to unpack. Since there was to be a family dinner tonight, he figured he might as well wear his new suit. Alex always dressed like a banker—pinstripes, vests, button-down collars—and made Danny feel like a schlump in his jeans and sweaters. Danny figured that wearing a power suit tonight might give him just the edge he needed. It would make him look substantial. Well-off. A man of the world, with knowledge and insights that deserved to be considered. While lecturing at a college campus, or being interviewed on TV, he *was* all of those things. But at home, he was just Danny, the baby of the family, the crazy kid who'd written a couple of books. Nobody in his family read fiction, not even his.

After taking a nap and then showering, he sat down on the bed and picked through the socks his wife had packed for him until he found the ones he wanted. He thought about calling Ruth but decided to wait. If he was able to talk to his mother privately tonight after dinner, he might have something interesting to report. Ruth didn't know why he'd come, nor would she have agreed with his plan. Danny had worked out a progression in his mind. One step at a time. Maybe he'd been wrong about his mother. Time would tell. The problem was, he wasn't sure how much time was left.

As he stood, he glanced out the window. Directly below him was the patio and the pool house. The patio was empty now, which meant that everyone was inside, getting ready for the evening.

Danny laughed to himself, remembering how much trouble the pool and the tennis court had caused his mother. The tennis court was built first, but nobody took into consideration the amount of wind on the prairie. His mother had built a windbreak after a couple of years of never using the court. Danny and Elaine would try to hit balls back and forth, only to have them blow into the next county.

Once the pool was complete, it had the same problem. When it wasn't covered by a tarp, leaves, dead grass, and general prairie debris blew into it and clogged the filters. It was like swimming in a swamp. In frustration, Danny's mother had consulted a builder and a plastic dome was eventually affixed over the top. It worked pretty well until a tornado came through one summer, lifting the dome off its moorings and tossing it on top of the garage. It cracked into six huge pieces. Now the pool was enclosed in a brick building. Floor-to-ceiling windows allowed a view of the outdoors without letting the outdoors in. So much for the little house—or, in this case, the log mansion—on the prairie.

Glancing at the time, Danny saw that he'd better get moving. As he opened the closet door to get his suit, he heard voices. Stepping deeper into the closet, he bent down, pressing his ear to a crack in one of the wallboards. He remembered now that, as a kid, he'd crawled into his closet once or twice a week to listen to his sister talk on the phone. The bedroom next door had been Elaine's. God, but she was full of shit. Always angling to draw some poor sap into her web of romantic excess. Listening at that crack had been a rite of passage for Danny. He'd learned about sex and the intricacies of the mating dance in that closet. The room appeared to be Tracy's now. She was talking to her boyfriend Mick.

Danny listened:

"Are we gonna eat dinner with your family?" asked Mick.

"No."

Tracy's voice sounded as sullen as ever, thought Danny. Nothing had changed.

"Won't your mother want us to come down?"

"I don't know. Maybe. But I'm not going. You can if you want. If you're *that* hungry."

"Not without you." Silence. "Tracy, are you worried about something?"

"What makes you think that?"

"I don't know. The way you're acting."

"I'm just tired."

"Is that all?"

"What do you want from me? Yes, that's *all*."

More silence.

"I don't believe you. Something's been eating at you ever since we got here. I think you're scared."

"You don't have a clue so just shut up."

"Look, you may not believe me, but I care about you."

"You mean you care about my family's money."

"No. I care about *you*. If my life was about money, do you think I'd be selling hot dogs at a ballpark for a living? I care about time. Time is all we've got. That's why I don't want to sell it for some asshole job. Look, if you were upset because of what we did yesterday, I'm sorry. I never meant to hurt you. You could have said no."

"You didn't hurt me. I wanted to."

"Then why did you freak out last night?"

"I told you. I was drinking. I got depressed. I saw the razor blades in the medicine chest and I just *did* it, okay? It was an impulse."

"A stupid one."

"Okay, *okay*. I won't do it again."

Another silence. This one longer.

"Don't look at me like that," said Tracy.

"You're up to something."

She lowered her voice. "I'm not staying here."

"You've got to stay here. Otherwise, your mom said it's the psych hospital, Shady whatever." He laughed.

"Screw her. Screw all of them. I've got stuff I need to do. I'm not sticking around."

After a few more seconds: "Tracy?"

"What?"

"I take that back about you being scared. It's more like you're really pissed off. You seem . . . stronger. More sure of yourself."

"Whatever."

"Tell me the truth. Is there another guy? If there is—"

"No. Just drop it."

"Did he try to hurt you? If that's what you're so angry about, just tell me who he is and I'll wipe the floor up with him."

"You mean violence isn't against your principles?"

"Shit, no."

Danny could hear rustling.

"I've got to get out of here," said Tracy. "I'm going stir crazy."

"It won't be easy. What am I saying? With that guard service your mother hired, I'd say it's fairly impossible."

"If I can figure out a way, will you help?"

"You mean tonight?"

"Hell, no. Not with everyone watching me like a hawk. In a few days. I'll make my break then."

Their voices dipped to a whisper.

Danny pressed his ear hard against the board, but they were talking too softly. He couldn't catch it. And it was getting late. If he was late for dinner, it would only tick off his mother. He didn't want to start the evening on a negative note. Even though it might end that way.

9

It was chaos theory, pure and simple. A butterfly flapped its wings in Japan and altered the atmospheric pressure in Seattle. Or at least that's what Elaine was thinking as she hurried down the central stairs in her mother's house, carrying a tray of dirty dishes. She'd spent the last few minutes trying to convince Tracy and Mick to come downstairs for dinner. When Tracy ripped open a bag of potato chips and turned on the TV, she knew it was a lost cause. And then, as she passed into the front foyer, Alex walked in. She was glad to see him and would have said so if it hadn't been for the man accompanying him. Elaine couldn't believe her brother would bring Roman Marchand to a private family gathering, but there he was, standing in the front hall with his lopsided grin, wreaking of smarm.

Yup, it was chaos theory all right. Life had too damn many variables.

Marchand was the president of Kitchen Visions, a division of Veelund Industries, and a man Elaine loathed for a multitude of reasons.

Alex must have noticed the disgruntled look on her face because he rushed over and whispered, "Just chill, okay? I need him to be here. Don't make a scene."

"I never make scenes."

"You live for them, Elaine."

She turned her back on them both and continued into the pantry, where she set the tray on the granite counter and then tried a couple of deep-breathing exercises to calm herself down. Exhaling slowly through her mouth, she counted to seven. She heard Alex urge Roman to make himself a drink, that he'd be right back. A minute later, he pushed into the small butler's pantry.

Elaine was hurt and angry and she wasn't about to let her brother off the hook. When she was a kid, she always thought that having a brother was a lot like having a gerbil. They were fun, but they were also kind of useless. She wasn't sure her opinion had changed. "In case you've forgotten, my daughter just tried to end her life. Do you think I want to sit across the table from that buffoon?"

"Lower your voice, okay? Your jealousy is showing."

"Why do you always defend him?" She figured she knew the answer, but it wasn't the time or place to discuss that now. "He's a weasel, Alex, with a ridiculous French accent. He sounds like Pepé Le Pew." And he looked like him, too, with his slicked-back silver gray hair and thin mustache. As far as she was concerned, Roman Marchand gave French Canadians a bad name. Maybe that's why he'd been run out of Toronto on a rail—or was that just one of her daydreams?

"How's Tracy doing?" asked Alex. He looked fresh and tanned, recently showered and shaved, dressed in a yellow polo shirt and khaki cargo pants. Apparently, celebrating an unsuccessful suicide attempt wasn't a formal occasion.

"She's . . . okay."

"Just okay?"

"She's peachy keen. What do you want me to say?" The tension between her shoulder blades was growing worse. She needed a glass of wine. Or maybe someone could just put a paper bag over her head and tell her when it was over. Glancing into the kitchen she saw Mrs. Knox, the cook, frosting a chocolate cake with whipping cream. Just what she needed. Empty calories.

Alex stepped closer and gave her a hug. "Come on, Lanie. It's going to be okay. If that therapist can't help her, we'll find someone who can."

She relaxed against him. It felt nice. If nothing else, he was a sturdy gerbil. "I wish it were that simple. By the way, Danny's here."

Alex backed up, holding her by her shoulders. "Did you call him?"

"Nope. He just arrived out of the blue. Said he needed a break."

"That's weird. I wonder if he and Ruth are having problems."

"He didn't say anything about it. On the other hand, I only talked to him for a couple of minutes. Actually, I'm glad he's here. It gives me one more pair of eyes to watch Tracy."

"Do you think she'll try it again?"

"She says she won't."

He slipped his hands into his pockets. "I wish someone would tell me what's wrong with that kid, why she's in therapy in the first place. I mean, maybe I could help."

"It's her decision, Alex. Her life. I have to respect that."

"Yeah, I suppose. Look, Elaine, just so that you know. I'll do anything—and I mean anything—to help. Just name it. Day or night. I'm your man."

She brushed a lock of blond hair away from his forehead. "Thanks."

He ducked his head and whispered, "Where's the dragon?"

"In her study."

"You doing okay with her? She hasn't been breathing too much fire at you today?"

"She's been in one of her more sanguine moods. She did a fifteen-minute rant on modern psychology, but that's about it."

He offered her his arm. "Shall we present a united front?"

At this moment, Elaine adored her older brother. She wished they could always be this supportive, this connected, but she knew that life had a way of messing up relationships. "You're on," she said, linking her arm with his.

Together, they bumped their way, laughing, out of the pantry. They were met in the living room by Danny and Roman, who were standing by the fireplace, drinks in hand, talking quietly.

Danny was all dressed up. With his graying blond hair and trim build, he looked terrific. He was a good foot shorter than Alex. Shorter and leaner. Alex was into his body in a way Danny never had been. Elaine knew that Danny, as a New Yorker, walked a lot. Alex, on the other hand, worked out at the gym, keeping himself not only fit but buff. She also had a sneaking suspicion that he was dyeing his hair these days. The blond had changed slightly from the blond of old. The new color had more red in it. All in all, they were a good family, a good-looking family—and a family of total opposites. That last part was the rub.

Before Elaine sat down to dinner she puffed back up-stairs for the umpteenth time to check on Tracy. She and Mick were lying on the king-sized bed watching a horror flick, laughing hysterically at the dialogue and hokey sets. So far, so good.

Returning to the dining room, Elaine found that the family had gathered around the table. A sixth member of the party had been added while she was upstairs. Dr. Walter Holland, otherwise known as Doc, was seated next to her mother. He was not only her mother's best friend, but he was her only confidant as well.

Doc Holland was in his late seventies, plump, with thinning white hair and thick glasses. He'd retired from his medical practice long ago. He needed a cane to help him get around these days, but other than that, he seemed to be in good health. Everyone treated him like an uncle, and he seemed to bask in the attention. He'd never married and he had no children. As far as Elaine knew, he was also the only man who could make her mother giggle. The two of them played canasta together nearly every night.

Even though Elaine was surrounded by friends and family, dinner was a struggle. She didn't talk much, but listened as others carried the conversation. Alex and Roman struck her as unusually secretive tonight, passing meaningful looks back and forth. At the same time, they came off as extremely upbeat—too upbeat for the occasion. Danny was almost as subdued as Elaine. His comments seemed occasionally biting. Not that he wasn't a master of sarcasm when he wanted to be, but this seemed different somehow, almost as if he was trying to distance himself from everyone at the table. Elaine didn't get it and thought that, in her present condition, she must not be reading him—or anyone—correctly.

"You look so pretty tonight, Mom," said Alex, taking a sip of coffee.

"I concur," chimed in Roman, wiping his bright red little mouth with a napkin.

What an asinine, thoroughly tight-assed way to put it, thought Elaine, searching the table for the wine bottle.

"Nobody at my age looks pretty," said Millie.

Elaine knew her mother hated being around old people. It was one of the main reasons she was so concerned about money. She refused to end up in a nursing home, drooling along with the riffraff. If she was going to drool, she wanted to do it in the privacy of her own home, with a staff to wipe her chin—and anything else that needed wiping. She often said that she found old age ugly and generally pathetic, which meant, of course, that that's how she viewed herself. Elaine, on the other hand, truly believed that there was something almost beatific in the faces of old people. She'd always been drawn to the elderly, far more than to the other end of the spectrum: children. But when she tried to explain this to her mother, her mom just brushed it off by saying "Wait till you get old. You won't find it so 'beautiful' then."

Maybe her mom was right. Elaine wasn't feeling very sure about anything tonight, especially her own judgment. She returned her attention to the filet of sole, which was suitably blah. The roasted brussels sprouts were okay. Mrs. Knox had made them in honor of Danny's arrival. Incomprehensible as it was, brussels sprouts were Danny's favorite vegetable. He craved them the way other people craved chocolate.

Nobody talked much about Tracy, and for that Elaine

was grateful. She'd spoken of little else since last night and desperately needed a break. She'd already had too much wine, but she figured she was allowed. Actually, as she looked around the table, everyone, except for her mom, was drinking more than usual. Coming face-to-face with suicide was probably taking a toll.

As the dessert plates were removed and the final round of coffee poured, Alex cleared his throat and said that there was something he'd like to discuss with everyone. He said he knew it was bad timing, but he'd started a process in motion many months ago and now needed to talk about it. All he needed was ten minutes.

Elaine had been planning to hit the couch in the music room and check out for a few hours, but Alex seemed so keyed up, she felt it was only fair to stay and hear him out. She glanced at Marchand and saw that he was chewing his bottom lip, looking nervous.

"Okay," began Alex, pushing back from the table and crossing his legs, "this may sound like it's coming out of the blue, but I've been thinking seriously about this for almost a year. Mom, everyone, I believe it's time to take Veelund Industries public."

"Public?" repeated Danny. He seemed puzzled by the proposition.

"Just listen, all right?" said Alex. "Let me explain. This past winter, I had our annualized revenues pulled for the last five years. I gave them to a financial service company—P.J.I. in Boston. In today's market, you can't just tread water. You either grow or you die. We need to expand, add to our visibility, but to do that we need money. I want to build on Dad's dreams. Not just with the Log Lodges, but with all our divisions. Going public would allow us access to new capital through both equity and debt financing. We'd be able to attract better people if we could offer stock options. We convert our debt to equity and strengthen the company's balance sheet. It's win win."

Nobody said anything for several long moments.

Finally, Danny crossed his arms. "You want to do this through an IPO?"

"Possibly. We could do it more quickly through a reverse takeover."

"What's that?" asked Elaine. Her head was throbbing.

"It's complicated," said Marchand.

"Meaning what?" said Elaine. "Women can't possibly understand?"

"No, of course not," said Alex. "If you want me to take you through it step by step, I will. But for now, let's just address the basic concept. Should we take the company public? I think the answer is yes."

Danny looked over at Elaine. "There's a significant cost associated with going public, I believe. I've spent a lot of time studying the stock market, as well as investing in it. This last downturn has nearly finished me off. I'm not sure that's where we want to be."

"Wall Street will kill you," muttered Doc, adjusting his glasses, "if you miss."

"I'd like us to take the next step," said Alex, ignoring them both. "I want to hire P.J.I. to help us with the process. As far as I'm concerned it's no guts, no glory. We need to hire additional key personnel, possibly even start looking to acquire additional businesses to complement our core company."

"We already have good employees," said Elaine, still chewing on the no guts, no glory comment. Who did he think he was? General Patton? If the company went public, it would change everything. Veelund Industries would suddenly be responsible to a bunch of faceless shareholders who would demand to be informed about business practices, financial stats, budgets, changes in management, or anything else that might materially affect the cost of the stock. It sounded like a nightmare—not at all like the company her father had begun in the sixties.

"We need someone who can speak to the public," continued Alex. "I, for one, would like to nominate Roman for that job."

"You've *got* to be kidding," said Elaine. She couldn't believe her brother was that stupid. "Have you lost your mind?"

Marchand stiffened.

"The main problem I see," said Danny, glancing at his mother, "is that the family would lose flexibility, particularly with actions that would require shareholder approval."

Bingo, thought Elaine. Give that man a cigar. She poured herself more wine.

"You mean *control*, don't you, dear?" said Millie. All through the discussion, she'd remained silent. But everyone knew she had the final say.

"That's too simplistic," said Alex. "You need to come to the office, let me lay it all out for you."

"That won't be necessary." Her eyes traveled slowly from face to face. "I'm sorry you did all that work. You should have consulted me first. Not only are we not taking Veelund Industries public, I'm planning to sell the company."

"What?" Had Elaine heard her correctly? *"Sell?"*

"Yes."

"Why?"

"For a multitude of reasons, not the least of which is

the uncertainty in the American economy. After what happened on nine-eleven, I made a decision. Who knows what crazy thing could happen to this country? The world has grown too precarious to have major assets sitting out there without protection. Even a small terrorist attack could send us into deep recession, possibly even a depression. I want all my investments as safe and secure as possible, and that means I intend to sell the company within the year. I already have two buyers waiting for my decision, and one is about to put in a bid." She turned to Alex. "Your going ahead with your plans without consulting me only further proves my point. Veelund Industries belongs to me, Alex. Your father wanted his fortune passed on to his family, and I'll make sure that happens. But he gave the company to me because he trusted my judgment. After I'm gone, you'll all be quite rich. I promise that none of you will be hurt by my decision to sell. If you'd like to continue working for the new company, we'll make that a provision of the sale. One day you'll all understand why I did this, and you'll thank me."

"You can't be serious," said Alex. He looked dumbfounded.

"I'm perfectly serious."

"But . . . what about my company?" asked Roman. "I'm not one of your children. What happens to me?"

"I'm afraid your division has complicated this sale, Mr. Marchand. It was a bad decision to buy Kitchen Visions. I'm sorry I ever agreed to it. Alex felt it would be an interesting experiment, and I agreed. But it hasn't turned out well."

"But, as you said, the entire economy is in a downturn."

"At this point, it's all moot. Decisions have been made.

I'm sorry this couldn't work out to everyone's benefit, but that's the way it is sometimes. Alex, next week we need to set up meetings with all our division heads. My legal team will brief everyone on what's about to happen."

Alex looked as if he'd been hit over the head with a shovel. "You can't do this to me, not after all the hard work I've put in."

"Mom," said Elaine, her head drooping into her hands, "I can't talk about this tonight."

"We don't need to," said Millie, struggling to push her chair back from the table.

Danny stood and helped her. Quietly he muttered, "I was hoping we could talk privately for a few minutes."

"This discussion is over."

"No . . . I don't want to talk about the sale. It's something . . . more personal."

Millie sighed, patting his arm. "I'm too tired, dear. I'm going to turn in early." Addressing everyone, she said, "Will someone tell Zander to bring my medication up to my room? Doc, I'll see you tomorrow. The rest of you, well, I suppose you can take another crack at me in the morning, but it won't change my mind."

On that note, she turned and walked out of the room.

Elaine's head sank down farther against her hands. In twenty-four hours her daughter and her mother had managed to blow her entire life to smithereens. All this talk about terrorists seemed like nothing but a red herring. Why did you need a terrorist to create chaos when you had the love of a good family?

10

An arm waving a white silk handkerchief oozed inside Sophie's office door. The cuff links on the shirt belonged to Bram, so Sophie assumed the body did, too.

"What are you doing?" she asked, tossing her pen on the desktop. She'd been at work since seven A.M.

"Asking for permission to enter," came his deep voice.

"Do you need permission?"

"You tell me." He opened the door, a strained smile on his face. "I've come to grovel."

"Well then, better sit down. It's no fun groveling and standing at the same time."

Sophie had been working on a new program she was designing for the Maxfield. She called it the Corporate Connection. It was meant specifically for frequent business travelers and she hoped to have it up and running by the time her father returned, though that seemed optimistic.

"You got up awfully early this morning," he said, pulling up a chair. He unbuttoned his herringbone sport coat, then straightened his tie.

"I couldn't sleep."

"Because of me?"

"You? Why would you prevent me from sleeping?"

"You're upset with me. Because of Margie."

"I am?"

"You don't think I should have offered her one of the Maxfield's apartments. If I've overstepped, Sophie, I'm sorry. I know, in theory, the hotel belongs to both of us, but it's really yours. We both know that. I just thought, having her here would be so fantastic. I'd actually get to see her every now and then."

"I think it's fine, sweetheart. Really. I'm just not sure—" She could hardly say that she knew he'd written Margie a sizable check. After all, she shouldn't have been snooping, and if he gave his daughter money that was up to him. Sophie simply felt uncomfortable around Margie, and being a sensitive sort of guy, Bram had picked up on it. "Look, I'm happy that Margie's here, truly I am, particularly because it makes you happy."

"But not you."

"No, it's not that." She'd been dreading this conversation, though she knew it was coming.

"You two have never really bonded, Soph. That's the problem."

"I agree. But I'm not sure how to change it. I mean, I tried years ago, but Margie resisted. I hoped we could be friends, but it never happened."

"But it could, if you spent time with her. She's grown up a lot since high school. She's not the same person. We're a lot alike. You love me. I think you could love her, too."

Sophie's take on Margie was a little different from her husband's, but she knew he was right. She had to try harder. Bram had been so generous when Rudy, Sophie's son, had come to stay with them. It was right before his freshman year at the university. Against his father's wishes, he'd left Montana. Rudy was gay, and he knew that if he stayed, he'd have to hide his sexuality. He needed a safe place where he could figure out his life. That had become Sophie and Bram's home. Bram had done his best to make Rudy feel welcome. And that's why Sophie needed to make a greater effort when it came to Margie. The tension in the air between them was probably all in Sophie's head. She just needed a little time to smooth things out.

"I've got the perfect opportunity for you," said Bram, stuffing his white silk handkerchief back in the breast pocket of his sport coat. "I know it's Saturday, but something came up at the station and I need to run over there."

"Will you be gone long?"

"Actually, next Thursday, I was supposed to interview a woman about her new book. She's an ornithologist with a pet parrot. The book's about the woman's relationship with the parrot. It's pretty bizarre stuff. Anyway, her tour got rearranged and she's coming through town today. I tape the interview this morning or I don't get it at all."

"I thought you'd made plans to take Margie shopping for a new couch."

"I had." He lifted his eyebrows and gave her a slow smile.

"You want me to do it?"

"Your taste in furniture is almost as good as mine."

"Gee, thanks for the vote of confidence."

His smile widened.

"Actually—" She glanced at her watch. "Elaine invited me out to Prairie Lodge for lunch. Remember? I told you my dad wants a log house built up on Pokegama Lake. There are several models on the Veelund property I'm supposed to look at."

"Fine," said Bram. "The couch can wait. Why don't you take Margie with you? I'm sure she'd love to see the log houses. And you two could do a little . . . bonding . . . in the car on the way."

He was pushing, but she couldn't blame him. "Do you really think she'd want to? I doubt log houses are really her thing."

"She'd love it."

"You know, Bram, sometimes I think she wishes you'd married someone else."

"Nonsense." He retrieved a cell phone from his pocket. As he punched in the numbers, he said, "You're sure you're okay with asking her to come along?"

"Fine with me," said Sophie, trying not to look trapped.

Sophie hadn't visited Prairie Lodge in almost eight years, not since Elaine's last wedding. It was a good hour's drive from St. Paul—freeway about a third of the way, and then two-lane country roads heading southwest. Margie and Sophie managed some small talk at first. Margie thought Sophie's short, strawberry blond hair was a dye job and wanted to know the name of the color. Sophie assured her it wasn't. Margie talked a little about how much she used to hate Minneapolis. In high school, she thought it was sleepy and dumb and couldn't wait to go live someplace else. Just as they were leaving the St. Paul city limits, Margie asked, "Who's Nathan?"

Sophie turned to look at her. "Nathan?"

"I don't know his last name. Dad just said 'Nathan.' "

"In what context?"

"That he was an old boyfriend of yours. That he owns some big fancy restaurant in town."

"It's in Stillwater. What else did your father say?"

"Just that he was back in town. He's a chef, right?"

Sophie nodded.

"Dad said he didn't like him."

"Why was he talking to you about Nathan?"

Margie shrugged. "I guess maybe he needed to vent a little. He knows I care about him."

And I *don't*, thought Sophie, gripping the steering wheel more tightly. Margie was the last person Bram should be confiding in about any perceived marital problems. Not that Nathan was a problem.

"I guess maybe he's kind of jealous. Do you see this guy a lot?"

"No, certainly not."

"Well, whatever. I suppose that since he's still around it sort of bothers Dad."

This was all news to Sophie. Bram hadn't even mentioned Nathan's name in over a year. She hated herself for thinking this next thought, but what if Bram had asked Margie to feel out the situation? What if he was using her as a go-between, a way to ferret out information? Suddenly, the earth under Sophie's feet seemed to shift.

"Nathan Buckridge and I are just friends—not even friends, really. We used to be friends."

"But you had dinner at his restaurant the other night."

"Yes, it's my job. I review new restaurants, Margie. I can't ignore Nathan's just because we once had a relationship."

"Dad said you almost married him."

"I was eighteen. That was a long time ago."

"So, you don't have a thing for him anymore? You and my dad are still tight?"

"Of course we are. Where's all this coming from? Does your father think I'm still involved with Nathan?"

"No, not really. Actually, he didn't say all that much about him. I was just reading between the lines."

"Well, there's nothing to read."

"Okay."

Sophie wasn't sure it was okay, but she couldn't let it show. That would only add more fuel to a fire Sophie wanted to douse. And yet she realized that Margie's comments had left her shaken. What if Margie had picked up on something Bram was really worried about? Sophie thought Nathan was a dead issue between them. But what if Bram was still chewing on it, still in doubt about her affections?

Sophie figured it was best to change the subject, so she took a few minutes to explain about Elaine's daughter's suicide attempt. It seemed to both horrify and intrigue Margie. They talked about death for a while, but Margie eventually grew tired of the topic and slipped in a CD. She spent the rest of the drive humming along with Counting Crows as she gazed out the side window. Sophie was relieved to be able to sink back into her own thoughts. She had the impression that Margie hadn't really wanted to come along, but that, like Sophie, she'd succumbed to Bram's pressure.

It was close to noon by the time Sophie's Lexus rolled onto the paved drive in front of the four-car garage. Like everything else on the property, the garage was made of logs. Elaine was sitting on the front porch, but rose when she saw the car, padding barefoot down the front steps and across the wide lawn to greet them. Sophie introduced Margie, and after a short conversation about how hot the weather was for mid-September, the three of them entered the house.

Sophie had always loved Prairie Lodge. The log walls made the interior look like it was bathed in honey. The faint smell of cedar was deliciously rustic, and took Sophie back to another place and time. Her grandparents on her father's side had owned a log cabin up on Deer Lake in northern Minnesota. As a child, Sophie had spent many wonderful fall nights there, sitting in front of the fire. The Veelund home was far more grand, and yet the construction had a simplicity that appealed to her.

As they walked into the cool of the kitchen, Elaine explained that Tracy and Mick were about to take a swim. She wondered out loud if Margie would like to join them. There were extra swimsuits in the pool house.

When Mick breezed into the kitchen to grab some drinks from the fridge, he nodded to everyone, but stopped when he saw Margie. "Baldric?" he said, a slow grin forming.

"Frye?" Margie responded.

"Shit, lady, get over here and give me a hug!"

Sophie and Elaine stood in surprised silence as Mick and Margie slapped hands and then embraced.

"What are you doin' here?" asked Mick.

"I came with my stepmom," said Margie.

Sophie had never heard Margie call her by that name before and it caused a moment of pure panic. Stepmothers were horrible creatures with hair on their chins and warts on their faces, fairy-tale crones who baked their children in gingerbread ovens. Sophie couldn't possibly be a *stepmother*.

"Do you have to stay . . . in here?" asked Mick, glancing at Elaine. "Why don't you come out to the pool, meet my girlfriend."

Margie turned around to look at Sophie. "You don't mind, do you?"

"Fine with me," said Sophie. "But first, tell me, how do you two know each other?"

"High school," they both answered, almost in unison.

"Actually," said Margie, "we both liked this one local band, so we met for the first time in a bar. We kind of followed them around town and struck up a friendship along the way."

They both seemed anxious to leave the kitchen.

"You go have fun," said Elaine, waving them off.

After they'd gone, Sophie saw that Elaine had set fresh bagel sandwiches out on the kitchen counter next to a bowl of cut-up strawberries and cantaloupe. The coffee had already been brewed. But Elaine, too, seemed anxious to leave.

"What's up?" asked Sophie, picking up a sandwich.

"Let's get out of here." On the way out the back door, Elaine whispered, "You'll never believe what happened last night."

As they crossed the patio and headed for the garage, they ran into Elaine's mother and Doc Holland, who looked as if they'd just come back from a walk. Doc's big, good-natured face was red and damp. He carried a handkerchief balled up in one hand and used it to wipe the sweat away from his forehead.

"Sophie," said Millie, coming to a full stop. "What a nice surprise. Elaine told me you were coming today. Something about your dad wanting us to build a log house for him."

Millie had aged since the last time Sophie had seen her. Aged and put on weight. Even with a smile on her face, she looked dour.

"You know, Sophie," said Millie, steadying herself by taking hold of the fence. "An idea came to me last night, one I'd like to talk over with you." She glanced up at the house. "I'm thinking of turning my home into a bed-and-breakfast."

Elaine's jaw dropped.

"I spoke to my granddaughter about it this morning, and—"

"What's Tracy got to do with it?" said Elaine, cutting her off.

"I'm doing it for her. She would be the person to run the business and eventually own it. Why not get some use out of the old place? It's a good idea, Elaine, so stop looking like you just swallowed ground glass. It will give Tracy something to focus on, something other than her problems. In case you're interested, she really took to the idea. This house would make a perfect bed-and-breakfast. We have a tennis court, a pool, a lovely garden, and twelve empty bedrooms upstairs. If Mrs. Knox doesn't want to stay on as the cook, we'd find someone else. Sophie, you run a hotel. I thought you could give me some pointers on how to put my idea to work."

"Well," began Sophie. She wasn't sure where to go from there.

"I know you're here to see Elaine today," said Millie, taking hold of Doc's arm, "but come back first thing Monday morning. I'm happy to pay you a consulting fee. Just name your price. Tracy and I will both meet with you."

Sophie and Elaine exchanged glances.

"Fine," said Sophie.

"Good. We'll see you then." Millie and Doc continued on their way to the back door.

Elaine eyed them for a moment, then turned and stomped off toward the garage. Sophie took another bite of her sandwich and hurried after her. By the time she caught up, Elaine had opened one of the doors and was backing up what looked like an electric golf cart, complete with front and back seats, and a yellow canvas canopied top with the words *Veelund Log Lodges* stamped on the side in bold black letters.

"Get in," said Elaine.

"Your mom's full of surprises."

"You don't know the half of it."

"Where are we going?"

"I'm taking you on a tour of the cottages."

As they bumped along a dirt road, Sophie nibbled on her sandwich. "How's Tracy doing today?"

Elaine stared straight ahead. "It's hard to say. She sounds fine. She's eating normally, which means with no interest in nutrition. She promised to stop drinking, although her therapist doesn't think she has an actual drinking problem. She talks and acts just like she always did. But . . . trying to end your own life has to change a person, right? Except, I don't see any changes. She acts like it didn't happen. That worries me."

"Is she still talking to a therapist?"

"Absolutely. The woman was here most of the day yesterday, and she's stopping by later this afternoon." Elaine grew silent.

As they came down the rise behind the garage, Sophie could see three log cabins in the hazy distance. Now that they were away from the tended grass around the main house and into the higher prairie grass, the hot scent of baked earth rose up all around them.

Glancing over at Sophie, Elaine said, "Tracy doesn't

want anyone to find out what happened to her when she was a teenager." Stopping the cart, she turned her head away. "If I tell you a secret, Sophie, will you promise to keep it to yourself?"

A swarm of bees suddenly materialized inside Sophie's chest.

"You were always good at keeping secrets."

"I still am," said Sophie.

"Then listen to this."

11

"I feel like . . . like I'm going to explode if I don't talk to someone about it," said Elaine, her eyes scanning the high grass. "Normally, I'd confide in my family, but that's just it. They're part of the problem. Not that that's anything new." She hesitated, then started again. "I'm sorry to dump all over you, Soph, but I need to vent. I need someone I can trust."

"You can trust me," said Sophie. She'd been Elaine's vent-ee many times before. As far back as high school.

"I know," said Elaine, reaching over and squeezing Sophie's hand. "You're a good person. I should be more like you."

"I wouldn't go that far."

Heat rose off the land in waves.

"This is hard to talk about," began Elaine. "As a mother, I should have known what was happening. I should have protected my daughter."

That sounded ominous, thought Sophie. She could just about guess what was coming next.

"Apparently, when Tracy was eight, she was . . . molested."

"My God, Elaine. I'm so, so sorry."

She held up her hand. "It didn't just happen once, but

over a period of years. I don't know a lot of the details. The man who did it warned her that if she ever told anyone, he'd kill her. She believed him."

"How awful!"

"Tracy still refuses to say who did it."

"You mean she hasn't even told you?"

"She hasn't told anyone, not even her therapist. I think she's still frightened by him."

"He's still around?"

"Tracy said he is. The only thing I know for sure is that it wasn't her father, and it wasn't my third husband. My first husband died before she turned eight, so it couldn't have been him."

"Maybe it was a teacher, or—"

"It wasn't. She said it always happened in the grove just south of the tennis court. For years, Tracy wouldn't go near the tennis court and I never understood why. Now I do."

"Do you think it was a member of the family?"

"That's a pretty small group, Sophie. Two people. Alex and Danny." She covered her face with her hands. "How can I think something so terrible about my own brothers?"

Sophie rubbed Elaine's back, feeling a rush of tenderness toward her.

"It's like . . . like I'm standing next to something so huge I can't even see it."

"There had to be other men around," said Sophie.

"Not many. Mom always kept her work life separate from her private life. The only other men who've been around consistently are Zander—he's lived at the house since before Tracy was born—and then Doc Holland. He's been a friend of the family since before I was born."

"You can't think of any other men who—"

"The mailman?"

The suggestion was such a ridiculous stretch, they both laughed.

"Tracy won't say a name, but the vibe I get is that it's someone we all know. And that's part of the problem. Could this monster still be tormenting her? What kind of a mother allows something like that to happen?"

"You've been a good mother, Elaine. But you don't have eyes in the back of your head. No mother does."

"Except for my mother."

"And mine."

Sophie tossed her sandwich away. She'd lost her appetite. "Under the circumstances, maybe your mom's house isn't the best place for Tracy."

"But that's just it. Tracy's the one who suggested it. Of course, that was after her doctor and her therapist insisted she be admitted to Langston Hills."

"The private mental hospital?"

"Tracy nearly went berserk. I thought the doctors would have to sedate her. The idea of being locked up terrifies her, Sophie. How could I do that to her? She's already been horribly injured. When she suggested coming to Mom's place to recuperate, I gave in. Mom thought it was a perfect idea. She doesn't know anything about the molestation, and I promised I wouldn't tell. Mom has staff around to help out, and I've hired a private bodyguard to watch over Tracy. That way she'll be safe. As safe as I can make her."

"You're really in a bad spot."

"Don't I know. The thing is, Tracy used to come and stay at Mom's place all the time, especially during the summers. I thought she loved it out here. But when she started getting a little older, all that changed. I get it now, but at the time I thought it had something to do with Mom—that she was being her old pushy, obnoxious self and that Tracy was sick of it. But you know Mom. She insisted that Tracy come for two weeks every July. And you know that when my mother insists, even Tracy had to give in. But neither of us knew what was happening behind the scenes. If we had—" Her mouth trembled and she looked away.

Sophie's heart went out to her.

After a few moments, Elaine shook off the emotion, pulled a tissue out of the pocket of her shorts and blew her nose. "I have to be pragmatic, Soph. I can't fall apart. As I see it, this pedophile has to be one of four people: Alex, Danny, Zander, or Doc. Maybe I'm wrong. Maybe it was someone else, some stranger, but until Tracy tells me the man's name, I'll never know for sure. And that means every time I see one of those men I wonder. I'm angry at them all and I *hate* that."

"None of this is fair."

"I want to shake every one of them, demand to know the truth, but if I did, I'd be betraying Tracy's confidence. Maybe, in the end, it would be worth it. I just don't know anymore."

"When did the molestation stop?"

"When Tracy was thirteen."

"Why did it stop then?"

"I figure the guy's a classic pedophile. She was getting too old. He wasn't attracted to her anymore."

"How does Tracy act around her uncles—around Doc and Zander?"

"Aloof. But she acts aloof around everyone. She doesn't like men. That's been clear since her teenage years. Can you blame her? It's why I brought Mick into the picture. I thought having a safe guy around might help."

"You *brought* him into her life?"

She nodded.

"How? And how do you know he's safe?"

"I'm paying him to be Tracy's friend. He does what I tell him to do."

Sophie wasn't shocked by much, but she was by this. And Elaine thought *her* mother was controlling. "What if Tracy finds out?"

"She won't."

Sophie couldn't fathom how she could be so sure. "Has his presence helped?"

Elaine squinted up at the sky. "I don't know." She sat silently for a few seconds, then pressed her foot to the pedal and drove on. At a fork in the road, she turned right. "As if Tracy's problems weren't enough," she continued, tapping her fingers nervously on the steering wheel, "my mother announced last night that she's selling the company."

Sophie turned to stare at her. "She what?"

"Before the grand announcement, Alex made this big pitch to take the company public, but then Mom nixed it all by saying she'd already found a couple of buyers."

"How . . . how do you feel about that?"

"Like I've been sucker punched. But what can I do? Rip my hair out? Pitch a fit? Mom's mind is made up. I blame Alex for this. It's all his fault."

"Why?"

"Because the company hasn't prospered under his leadership. My division, as I told you the other night— the log lodges—is the only reason we're still in the black. Mom knows it, but she'd rather sell the company than give me the top job, even though I've earned it."

Talk about kicking someone when they're down, thought Sophie. She didn't know what to say.

"When Alex took over the company, he listened to the men my father had hired. He took their advice. Everything went okay for a long time. After I'd been around for a while and felt I had a firm footing, Alex and I formed a kind of partnership. You remember how close we used to be. As the men my dad had placed in positions of authority retired, we took over. Of course, Mom always had the final word. She blew in every morning and arranged her desk for a few hours. But then she'd leave for her usual three-hour lunch. If she got involved in shopping, she wouldn't come back at all."

"Your mother is a study in contradictions."

"Tell me about it. Anyway, Alex and I would talk to everyone, then we'd take our decisions to Mom. She generally went along with what we wanted. But when Roman Marchand came on board in the spring of 1999, everything changed. Suddenly Alex was listening to *him*, going to *him* for advice. Eventually I was edged out."

"I didn't know," said Sophie.

"I opposed buying Kitchen Visions and Roman knew it, so he didn't like me from the get-go. About a year after Marchand arrived, Alex began bellowing like he was some kind of business genius. I realized immediately that it was all the crap Marchand had been feeding him. We were doing so well with the log lodges, and everything associated with that side of the business, that Alex thought he had the magic touch. A year after he bought Kitchen Visions, he acquired a wood-flooring company. Neither have done well. But the real epiphany for me came when I realized that Alex and Marchand's relationship might be more than just business."

"Meaning what?"

"I'm a little slow on the uptake sometimes, Sophie. Marchand is a predator, I get that now. He must have seen Alex coming a mile away. His company needed money to survive. When Veelund Industries bought it—leaving him, I might add, in the top position—he started working on Alex. Flattering him. And more."

"More what?" asked Sophie, not sure where Elaine was headed.

"We're still keeping confidences, right? This stays between us?"

"Sure."

"Okay. I don't know this for an absolute fact, but . . . actually, I think Alex is gay."

"Alex?" Sophie couldn't believe her ears. "He's about as homophobic as they come. Ever since he was a kid."

"He's a cliché. The guy who talks the loudest about hating fags—"

"But he was married."

"Yeah, for about five minutes. And besides, you and I both know being married means nothing. And it threw Mom off the track. I think that's why he did it. He's gotten a lot of mileage out of that five-minute marriage."

"What would your mom do if she found out he was gay?"

"What do you think? He'd be out on his ass. Out of the company and erased from her life. And beyond that, it would kill her. Alex has always been her favorite. That's hard for me to say, but it's true."

"You think he and Marchand are lovers?"

Elaine looked over and gave Sophie a heavy-lidded nod. "I have no proof, but yes, that's exactly what I think. I also believe he's the motivating force behind this idea to take Veelund Industries public. Alex wants to make him the spokesperson for the company. Can you imagine anything more ridiculous?"

"You make Alex sound like a puppet, with no will of his own."

Elaine groaned. "He's in love, Sophie. I've seen it in his eyes. And he looks up to Marchand. Ever since Dad died, Alex has been looking for a mentor. Maybe it's because Marchand is older. It can't be because of his business savvy, because he's a failure, in anyone's book. But aside from all that pop psych crap, if Alex is anything like me, being in love means he's lost his mind." She paused, then shook her head. "And they say *I* have bad taste in men."

"You make love sound like an illness."

"It is."

"That's a rather dark view."

"Maybe so, but that's my experience. And besides, everyone knows testosterone rots the brain."

Sophie couldn't help but laugh.

"Once Mom is gone—"

"After she dies."

"I suppose she could live another fifteen years. Who's to say? But if Marchand can just wait it out—"

"Alex is just a glorified meal ticket?"

Elaine shrugged. "That's the way it looks to me."

"Marchand doesn't care about your brother, even a little?"

"If I'm reading him right, he cares about one person and one person only. Himself."

"Then I feel sorry for Alex."

"I do, too. It must be hard to find a decent guy when

you're hiding in a closet. I'm out there in the world every day and I've never found one."

Sophie had met Marchand once. She remembered a short, compact, rather swarthy man. Tiny mustache. Slicked-back salt-and-pepper hair. Not bad-looking. His taste, as Bram would call it, was "corporate corporate." Expensive business suits. Essentially conservative appearance, but wearing too much heavy gold jewelry to be considered entirely tasteful.

"But if your mother sells the company, then all of Marchand's plans are out the window."

"Exactly," said Elaine. "And so are mine. You think I want that company sold? I could strangle her with my bare hands."

"What does Danny think of all this? Has anyone called him?"

"He's here. He arrived at the house yesterday afternoon."

Sophie brushed bagel crumbs off her khaki slacks. "Because of Tracy?"

"No, he said he just needed a break."

"Interesting timing."

"I suppose. I mean, he never just *drops in*. Leaving New York is always this big production number. He usually brings his wife and kids and about thirty suitcases. I think he's got something on his mind."

"But you have no idea what."

Elaine sighed. "I can't take on any more problems right now, assuming it is a problem." She turned off the dusty dirt road and headed up a gravel path toward one of the log houses. She pulled the cart up next to a dark gray BMW convertible and turned off the motor. "Alex lives in this one." They sat for a few moments looking at it.

"It's beautiful," said Sophie. She remembered when Elaine had built the model homes, but she'd never been in them. "But it's kind of . . . western. Feels like Annie Oakley should meet us at the front door." It was a one-story structure, just a simple rectangle, with a picture window to the right of the door and two smaller windows to the left. The roof swooped down low over a narrow deck that ran the length of the front.

"That's the style. We call it The Ranch House. Alex has lived here for six years. Seems to suit him. The one I moved into five months ago has more of an English country house feel to it. Two-story. We call it Wisteria Cottage. And then the third one is Morningstar House. That one's empty. It's more modern, not my favorite. But we can build to any specifications. All your dad needs to do is tell us what he and your mom like."

"Alex must be home," said Sophie, slipping out of the cart and stretching her arms above her head.

"That isn't Alex's car," said Elaine. The cell phone in the pocket of her shorts gave a ring.

"Whose car is it?"

"Three guesses."

Clicking the phone on, Elaine said hello. "Who?" she asked, still sitting halfway in the cart, halfway out. "Oh, hi. Sure I remember." She turned away from Sophie.

Sophie leaned against the rear fender.

"No, I thought the food was wonderful. Who would have thought an old monastery would make such an amazing spot for a restaurant?"

It had to be Nathan, thought Sophie. She was instantly annoyed. Why was he calling Elaine?

"Sure, I'd love to. But today isn't good. My daughter is . . . ill, and well . . ." She paused. "Really? You know, I have a friend who sells pleasure boats. If you twist my arm, I might even be able to get you a deal." She laughed. "Well, what are friends for?" Silence, then, "Look, I'm in the middle of something. Can I call you later? I'm sure we can figure out a time." Again, she laughed. "I'd forgotten how funny you are. Good, we'll talk this afternoon. Thanks for calling. Bye." She clicked the phone off, then socked the air. "Score!" Swinging out of the cart, she turned to Sophie, a Cheshire cat smile on her face. "You'll never guess who that was."

"Who?"

"Hunky Nathan Buckridge."

"Really?"

"Wasn't that nice of him to call?"

Sophie wanted to ask what he'd said, but knew it was none of her business. Not that she couldn't guess what the gist of the conversation had been about. Nathan had called Elaine to ask for a date.

"Maybe he's just what I need right now. A little diversion."

Sophie hated to think that Nathan would be Elaine's "little diversion." He deserved better. But then, that was his concern, not hers.

As they trooped up the paved walk, Roman Marchand stepped out on the front porch, ending any further discussion.

"Morning, Elaine. Hot day." He nodded to Sophie. "Mrs. Baldric."

He never seemed able to get it that Sophie hadn't taken Bram's last name. She let it pass.

Returning his attention to Elaine, he added, "If you're looking for your brother, he isn't here."

Marchand was wearing a pair of black cotton shorts, sandals, and a black T-shirt. Not his usual business attire.

"Where is he?" asked Elaine.

"Your mother phoned him early this morning. Asked him to come up to the house so they could talk. Alex assumed she wanted to speak to him privately about her plans to sell the company."

"That's funny," said Elaine. "She never mentioned anything to me about it."

"Well, as I said, I believe the conversation was private. Just between the two of them."

His comment seemed to make Elaine angry. "I'm here to show Sophie the house."

Marchand moved in front of the door. "This . . . is not a good moment."

"Alex knows the drill. So do you. I bring people by all the time. Alex keeps the place picked up. It's the price he pays for living here."

"But you always call first."

"Well, I forgot," said Elaine, trying to push past him.

He stood his ground.

"If you don't get out of my way, I'll call the police and have you forcibly removed." There was acid in her tone.

"You would not do that."

"Want to try me?"

"Alex will be angry, Elaine."

"Do you think I care?"

They stood eye to eye. Sophie wasn't sure who would blink first.

Finally, Marchand backed up. "Will you give me a minute to clean up?"

"No." Elaine bumped past him.

As Sophie entered the house, she saw that the dining

room table was cluttered with dirty breakfast dishes. The door to the bedroom was open. Elaine was already standing by the bed, looking down at a bunch of clothes on the floor. It seemed pretty obvious that Marchand had spent the night. Both sides of the king-sized bed looked rumpled. A bottle of wine and two glasses sat on the nightstand.

Elaine kicked the clothes out of her way as she returned to the living room. "I demand an explanation."

Marchand sat down on the couch. He'd obviously cast himself as the reasonable one in this interaction. "What should I explain, Elaine?"

"Are you sleeping with my brother?"

He looked up at her with innocent eyes. "I do not think that is any of your business."

"Are you?"

"I will not respond to such a question." He pressed his lips together tightly and looked away.

"If I tell my mother what's going on between you two—"

He stood to face her. "You know nothing."

"I know you've single-handedly ruined my father's company. If it hadn't been for you and your destructive influence on my brother, my mother wouldn't be forced to sell."

"Are you so sure that's the reason, Elaine? Have you ever thought that maybe there's another one?"

"Like what?"

"Your mother is not a stupid woman. She can see what's happening. She's trying to head off an all-out war between you and your brother."

"You're wrong."

"Am I? It is *you* who has caused her to make this sale. I'm surprised you cannot see it." Poking a finger at her, he added, "I hold *you* responsible for the destruction of *my* company."

They glared at each other.

The ring of Sophie's cell phone broke the strained silence. "Excuse me," she said, retrieving the phone from her pocket. She stepped out on the front porch. "This is Sophie."

"Hi, it's Glen Mortonsen—from the station."

Glen was Bram's producer. He sounded agitated.

"Is something wrong?"

"It's Bram. The paramedics just took him to the hospital."

The ground beneath Sophie's feet vanished. "Is it his heart? Is he okay?"

"He was doing this interview with the parrot woman, Sophie, when he suddenly got dizzy. He said he had some chest pain, so I called the paramedics. I said I'd call you. He wants you to meet him at the hospital."

"I will. Thanks, Glen." All she could think of was that she was an hour away from the city. Too far. She had to get back to the main house, grab Margie and leave right away.

Hurrying back inside, she saw that Elaine and Roman were still sparring, but she couldn't focus on anything but her husband. "Elaine, Bram's been taken to the hospital. I've got to get back."

Elaine seemed startled. "Oh my God."

"You've got to drive me back to your mom's house so I can get my car."

"Sure. Right away."

As they rushed out, Elaine called, "We're not done, Marchand."

12

Sophie dropped Margie off at the emergency room entrance, then parked the car in the lot. When she finally made it to Bram's room, she found him sitting up on the gurney, fully clothed except for his sport coat. Margie was sitting next to him, holding his hand. A nurse stood on the other side of him taking his blood pressure.

Sophie gave Bram a kiss on his forehead. She wished Margie would move so she could sit down with him, but she didn't look like she was about to vacate her spot anytime soon. "What do the doctors say?"

Bram's expression was full of irritation. "This has all been a stupid overreaction. I had some indigestion, that's all. I felt a little dizzy. So what does my producer do? He has a meltdown. Baldric's on his deathbed again. Call the National Guard."

"It's important to be careful, Dad," said Margie, slipping her arm around his back. "You're a pretty important guy. I don't want to lose you."

He smiled at her. "Thanks, sweetheart."

The nurse stepped in front of him.

"That goes for me, too," said Sophie, waving her hand to get his attention. She couldn't help but feel as if her comment was somehow lessened because Margie had said it first. Get a grip, she told herself. She was being entirely too touchy. What mattered was that Bram was okay. "You *are* okay, right?" asked Sophie.

"He had an EKG," said the nurse. "Everything was normal."

"See," said Bram. "I'm fine. Can I get out of here now?"

The nurse checked the chart. "Your doctor's in the hospital. She wants to see you before you leave. I think she may have ordered one more test."

"Oh, just great," said Bram, hanging his head. "Some new form of Chinese water torture, no doubt." Looking up at her, he added, "Whatever it is, does it hurt?"

"*Daaaad,*" said Margie, her voice growing nasal. "You're such a baby."

"It's part of my charm."

"No, Mr. Baldric. It won't hurt."

Bram glanced at Sophie. "How's Elaine?"

"Long story."

"Oh, goodie. Save it for bedtime. I love juicy bedtime news."

"If you ladies will step out to the waiting room," said the nurse, pulling the curtain around the bed.

"Sophie, will you take my sport coat with you?" asked Bram. "One of the paramedics stuffed it in that bag over there. It's probably wrinkled beyond repair."

Margie hopped off the bed. "I'll get it."

As they were about to leave, a petite, attractive, brown-haired woman pushed her way in through the curtain. "We've got to stop meeting like this, Baldric. You're wife's going to catch on." She winked at Sophie, then smiled at Bram, taking the chart from the nurse and giving herself a moment to study it.

Dr. Anne Schaefer had always reminded Sophie of Debra Winger. Throaty voice. Nice-looking—and with a great deal of intelligence behind those dark brown eyes. Sophie liked her. Most important, she thought Schaefer was a good doctor.

"Hmm, well, everything looks fine. Your EKG was normal. Blood pressure is good. Tell me about the pain. Where was it?"

He pointed to a spot closer to his stomach than his heart.

"Do you feel it now?"

"No. It's gone. But earlier, it was like I'd eaten one too many bowling balls."

"Have you eaten any bowling balls today?"

"No."

"Have you had this same feeling before?"

He nodded.

"Recently?"

"Yes, but this was a little worse."

"Instead of a one-bowling-ball pain it was more like a three-bowling-ball pain?"

"Exactly."

"You don't make my life easy, Baldric."

"Haven't you ever felt like you'd eaten a bowling ball?"

"Not that I recall." She stepped behind him, pulled up his shirt, and pressed her stethoscope to his back. "And the dizziness. Have you had that before?"

"Never."

"Breathe deeply."

He rolled his eyes, but did as she asked.

"Yup, I can hear it."

"Hear what?" asked Sophie.

"His heart. It's still there." She moved around to the front and listened to his chest again. "Sounds good." Taking off the stethoscope and wrapping it around her neck, she added, "But there is another test I want to do. It won't hurt and it won't take long."

"What do you think the pain was all about?" asked Sophie.

"It could have been gas. Or indigestion. But combined with the dizziness, we need to be sure this gets checked out thoroughly." Narrowing her eyes at Bram in mock seriousness, she said, "So you can live to flirt another day."

"It's my raison d'être."

"We'll be in the waiting room," said Sophie, giving Bram one last kiss. "Thanks, Anne."

"I'll have him back to you in less than an hour."

Sophie and Margie found a couple of empty chairs near the windows. Margie asked Sophie if she wanted a cup of coffee, but Sophie was already so nervous, she didn't want to add to it. She couldn't believe this was happening. Bram had been feeling so well. She was glad Dr. Schaefer tended to be conservative, always erring on the side of caution. If there was a problem, she'd get to the bottom of it.

Margie returned with her coffee, grabbing a *People* magazine before sitting down. She flipped it open, looked at a couple of pictures, then turned to Sophie and said, "Dad looked a little pale this morning, didn't you think?"

"Pale," repeated Sophie. "No, not really."

"He seemed upset. Stressed. I'm worried about him. Maybe he's exercising too much."

"I think he's discussed all that with his doctor."

"You mean that woman we just met? She's his doctor?"

Sophie nodded.

"She's really cute. I could tell Dad thought so, too."

"Really."

"Yeah." Margie flipped to the next page. "Do you feel threatened when Dad finds other women attractive?"

"Excuse me?"

"I just wonder how it will be when I get married and my husband is so obviously flirty with someone who's younger or prettier than I am."

"I'm sure you'll cope."

"I suppose." Margie read for a moment, then continued, "For an old guy, Dad's pretty cute. He's got that Cary Grant thing going. People used to tell him all the time that he looked like Cary Grant."

"They still do. I think he's sick of hearing it."

"Oh, don't kid yourself. He loves it."

Sophie would have preferred a few peaceful moments, but Margie obviously wanted to talk. Perhaps it was the way she expressed her nervousness. Whatever it was, the inevitability of a lengthy conversation led Sophie to change the subject. "Did you and Mick and Tracy have a nice swim?"

"Yeah, it's a great pool. Mick's really lucked into a sweet situation, if you ask me. He's not a terribly motivated guy, so hooking up with a rich girl was a stroke of luck."

"I thought they were just friends."

Margie snorted. "Hell, no. He's head-over-heels in love with her. I mean, he is *totally* gaga, treats her like a princess. I don't think she's quite as hot and heavy for him as he is for her, but she's lucky. He's a great guy."

"How well do you know him?"

"I haven't talked to him in years." She picked up her

coffee, blew on it, then took a sip. "But the summer after high school, we were pretty close. I'd say we talked probably every day. I was dating Lance Crawford at the time, and Mick was dating a girl named Janna Eberly. The four of us did a lot of stuff together. Bars. Concerts. Janna loved to play miniature golf late at night. Sometimes we'd just sit on a bench by Lake Harriet and talk, or go back to Janna's place and drink beer. Mick had a motorcycle back then and Janna and I would take turns riding it with him."

"And what did you think of Tracy?"

Margie considered the question, taking another sip of coffee. "I liked her. It took her a while to warm up to me, but when she did, we really hit it off."

"Did she talk about—"

"Her suicide attempt? Yeah. She said she'd been drinking. That it was totally dumb and she'd never do it again. She struck me as kind of young, you know, but she's no dummy, that's for sure. Actually, she did say something really interesting."

"What?"

"Well, when she woke up in the hospital, she said it was like she'd become this new person."

"In what way?"

"Like . . . she wasn't going to be anybody's victim anymore. She was going to take charge of her life. She said she didn't know where it came from, but she felt this surge of power. Personal power. Mick's into Eastern religion, and he had some name for it—I don't remember what it was. But he said he was proud of her." Margie paused, chewing on her lower lip.

"What?" said Sophie, sensing that there was more.

"Well, Mick saw Tracy's change as positive. And, I mean, it is. But my take on what she was saying was a little different. When I looked at her, I saw—and I know this might seem melodramatic—but I thought she seemed dangerous. Like, not only was nobody going to mess with her, but she had plans for some major paybacks."

"Did she give you any details?"

"Not really," said Margie, her voice fading as she looked down at the magazine in her lap.

It was a tease, thought Sophie. Margie knew Sophie was dying to know more about what Tracy had said. Holding a piece back allowed her a sense of power. If Sophie pushed, it would only add to Margie's general amusement.

Sophie hated herself for thinking such negative thoughts about Bram's daughter. She wondered briefly if she was jealous of Margie's relationship with him.

Leaning her head back against the wall, she closed her eyes. She was being too hard on the girl. Too analytical. She was seeing motivations that weren't there. Sophie thought of herself as a good person. Giving. Generous. Generally patient. For some reason, Margie brought out the worst in her. She would simply have to turn over a new leaf, show Margie a kinder, gentler Sophie. In turn, Margie would respond by being kinder and gentler herself.

Right. And the earth was flat.

Pearl's Notebook
March 29, 1972

On our way back to the house that last night, we were met by a succession of cars going in the opposite direction. The bad weather had cut the evening short. Guests were leaving the party. Everyone seemed to be crawling along at a snail's pace, trying to avoid ending up in the ditch. I hate driving in treacherous weather, especially on narrow country roads.

"Rats leaving the sinking ship," Carl muttered, shielding his eyes from the oncoming headlights.

When we arrived at the house, Carl told me to park the Cadillac across from the front door. We stayed in the car for a few seconds, watching people trickle out. Some stood beneath the porch's overhang, waiting for the attendants to bring their cars around. It wasn't a mass exodus, but it was steady.

Carl didn't seem to be in any hurry to get inside. On the drive back, he'd grown quiet again.

"What are you going to do now?" I asked, studying his face. "You won't . . . hurt Millie, will you?" It nearly killed me to ask him that, but his emotions were all over the place.

"I'm going to ask her for a divorce," he said.

"Tonight?"

"Yes, tonight."

127

"But . . . this was supposed to be such a special evening." I said it more to myself than to him. He was already well beyond the gala celebration for his new house. I looked past him out the window at his grand log mansion, wondering if Millie and the children would live there without him when all the dust settled. It seemed like just one more piece of bad luck. But a house was a house. He could always build another. I knew that what had truly gone wrong in his life had nothing to do with a piece of property. He'd admired his wife once upon a time, but he'd never loved her. I was amazed that they'd stayed together this long. But divorcing Millie was just the end product of something far more serious. I thought I knew what it was. *"Millie's been cheating on you, hasn't she."* Knowing Carl, that would have been the last straw.

He glanced over at me. *"Pearl,"* he said, *"she's been lying and manipulating me from the day we first met. I saw it . . . but I didn't see it. Do you understand? She's a black widow spider. She eats her young."*

I gathered from this that she'd hurt him and the children in some profound way, not that it was a direct confirmation of my suspicions. I believe that he might have forgiven Millie if it hadn't involved his kids, but since it so obviously did, I was starting to understand his anger. I asked him how she'd hurt his children.

He looked back at the house. All he said was, *"She's hurt them beyond anything I could ever imagine."*

We sat silently for a few moments.

Finally, he said, *"I'll get them away from her one way or the other."*

I shivered at his words.

"Come on," he said, climbing out of the front seat. *"It's time to divest myself of that monstrosity."* Crossing the

drive in front of the house, he said, "You and Henry might as well go home. The party's over."

Once back inside the warmth of the house, I tried to brush the sleet off my dress. It was coming down pretty hard now, starting to accumulate on the grass. As I was looking around for Henry, I noticed that Carl had once again made his way to the bar. He was downing another drink—this one looked like a double. His speech had never seemed slurred to me, but as he walked through the thinning crowd, he looked like a man lurching across the deck of an unsteady boat. A few of his guests seemed a bit startled by his red face and his uneven gait, but nobody said a word to him, or tried to stop him.

Millie was sipping from a glass of champagne in the dining room. A group of people were gathered around her. Her admirers, I thought to myself. Most of them were men. I'd never found Millie terribly attractive, but in the soft interior light, she looked radiant, a woman on top of the world. Carl pushed his way into the group and grabbed her by the wrist, pulling her with him as he made his way to a door at the back of the room. She seemed both shocked and embarrassed by his behavior, but she didn't struggle. She must have figured it was better to go quietly, indulge his little tantrum, than to make a scene.

Just then, Henry came down the stairs arm in arm with Sophie. He asked me where I'd been, said he was starting to get worried. He wanted to leave because of the weather. Leaning close to give me a kiss, he saw that my hair was wet, and my evening gown was spattered with watermarks.

"Have you been outside?" he asked.

I guess I felt a little guilty about leaving with Carl and not telling him. "I was just coming to tell you about the weather," I said.

"March is the cruelest month," he said, smiling at me.

"I think that's April, Dad," Sophie said, adding, "Mom, come upstairs with me for a minute. There's something you've just got to see. It's really really really important." She was so excited, I couldn't say no. While Henry went to say good-bye to a couple of new friends—and to get our coats—Sophie led me up the long stairway to the master suite. Elaine was waiting for us, sitting on the edge of the bed. She ushered me into the bathroom and opened a closet full of cosmetics.

"Look at this," Sophie said, removing one of the bottles. "It's French. Elaine's mom uses it all the time." She couldn't pronounce the brand name and neither could I. "There's shampoo, triple-cream conditioner, a special skin lotion, an after-bath splash, and perfume. Here, smell." She twisted the cap off one of the bottles.

"It's nice, dear," I said. I wasn't really concentrating. I was thinking about Carl, about what he was saying to Millie.

"Nice? It's divine! This is what I want for my next birthday."

"Your birthday isn't for another six months," I said.

"Yeah, but, see, I wanted you to look at it so you'd know what to get. It's pretty expensive, otherwise I'd buy it with my allowance."

"We'll see, honey."

Sophie was heavily into makeup and body lotions at the time, although I'd never seen her this excited. As Elaine pointed out some other "exclusive" products, my concern was elsewhere. In another part of the house, a dramatic scene was unfolding. I didn't realize how dramatic until later.

"Okay, then, Mom. Mom? Are you listening?"

I smiled, said that I was.

"Okay, the body splash for sure. Oh, and the shampoo."

I agreed to whatever she wanted.

On our way back downstairs, Sophie remembered one more thing she'd forgotten to tell Elaine. *I said she could phone her when we got home, but she insisted she had to tell her in person.* As she bounded back upstairs, I went to look for Henry. *He wasn't in the living room so I thought perhaps he'd already gone outside to ask for our car to be brought around.* I crossed the front foyer and walked out onto the porch. *I looked around, but couldn't see him anywhere. I was about to go back in when I noticed that Carl's Cadillac was missing. I walked down the outside steps and asked one of the attendants if it had been taken to the garage.*

"No," said the young man. He explained that Mr. and Mrs. Veelund had driven off together a few minutes before.

A tiny chill ran down my back. "Are you sure?"

To the best of my knowledge, he said, "Mr. Veelund came out first. He looked kind of funny. You know, kind of upset. Then, as he was about to drive off, Mrs. Veelund rushed out of the house and jumped into the passenger's seat."

I asked him if they said where they were going.

He responded that he figured it was some kind of emergency, otherwise, why go out?

There was only one way they could have gone.

"Will you bring my car around? The name's Tahtinen. It's a green Buick."

"Sure thing, ma'am," he said. He took off running toward a field north of the house where most of the cars were parked.

As far as I was concerned, he couldn't find the car fast enough.

13

Danny stood before a grouping of framed family photographs, the ones his mother had placed on top of the grand piano in the music room. He'd spent the last few minutes examining each and every one. In fact, he'd spent the last hour wandering through the house, looking at all the family photos. There was the line of wedding pictures hanging on the wall in the upstairs hallway. The pictures in his mother's bedroom and the small framed snapshots in her study. He'd gone down to the rec room in the basement, glancing through a picture album he found under the bar. And he'd scanned all the miscellaneous photos tucked here and there, on bookshelves, on end tables, atop bureaus and dressers in the unused bedrooms.

His wife had been right. She'd pointed out something curious to him a few weeks before and at first he was positive she was mistaken. His mother couldn't be *that* hateful. And yet if his wife had been right, if it *was* true, he couldn't understand why he'd never noticed it. Then again, his ability to erase his mother's troubling behavior from his mind was a survival mechanism he'd adopted years ago.

Ruth's comment had eaten away at Danny. He knew that coming home simply to inspect the family photographs was a strange mission, and yet he needed to do it. Danny saw himself as a good-natured, adaptable man, and that good-natured adaptability had always been a source of comfort. He might scrutinize other parts of his life, but he rarely scrutinized his family of origin. He now saw that lack for what it really was—a way to prevent the match from ever touching the fuse that would ignite the bomb of fury he'd always held deep within.

Danny had been waiting all morning for Doc Holland to leave because, once he was gone, his mother had promised him an audience. Oh, she hadn't put it quite that grandly, but that's how Danny felt. He was being allowed into her inner sanctum for a chat. She probably assumed he wanted to talk about her decision to sell the company. If she wanted his opinion, he thought it was a fine idea. He knew it would hurt Elaine, and for that he was sorry, but the family business had always been a source of contention. Alex would be just as happy being an unemployed millionaire, off doing his charity work. Not that he'd be a millionaire right away. The family largesse would become available to one and all only upon their mother's demise. Danny wondered if she only knew how loudly that clock ticked in her children's minds. It must be an awful feeling knowing your children were waiting for the moment when the clock would stop. Nobody deserved that. Not even Mad Dog Millie.

Danny felt momentarily sorry for his mother, but as his eyes took in the photos, the feeling passed. When he heard the door open behind him, he turned around, expecting to find his mother. Instead, Alex walked in.

"Hey, bro," said Danny. It took a moment for Alex's strange appearance to register. He looked like a man who'd been sleepwalking until a voice had startled him back to consciousness.

"Danny, hi. I forgot you were here."

"That's flattering."

"Huh? No . . . I mean—"

"You okay?"

He lowered himself into a chair, looking around at the room as if it gave off a painful light. "Yes, I'm fine."

"You don't look fine."

He massaged his forehead.

"You want to talk?"

Alex had no particular gift for conversation. Even though Danny was his brother, he felt he could know him only generally. Danny's penchant for adaptability had made that seem okay, up until now. Alex was his brother, his closest biological bond. Treating each other like former college roommates who had lost their grip on an old intimacy but were unwilling to admit it didn't cut it anymore.

"How about a drink?" asked Danny.

"It's kind of early."

"Let's live dangerously."

He left the room and proceeded to the kitchen, where he grabbed a bottle of brandy from a low cupboard and two juice glasses from the dishwasher. Returning to the music room, he poured them each a full glass.

"Here," he said, handing one to Alex.

"Huh?" Alex looked at it without comprehension. "Oh," he said after a couple of seconds. "Sure. Why the hell not." He took it and downed it in two gulps.

Danny raised his eyebrows, but didn't say anything. His brother had always reminded him of the squeaky-clean blond in the toothpaste commercials. But Alex had aged, as had they all. Sitting down on the piano bench, Danny said, "You look like shit. Something happen?"

Before he responded, Alex got up and poured himself another drink. "Mom happened."

"Ah. This is going to be a conversation about Mother."

Alex tossed back another shot of brandy. "I don't even know where to begin. It's like she took a sledgehammer to my life."

"You're talking about selling the company."

Alex looked over at the windows. Suddenly, his face puckered and tears leaked out of his eyes. He made no sound, nor did he make a move to wipe the tears away. He just stood there, the bottle in one hand, the glass in the other.

Danny hadn't expected this. He'd never seen his brother cry before. Not even when he was a kid. His senior year, Alex had been the star running back on the high school football team. The last game of the season, the last play of the game, he broke his shoulder. Danny remembered seeing the pain on his face, but no tears.

"It's just a business, Alex. We won't lose money, we'll probably make money."

"It's not about money." He poured himself another drink, then sat back down.

"Okay, I admit you've got ties to the business that I don't. But you'll survive. It's not as if someone died."

"It is. It's exactly like that." He finished his drink, then, holding the glass sideways, as if he'd already forgotten it was in his hand, he rose from his chair and left the room.

So much for their intimate brotherly dialogue, thought Danny. He checked his watch. When he glanced out the window, he saw that Doc Holland's car was gone. It was time.

Passing quickly through the gloomy back corridor, he reached the study. The door was standing open. His mother was sitting behind her desk, her face turned to the side, leaning over the lower drawer looking for something. Instead of announcing his presence, he just stood and looked at her, realizing he would be forever bound to her by an endless snarl of memories, of love and of loathing. Were his knees actually beginning to tremble?

Danny's family had never been confrontational. Well, not the kids. Their M.O. was to cast a blind eye on the outrageous opinions of their mother, treating her behavior and prejudices as a kind of family joke. It was both a way to defuse the vitriol and an opportunity to bond against her. Danny hated confrontation in any form, and yet that's why he'd come. No joke would clear the air this time. He gave a soft knock on the open door.

His mother's head popped up. "Daniel. Come in. I was just looking for a copy of my will."

"Why? Are you going to change it?"

"No, of course not."

"Am I mentioned in your will, Mother?"

She blinked at him. "Of course you are. I sent you a copy. My estate is divided equally among my three children."

He sat down. "Speaking of wills—" He let his voice trail off.

"Yes?" She continued her search.

He waited until his silence caused her to look up.

"You're in an odd mood today, Danny."

"Am I?"

"You haven't really weighed in about my decision to sell Veelund Industries."

"I don't care what you do with it."

She patted the curls at the back of her gray hair. "I assumed as much."

"Mother?"

"Yes?"

He waited a couple of beats. "Why don't you have any photographs of my family on your piano?"

She looked at him quizzically. "I do. There's that one of you when you graduated from college. And then I've got a couple of those wonderful professional photos you had done for your second book."

"Those are pictures of me, Mother."

"That's right." She seemed puzzled.

"What about my wife and kids?"

"What about them?"

"You have no photos of my family. Why is that?"

"Oh, you must be mistaken."

"Name one photo that includes Ruth, Abbie, or Zoe?"

"Well . . ." She fussed with some papers on her desk.

"There aren't any. I looked."

She stared at him, her mouth turning to a thin, grim line.

"I'll ask the question again. Why aren't there any pictures of me and my family? There are pictures of Alex and his wife of eight months. Pictures of Elaine and her seventeen husbands. Picture after picture of Tracy since the time she was a baby. Pictures of Dad. Pictures of every dog we ever owned. But no pictures of my wife and children. That can't be an oversight. You did it for a reason. I want to know what it is."

She leaned back in her chair. "Is Ruth making you do this? Did she send you here to pick a fight with me?"

"Ruth knows nothing about why I'm here. Answer the question."

"You won't like it."

"Just cut the crap and tell me!"

She adjusted the collar on her dress. "All right. Have you ever heard of the *Protocols of the Elders of Zion*?"

"Oh, God," he groaned, closing his eyes. He should have known it would be something like that. "You can't be serious, Mother. That piece of trash, that . . . anti-Semitic fantasy has been responsible for the death of more Jews than—"

"But have you ever *read* it? Do you know what it says? Daniel, the Jews have been conspiring for more than a century to gain control of all the major governments in the world, to destroy Christian civilization and to become masters of the earth. It's all there in black and white."

"The international Jewish conspiracy. You actually believe that trash?"

"It's not a matter of belief, dear. It's a fact. They start by controlling the money. Just look at our own country. Who were the big industrial financiers? All Jews! Andrew Carnegie."

"He was Scottish."

"A Scottish Jew! And Rockefeller—"

"Rockefeller was a Presbyterian."

She looked annoyed. "I can see the hand of your wife here, Daniel. If you weren't under her influence, you'd see that I was right."

He was so furious, he was shaking. He should have confronted her years ago. This horror should have been opened to the light of day.

"That's why I was so against your marriage, Daniel. I had such hopes and dreams for you. You were always my favorite."

Now she was trying to flatter her way out of it. "That's

bullshit, Mother. You've always loved Alex far more than you have Elaine and me."

"No, no. You don't understand. Your father and I . . . we planned to have two children. That's all. Your father wanted a boy and a girl. We were lucky enough to have Alex and Elaine. When you came along, you were—"

"An accident."

"No, a miracle. My. . . . redemption. When I watched you sleeping in your crib, my heart was filled with such love and joy. It was only then that I realized God was good, that there was a chance for me. Your birth brought me back to Him. And then you went and linked yourself to . . . to that woman. It was beyond my ability to comprehend."

"Do you actually hate my wife and children? Has this moral insanity caused you to sink that low?"

"Daniel, you miss my point. I don't hate your family, not specifically, not personally, but I hate what your wife's race is doing to the world. I will not have their pictures in my house."

"You're the worst kind of bigot, Mother."

She refused to look away.

"When Ruth comes to visit, you smile at her. You hide your hatred behind a *filthy smile*."

"I do not hate. That would be wrong."

"What do you think the *Protocols of the Elders of Zion* is? It's nothing but hate from beginning to end. Hate and lies. How can you live with yourself?"

"The Bible says that the Jews killed Christ. I didn't say that, the Bible did. The Jews cried, *Let His death be on our heads*. It's why the Holocaust happened. The Bible also says—"

He covered his ears to block out the sound of her

voice. As she talked on, he flashed to a crime story he'd once read. One of the men in the book, a police detective, said that with people like his mother, you either had to ignore them or kill them, because nothing you said would ever change their mind.

"Daniel, stop it. Put your hands down. Listen to me," she demanded.

He couldn't stay in the same room with her another minute. He got up, struggling simply to breathe. He felt frantic, wild, like his brain was bleeding. He had to get out before he did something he'd regret.

14

Alex spent most of the afternoon driving the back country roads around his parents' property, trying to make sense of the conversation he'd had with his mother. Her revelations had caught him completely off guard. He felt numb, disconnected from reality, or from what he'd always assumed was real. His mother had tossed a hand grenade at him and then assumed he'd go away like a good little boy and deal with it. But he wasn't dealing. Not at all. The longer he thought about it, the uglier the ramifications became.

When he'd entered her study this morning, he was certain that if he could present his case for taking the company public in just the right way, she'd see it for the incredible opportunity it was. But in one moment of truth-telling, she'd blown it all away. His hopes, his dreams, his life. Sure, he understood now why the company had to be sold, but that knowledge was little compensation.

The problem was, his mother had given him only a small piece of the puzzle. She was obviously embarrassed by her behavior. Alex should have asked more questions, should have demanded answers, but he'd always processed information slowly. When he'd walked out of her study, he was on information overload. He needed time to figure out what he really felt. It was during his afternoon drive that he'd come to an important realization. He'd never truly hated his mother before, but he did now—with an intensity that frightened him. He'd also formulated a plan. He would go home, shower and clean himself up, then return to the main house and demand that she tell him everything. He had no intention of harming the innocent, but the one person he knew for sure who *wasn't* innocent in this whole mess was his mother. Good old Mad Dog Millie. He wanted names. Dates. All the sordid details. If she refused to talk, well, his plan hadn't taken him that far. But when the time came, he'd know what to do. Of that he was certain.

As he trudged up the walk to his house, Roman met him at the front door.

"Why didn't you answer any of my calls?" asked Roman.

"I had my cell phone turned off." He didn't want to get into an argument right now. He'd already had one dreadful conversation today. But by the look in Roman's eyes, he could tell he was headed for another.

Roman was a mercurial man with a terrible temper. Alex never knew from one moment to the next what kind of mood he'd be in. By all rights, he should have been a business tycoon by now, but it hadn't happened. His lack of success in his chosen field had left him bitter. And yet he was still trying, still reaching for the brass ring that had always eluded him. His kitchen company had burned up the business circles in Canada for years, becoming a major player, as well as a major moneymaker. But a downturn in the Canadian economy at the same time

Roman was in the process of expanding had left him looking for cash just to keep going.

Roman and Alex had met at a building convention in Toronto in the summer of 1998. Over drinks that first night, they'd hit it off. During the next few days, they discussed Kitchen Visions' financial predicament in some detail. Their physical relationship also began during that week in Toronto. Roman was up front about his marital status. He said he'd been married for many years, but had never been happy. For the past year, his wife had been experiencing some debilitating emotional problems. Anxiety and depression. Leaving her while she was ill wasn't an option. Roman also told Alex that he'd had lots of affairs—with both men and women. He considered himself bisexual, although he was finding that, as he got older, he was drawn almost exclusively to men.

Four months later, when Roman came to Minnesota for a visit, Alex had begun to muse out loud about buying his company, bringing it under the wing of Veelund Industries. Alex saw it as a good business deal, and a way to continue his relationship with Roman.

Roman was initially skeptical. He didn't want to sell, he wanted a loan. Alex understood his hesitance, but Roman's financial problems were growing worse by the day. Over time, they were able to reach an agreement. Veelund Industries would buy the company, but Roman would retain the presidency and, in effect, control. In the bargain, Alex would get the chance to work with a businessman he'd grown to admire, and a man he'd grown to love.

Roman, who was nine years older than Alex, was a man full of ideas, constantly in motion. Where Alex tended to sit back and study an issue to death, Roman acted. Alex felt they made a good team, each tempering the other. In the beginning, they both needed to be discreet about their personal relationship, but Roman had left his wife at the beginning of the year. She'd returned to Canada, having recovered from the worst of her emotional illness, and seemed to be remarkably sanguine about their separation. Roman hadn't pressed her for a divorce, and that was fine with Alex. The fact that he was married put people off the track, specifically Alex's mother.

"Your sister stopped by with that friend of hers," said Roman, lighting a cigarette and sucking in the smoke as if it were pure oxygen.

"You mean Sophie?"

He nodded.

Pulling off his polo shirt, Alex headed into the bedroom. He sat down on the bed and began to untie his shoes and remove his socks. "When?"

"Shortly after you left this morning." Roman stood in the doorway.

"I thought you were leaving. How come you were still here?"

"I had some business calls to make." He took a drag from the cigarette. A tiny bit of ash fell to the wood floor.

"What did Elaine want?"

"Alex, look at me."

He stood up and unhooked his belt. "What?"

"Elaine always calls when she is about to bring someone over, yes?"

"Always."

"But she didn't this morning. This Sophie wants to build a log home. Elaine demanded to bring her inside."

"I don't understand—"

"Elaine knows about us."

Their eyes locked. "Don't be ridiculous."

"The bed was unmade. My clothes were strewn around the room. She could tell I'd spent the night. Do I need to give you the blow by blow of her reaction?"

Alex couldn't believe Roman had been so stupid as to let her in before he'd cleaned up. "You should have stopped her."

"Do you think I want her to know about us? I just handed her the means to blackmail you into doing whatever she wants. If your mother finds out that we are lovers, who knows what she will do?"

"Elaine would never use my personal life to blackmail me."

"You are blind, Alex. You do not see what is right before your eyes. Your sister has been jealous of my relationship with you from the very beginning. She hates me."

"You're not her favorite person, sure, but I think that's way too strong."

"She has much to lose when we take the company public."

Alex sat back down on the bed. Pinching the bridge of his nose, he said, "I'm sorry, Roman, but . . . that's not going to happen."

Roman didn't respond. "Meaning what?" he said after a few seconds. "That you could not convince your mother when you talked to her this morning?"

"Something like that."

"Then we will figure out another approach." He was smoking in quick jabs now, pacing in front of the bed.

"It's over. The company will be sold as soon as possible."

"I do not understand."

"And I can't explain it."

"But"—he smashed the cigarette out in an ashtray— "you cannot do that to me." He took a few steps closer to the bed. "We have made plans. Ever since I came on board, this was always our idea. How can you change your mind after such a short battle? You must not lose confidence, Alex. We are so close to realizing our dreams."

"I can't stop it."

"You are weak! You are a *weak* man to let your mother tell you what to do."

Roman's French accent had grown so thick, Alex could barely understand him.

"You do not love me!"

"I do. But it's out of my hands."

"It is your mother. She commands and you jump."

"It's a family issue. But when the company is sold, I'll be a very rich man. Richer than I am now. We can do whatever we want, Roman. Go abroad. Begin a new life together, one where we don't have to hide our feelings. I'm so sick of all this sneaking around."

Roman's face was full of disgust. "You lie to me. You use me and my company and then you toss us away. I do not know how I could be so wrong about you, but you have failed me, Alex. And there is nothing more to say." He stood waiting for Alex to respond. He'd played every card in his deck, but this time, it wouldn't be enough.

Alex felt sorry for him. He wished that Roman would get off the dime, stop with the temper tantrums and see that there was a rich, full life waiting for them. Alex got up and walked into the bathroom. But when the front door slammed a few seconds later, he grabbed his shirt, pulled it back on, then rushed to catch up. Cracking the door, he heard Roman holler, "You do not understand me at all. All I get from you is sex and greeting card sentiments."

Alex stepped out on the front porch. "Come back in and we'll have a glass of wine, talk some more."

"You are a pathetic mama's boy," spat Roman. He'd opened his car door and was ready to get in. But he waited. He was willing to be coaxed.

Picking his way barefoot though the white stones on the walk, Alex headed for the driveway. Before he got ten feet, he heard the report of a rifle. An instant later another shot rang out as the rear window of Roman's car exploded.

"Get down," screamed Alex. He sprinted toward the BMW and took a flying leap behind the car. Roman was on his hands and knees near the front tire.

"What the hell is going on?" said Roman, covering his head. "Who the hell is shooting at us?"

Alex wasn't positive, but he thought the sniper was in the grove to the south of the tennis court. The grove was a thick woods about two blocks long and maybe a block wide, clustered around a section of Dog Tail Creek.

"Just stay down," said Alex.

For the next few minutes, they waited. But as suddenly as the shooting had begun, it stopped.

"Do you think he's gone?" asked Roman finally, uncovering his head.

"He's probably waiting for us to show ourselves."

"Do you have your cell phone?"

"It's in my car."

"Mine is out of juice." He wiped the sweat from his eyes.

Alex was sweating, too. "Take off your shoe."

"Why?"

Alex reached over and yanked a loafer off Roman's right foot. He inched it upward until just the tip of it was showing. When nothing happened, he inched it up higher, moving it slowly back and forth. Either the guy was gone, or he saw the ruse for what it was.

"Maybe someone heard the shots and will call the police," said Roman.

Alex took a look over his shoulder, back toward Elaine's house. He couldn't see a car in her drive. She was probably still up at Prairie Lodge. "We better sit tight."

"What if the sniper moves, tries to shoot from a different angle?"

"If he wants to remain anonymous, he can't leave the grove," said Alex. His only way out was back toward the main house.

"What the hell does this guy want with us? What did we do?"

"Maybe he just wants to scare us."

"This is your property. Do something!"

Alex thought about it. "I'm going to make a run back to the cabin." They could wait until dark to make a break, but that was hours away. And darkness would provide cover not only for them, but also for the sniper.

"Good idea," said Roman.

Alex thought Roman might try to talk him out of it, but instead, he offered encouragement. Swell.

"Just don't run in a straight line."

Crouching at the front of the car, Alex peered out from behind the bumper. He couldn't see anyone in the woods, but that didn't mean anything. With all the trees and the dense underbrush, it was a perfect place to hide.

Pushing away from the car, he zigzagged his way to the front door, glad that he'd left it open. Diving inside, he hit the floor with a grunt. It took him a few seconds to catch his breath and then he was on the phone. His heart was pounding. "This is Alexander Veelund," he said when a man's voice answered. "I need help. The Veelund property is at the crossroads of County Road Thirty-one and Highway Fifty-nine. Send a police car right away. Someone just tried to kill me!"

15

The sound of banging woke Elaine. Moving up slowly from the depths of her dream, it took a few moments to get her bearings. She blinked open her eyes and glanced at the clock on her nightstand. It was three-twenty in the morning.

She was at home in her own bed for the first time since her daughter's suicide attempt. Nathan had left a few hours ago. After a swim in the pool at the main house, they'd walked back to her place and had dinner on the terrace. One thing led to another and they'd ended up in bed. The scent of his aftershave still lingered in the sheets.

The banging started up again. This time, Elaine realized someone was knocking on the front door. She could hear a male voice shouting her name. Switching on the light, she threw on a bathrobe and hurried to the top of the stairs. "I'm coming," she called.

Her thoughts turned instantly to the shooting at Alex's cabin on Saturday night. After a thorough search of the property, the police had found nothing but a few empty rifle casings to help them identify the sniper. When they finally left around seven, they promised to get to the bottom of it, but no one in the family had heard from them all day. Maybe they didn't do investigations on Sunday.

Squinting through the peephole, Elaine saw that Mick was standing outside. She threw the door open and he rushed in.

"You've gotta help me," he said. He looked like he'd run a mile through a swamp. His pants and shirt were soaking wet with leaves and twigs clinging to them.

"What is it?" she said, tying the robe more snugly at her waist. "Is it Tracy?"

He was so out of breath, he had to sit for a moment before he could continue. Sinking down on a bench by the front door, he said, "She's gone."

"Gone! Gone where?"

"I don't know." He coughed.

"She can't be gone. The bodyguard I posted outside her door—"

"Tracy drugged her."

"What?"

Now he looked terrified.

Elaine grabbed him by the shoulders and shook him. "Tell me!"

"Look, it's not my fault. It was all her idea. She wanted out, okay? She felt like she was in jail. I was supposed to tell everyone that I was going home for the night and then leave. That's what I did. But in reality, I waited for her in my truck about a mile past the house—out on County Road Thirty-one. She was supposed to stay until everyone had gone to bed and the bodyguard had nodded off, then climb out the window and down the trellis. She said she'd done it a thousand times. It was a piece of cake."

"Go on."

"She never came. I waited, but she never came. She was supposed to meet me between one and one-thirty. I waited and waited, and finally I got scared. I thought maybe something had gone wrong. So I left my truck and ran back to the house. I couldn't remember where the bridge over the creek was, so I had to wade through it. That slowed me down." He took a deep breath. "When I finally got to the main house, I saw that her room was dark and the window was open. I called her name a couple of times, but I figured that if I kept on calling, I might wake someone inside, so I climbed up. She wasn't there. The bodyguard was out like a light, so I knew that part had gone okay. I walked around the house, looking for her, but I couldn't find her anywhere. That's when I bumped into Zander."

"Zander? Why was he up?"

"He said he couldn't sleep. He'd gone downstairs to get himself a glass of milk. I ran into him in the pantry. I had to tell him what was up. I mean, I didn't have a choice. He saw me leave around eleven. He told me to wait in the kitchen, that he'd go wake Danny." Mick took another deep breath. "When Danny got downstairs, I explained everything to him. He told me to run to your place and get you up. He took the cart over to Alex's house to get him. They should be here any second. Zander said there was no point in waking your mother until we knew what was really going on."

Elaine's head was spinning, but she could agree with his last statement. She didn't want to upset her mother if this was just another one of Tracy's pranks.

"You should have told me what Tracy was planning!"

"I couldn't. I just . . . couldn't."

"For God's sake, that's what I'm paying you for! This could be a matter of life and death. What if she's off—"

"She's not. She promised. I love her! I'd never let anything bad happen to her."

Elaine wasn't sure she'd heard him correctly. "You *love* her?"

He looked up at her defiantly. "Yes."

Before she could ask another question, she heard a motor. She rushed outside just as Danny and Alex jumped out of the cart. Danny reached her first. Slipping his arm around her shoulders, he walked her back inside. Alex entered a few moments later and shut the door behind him.

"Let's turn on some lights," said Danny, moving into the living room.

Everyone followed, but no one seemed to want to sit down.

Elaine could see her brothers eyeing the dining room table. She hadn't cleared the dishes yet. They could see that she'd had company.

"She's for sure not at the main house," said Mick, pushing his hands into the back pockets of his wet jeans. "I checked everywhere. Well, except Mrs. Veelund's room. But I doubt Tracy would go in there. Besides, the light was off. Since Tracy's window was open, my guess is she did what she'd planned. She left. Maybe something happened to her on the way to my truck. Maybe . . . I don't know. Maybe she stepped in a hole and sprained her ankle."

"Did you check the pool house?" asked Alex.

Mick nodded. "Zander said he'd call me on my cell phone if she turns up at the main house."

A frightening thought struck Elaine. She backed up, then spun around. It was an involuntary response. She couldn't help herself. She felt sick inside. Panicky.

"What is it?" asked Alex.

"The grove. Did anyone check that?"

"No," said Mick, looking confused. "Why would she go there?"

"If you know something, tell us," demanded Alex, looming over Mick.

Danny leaned against the back of the couch. "What are you thinking, Alex? That her disappearance has something to do with the shots that were fired at you and Roman?"

"We need to check the grove right away," said Elaine. "There's not a moment to lose." Wearing nothing but her robe, she rushed outside. Everyone followed.

The early fall night was warm and windy. Sitting in the front seat of the cart as Danny drove over the moon-bleached land, Elaine felt a deep trembling take hold of her. In a matter of minutes, she could be facing a night-mare.

Glancing at Elaine, Danny said, "Is there something about the grove that we don't know? Something besides the sniper?"

As if in a trance, Elaine said, "It's where Tracy was molested when she was a child."

Danny stopped the cart and turned to look at her. *"Molested?"*

From the backseat, she could feel Alex's hand take hold of her shoulder.

"I didn't know," whispered Mick. "She never told me."

"She never told anyone," said Elaine. "Not until she started seeing a therapist."

"Who did it?" asked Alex. "I'll kill him. I'll kill him with my bare hands."

"She wouldn't tell me," said Elaine.

"So . . . what are you saying?" said Danny. "That this person, whoever he is, is still around? That he's still trying to hurt her?"

"I don't know," said Elaine. "Just keep going. I have an awful feeling."

Mick jumped off the cart. "I can run faster than this damn thing can move." He took off, disappearing into the darkness.

Danny pressed the pedal to the floor and the cart jerked forward.

"I wish we'd brought a flashlight," said Elaine.

"I've got one," said Alex.

"If she's not there, what do we do?" asked Danny.

Elaine hoped beyond hope that they wouldn't find her in the grove. But if they didn't, Danny was right. What did they do next?

"I think we should call the police," said Elaine.

"Tracy won't be considered a missing person until she's gone for twenty-four hours," said Danny, veering to the right at the fork in the road.

"Maybe if they know she just tried to—" Alex stopped before he finished the sentence.

Elaine knew what he was going to say. The police might respond more quickly if they thought the young woman was suicidal.

"I've got a friend who works for the Ahern County Sheriff's Office," said Alex. "I'll call him."

"Call him now," said Elaine.

"Might as well," said Danny. "If we don't find her, we'll probably spend the rest of the night looking for her out here in the dark. If the police are willing, they could help."

Alex made the call.

While he talked, Elaine tried to focus her thoughts. Both of her brothers seemed genuinely surprised and horrified by what had happened to Tracy. She desperately wanted to believe that their reaction meant that neither was the guilty party. They'd always been a team. The three of them against Mad Dog Millie. No matter what their problems had been over the years, what arguments they'd gotten into or what business frustrations they'd endured, deep down she believed they loved one another.

In the backseat Alex had just ended his conversation. "Andy says he'll swing by the house in about fifteen minutes."

"Good," said Elaine, feeling relieved. They'd finally have someone official on the scene, a cop who would know what to do.

A few minutes later they pulled up to the edge of the tennis court. Danny turned off the motor and the three of them got out. Since Alex was the only one with a flashlight, they followed him.

Danny called Mick's name a couple of times, but he didn't want to shout. They were too close to the main house for that. Mick didn't respond.

The grove was mostly elms and birch, with a number of paths cut through the brush. As a kid, Elaine used to play hide-and-seek in the grove with her brothers, sometimes late into the night. Once upon a time, she knew the paths like the back of her hand, but that was long ago.

They found Mick crouched on the bank of the creek, gazing up at the moon.

"I've looked everywhere," he said, breathing hard. "If she could hear me, she would have answered. She could see I was alone and she's got nothing to fear from me. That's why I don't think she's here."

"Then where is she?" demanded Elaine, her eyes searching the darkness. She was growing more frantic by the second.

He shook his head. "I think she ditched me. I'll bet she

took one of the bicycles from the garage and rode out to the main highway."

"Then what?" said Alex.

Mick slapped a mosquito on his arm. "I can't believe she ditched me."

Danny checked his watch. "It's nearly four. It'll be light soon."

"Not soon enough," said Elaine.

"I'll take the cart back to the garage," said Alex, handing the flashlight to Elaine. "It'll just take a couple of minutes. There are three bikes hanging up on hooks in the back. If one's gone, we'll have that much of an answer."

"I'll go with you," said Danny.

As the two of them sprinted off, guided only by the light of the moon, Elaine began to pace. Glancing down at Mick, who seemed more concerned with being ditched than he was with the notion that Tracy could be in grave danger, she said, "You're fired."

"Huh?" He looked up at her.

"I don't want you around my daughter. I'll write you one last check and then you're out of her life. For good."

He scrambled to his feet, but before he could protest, Elaine turned around. "Quiet." She listened. "Did you hear something?"

"Yes, you giving me my walking papers. Look, I—"

"Shut up!" Off in the distance she could hear Alex calling her name. "They must have found her!" Feeling her heart leap into her throat, Elaine pointed the flashlight at the path through the trees and rushed off in the direction of the sound.

16

Sophie was on the freeway headed west by seven-thirty on Monday morning. She'd promised Millie Veelund that she'd be out to the house by nine, and she didn't want to be late. Putting some distance between her and the hotel right now, spending some time alone, felt like a good idea. After Bram's health scare on Saturday, he was doing much better. No more indigestion or dizzy spells. All the tests had come back looking good, although his doctor had encouraged him to take a few days off just to rest. Fat chance, thought Sophie. But Bram had surprised her.

After the bypass surgery last year, Bram had returned to work on a part-time basis, but it wasn't long before he'd jumped back in with both feet. Sophie had tried to get him to cut back his hours permanently. They didn't need the money, so why push so hard? She eventually gave up, realizing that Bram loved his job, and doing what one loved was always the best medicine. In that respect, Sophie and her husband were a lot alike. When she left this morning, he was still in bed. Instead of his usual afternoon program, the station had agreed to run one of the *Best of Baldric* tapes. But tomorrow, he would be back on, live.

Margie had a meeting with her business partner today. They planned to look at office sites for their new wedding consulting business. Sophie was glad to think that Margie was busy with *anything* other than just hanging around the hotel. Sophie and Bram had barely had a minute to themselves since Margie arrived. They'd eaten every meal with her. Entertained her every evening. Discussed ad nauseum the ins and outs of her new apartment—the colors she wanted in each room. The bile green she'd picked out for the living room nearly took Sophie's breath away.

Sophie was sick of gritting her teeth and trying to be nice, sick of being told she seemed tense. As far as she was concerned, Margie was a master at ducking responsibility. Margie called it "delegating." Sophie had an endless list of phone calls she'd promised to make to "ease Margie's transition back to Minnesota." She wanted to tell her to make the damn calls herself, but parental guilt—and Bram's disapproval—prevented her. Sophie had decided that yes, Margie was indeed difficult, no matter what Bram said. On the other hand, Sophie also figured she wasn't trying hard enough. That's why spending time alone in the car seemed like such a godsend. For the next hour, she wouldn't have to force her lips into a smile she didn't feel.

Not that Sophie entirely understood what Millie Veelund expected from the meeting this morning. Sophie was hardly an expert when it came to bed-and-breakfasts, although running the Maxfield had taught her a great deal about the hotel business. Perhaps she could pass on something useful. And it would give her another chance to check in with Elaine and see how Tracy was doing.

What had started out as a thin mist in St. Paul had quickly thickened to fog. By the time Sophie reached the Veelund property, she could hardly see fifty yards in front of her. She hoped it would lift by the time she had to head home.

As she turned onto the private service drive, the three-story log mansion rose out of the fog like a haunted house in a Stephen King novel. Millie's idea to create a bed-and-breakfast in the middle of nowhere wasn't exactly the stroke of a business genius.

After parking the car by the garage, Sophie hurried across the lawn and up the steps to the screened porch. She pressed the front doorbell and then waited. The house seemed unusually dark and silent, especially after all of last Friday's activity. She peeked through the glass on the side of the door but couldn't see a single light on. She waited a few more seconds, then rang the bell again.

Still no response.

Thinking that perhaps everyone was out having a morning swim, she trotted back down the steps and followed the graveled walk to the pool house. But once again, she struck out. The pool house door was locked up tight. She checked her watch and saw that it was only eight-thirty. She was half an hour early. Maybe that was the problem.

Returning to her car, she decided to see if Elaine was home. On the way in from the highway, she'd noticed a sign that pointed to Wisteria Cottage. Backing out of the drive, she headed south along the private road. Once she found the sign again, she made a hard left onto a dirt road. She didn't see the house until it loomed suddenly in front of her. It was about an eighth of the size of the main house. There were two other cars in the drive—an old, beat-up Ford truck and a new Land Rover.

Before she could knock, the door swung inward.

"Sophie? What are you doing here?" Elaine looked exhausted, as if she hadn't slept for days.

"Remember?" said Sophie, feeling a bit unsure. "I

promised your mother I'd drive down this morning. She wanted to talk to me about turning her house into a bed-and-breakfast."

"Oh, God," said Elaine, running a hand through her uncombed hair. She backed up. "I completely forgot. Come in."

Once inside, Sophie was assaulted by the acrid smell of sweat mixed with stale cigarette smoke. She glanced into the dining room and saw Alex and Danny sitting at the table, along with that boyfriend of Tracy's. Zander was just coming out of the kitchen with a fresh pot of coffee. Everyone blinked at her so strangely, she felt like an alien.

"We've had a bad night," said Elaine, sitting down next to Danny.

"It's Tracy," said Alex. His blond hair drooped over his left eye. "She's missing."

"We found an overnight bag with her clothes in it," said Elaine, tapping a cigarette from the pack sitting next to her. "It was in the grove, right near the tennis court. We searched all night, but couldn't find her. I called everyone she knows, but nobody's seen her. The police helped us search, and they've put out an A.P.B."

Sophie was stunned. She sank down into an empty chair to listen.

"We figure she climbed out the window of her bedroom," said Danny, waving Elaine's cigarette smoke away from his face. "Sometime between one and two A.M. She drugged the security guard. When the guard finally woke up, she called Elaine right away to tell her what had happened, but we already knew. Tracy must have hidden in the grove. We're not sure why. We know she was there because she left her overnight bag behind." He went on to explain that Mick was in on it, but that Tracy had orchestrated the escape.

Sophie noticed that as Danny talked, Mick just stared at his hands.

"And then the damn fog rolled in around six," said Elaine. "We only had an hour of light to search." If a person could seem numb, exhausted, and frantic at the same time, Elaine did.

What had been left unspoken, thought Sophie, was that Tracy could also be dead—by her own hand. "I was just up at the main house," said Sophie. "I knocked, but nobody answered. I assume your mother must still be in bed."

Elaine looked up at the clock on the wall. "I suppose."

"Does she know about Tracy?" asked Sophie.

"We didn't find out ourselves until after three in the morning," said Danny, rubbing a hand over his beard, then adjusting his glasses as he glanced at his watch.

Zander, who'd been standing silently in the kitchen doorway, finally spoke. "I thought it was best to let Mrs. Veelund sleep. There wasn't anything she could do."

"But I wonder why she didn't answer the door?" said Elaine. "That's kind of odd. I think I'll give her a call."

"It's not a good idea to break the news to her about Tracy over the phone," cautioned Zander. "Maybe we should all go back."

Everyone looked disheveled, thought Sophie, except for Zander. With his fresh white shirt open at the collar and his gray linen slacks and black belt, he could have just stepped out of a *GQ* ad.

"I won't tell her about Tracy," said Elaine, setting her cigarette down on the ashtray. "I'll just make sure she's okay."

"Whatever you say," said Zander. "You know best." He

moved into the room and began pouring fresh coffee into everyone's mugs.

Alex pushed his cell phone across to her.

As Elaine pressed the numbers, all conversation died. She drummed her fingers on the table, then picked up her cigarette, tapped off the ash, and took a drag. Blowing smoke high into the air, she glanced from face to face. "She's not answering."

"Maybe she went for a walk," said Alex. "You know how much she loves her morning walks."

"In this weather?" said Zander. "I highly doubt it."

"But if she did, we certainly don't want two people missing," said Danny.

Elaine clicked the phone off.

"I think I better go over there," said Alex.

"Let's all go," said Danny. "No use staying here." He glanced at his watch again.

"Why do you keep looking at your watch every five seconds?" demanded Elaine, stubbing out her cigarette. "You're driving me crazy."

"Sorry," said Danny. "It's just . . . I booked a flight back to New York this morning."

"When did you do that?" asked Alex.

"After the heart to heart I had with Mom on Saturday. I found out what I needed to know. Now I can leave."

"And what did you find out?" asked Elaine.

"It's hard to have a heart to heart with someone who doesn't *have* a heart," muttered Alex.

Danny cracked a smile. "Tell me about it." Under his breath, he added, "*There was an old woman who swallowed a fly.*"

"Did you discuss her idea to sell the company?" asked Elaine. "I hope you talked her out of it."

"I didn't try. Our agenda was more . . . personal."

Elaine turned to Alex. "You had a conversation with her on Saturday morning, too, didn't you? How come she's talking to both of you and not me?"

"Just lucky, I guess," said Alex. His smile looked more like a grimace.

"Is there something going on I don't know about?"

Both men shrugged.

Zander raised his hand. "Why don't we have this conversation back at the main house?"

"He's right," said Danny, standing up and stretching. "We should go." Switching his gaze to Sophie, he added, "When Mom hears that Tracy's missing, I don't know how interested she'll be in meeting with you. You may have driven all this way for nothing."

"Don't give it another thought. Maybe I should just go. Get out of your hair."

"No," said Elaine with a sigh. "You never know what she'll want to do. If you don't mind wasting a little more of your time, why don't you come back to the house with us?"

"Of course," said Sophie. As she rose from her chair, she glanced at Mick. During the entire conversation, he'd remained silent. She had the distinct sense that his silence was related to guilt. She wondered if there was something he had to feel guilty about, beyond the obvious.

After turning off lights, they all trooped out to their cars. Mick headed off alone in his truck. Elaine and Zander rode with Alex and Danny. And Sophie brought up the rear. Everyone was driving so slowly, and the weather was so grim, that Sophie felt as if she she were part of a funeral procession. She thought about Tracy all the way to the main house.

After Elaine unlocked the front door, they all filed inside. Except for the tick of a grandfather clock in the hall, the house was still. None of the curtains had been opened.

"Your mother must still be in bed," said Zander, taking the stairs two at a time. Elaine followed. Danny and Alex headed into the living room to open up the house and turn on some lights. Sophie wasn't sure what to do, so she stayed in the foyer with Mick. He looked about as uncomfortable as it was possible for a person to look. His hands kept moving in and out of his pockets, never sure where they should be.

Suddenly, Elaine appeared at the top of the stairs. "Danny! Alex! Come up here. Now!"

Sophie stepped to the bottom of the stairway and looked up.

"It's Mother," said Elaine. Her face was ashen.

Alex brushed past Sophie on his way up.

As if in a trance, Sophie took a step up. Then another. And another. She was drawn irresistibly to the second-floor landing. As she approached the bedroom door, she turned around just as Danny rounded the stairs and rushed toward the room.

"What's wrong?" he asked, looking both frightened and intensely alert.

"I don't know."

"It's Mother," called Alex.

Sophie stood in the doorway.

Alex was holding Elaine as she cried against his shoulder.

The lifeless body of Millie Veelund lay on the bed, covered by a flowered satin comforter.

Behind her, Sophie could hear Danny whisper, "*There was an old woman who swallowed a horse. She's dead, of course.*"

17

"Hi, honey. It's me." Danny had taken his cell phone out onto the porch to call his wife. He needed to let her know that she wouldn't need to pick him up at La Guardia. He wouldn't be coming home today. "I'm sorry, but I've got some bad news."

"What is it?" she asked. "What's wrong?"

It was a few minutes after eleven. The police and the county coroner had just left. Since his mother's death had been unattended, an autopsy would need to be performed. Nobody doubted that her death was anything other than natural, but still, procedures had to be followed. Everyone in the family already knew her last wishes. She wanted to be cremated, her ashes scattered on the property by the creek. But that would have to wait until a death certificate could be issued. The coroner told Alex that he would perform the autopsy later in the day. Alex seemed to know the man. To Danny, it seemed as if Alex knew everyone in the county. The coroner assured the family that matters would be handled with the utmost care. As soon as a cause of death could be officially established, their mother's remains would be released and they could begin to make funeral arrangements.

"Mom died this morning."

"Oh, honey. I'm so incredibly sorry. How—"

"She died in her sleep. It was peaceful."

Danny couldn't believe how twisted his feelings were. He'd been so furious with her yesterday, and yet today, after her body had been removed from the house, he'd broken down, cried like he hadn't cried since he was a child. At first, when he'd seen her lying there in her bed, so still, so pale, so profoundly silent, he'd felt a moment of triumph. The greatest single source of irritation and anger in his life was gone. Ding dong, the witch was dead. But then he'd kissed her good-bye—kissed her cheek and touched her hair. That's when he began to fall apart.

He'd finally gone to his room. He was ashamed of the sick mixture of emotions that had plagued him ever since he could remember. But Elaine had heard him crying. She hadn't even knocked on his door. She'd simply come in. The two of them sat on the bed, holding each other. Through his tears, he told her what he'd been feeling. How could he hate someone and love them at the same time? Elaine said that she felt the same way. So did Alex. Their mother had been a confusing human being. Danny said that he thought she was a victim of her own lack of imagination. As soon as he said the words, he realized that the same could be said of him.

"Are you okay?" asked Ruth.

"Yes, I'm fine."

"But you won't be coming home."

"No. Not today."

"I'll pack and catch the next flight out. When's the funeral?"

"There won't be one . . . exactly. Ruth, listen. There's really no reason for you to come. Mom wanted to be cremated. She didn't want a funeral, just a, well, a sort of memorial service. And she only wanted her kids to be there."

"But I'm your wife. And Zoe and Abbie—they should have a chance to say good-bye."

"I know. But she was specific about her last wishes. It's just supposed to be Alex, Elaine, and me."

"I need to do *something*, Danny. It's only right."

He couldn't help but laugh. "We could send money to one of her pet causes, but they're all so off-the-wall. I mean, do you really want to support the Emanuel Swedenborg Society?"

"What's that?" said Ruth.

"Don't ask."

"I'll send flowers. A huge bouquet of whatever's in season."

"That would be nice." It was more than his mother would have done for her.

"How long do you think you'll have to stay?"

"Well, there's another bit of news I need to tell you. Tracy ran away last night. Nobody knows where she is."

"Oh, Danny, Elaine must be in a panic."

"She is."

"Why do tragedies always come in clumps? Are you sure you're okay? You're taking all your medication? This is a lot of stress for you, honey. If I were there, maybe I could lessen it for you."

"I'll only be here a few more days. I'll leave after the memorial."

"What about the reading of the will?"

"Everybody knows what's in it. Mom left everything equally to her three kids. We're rich, Ruthie."

"God, does that mean you can tell your publisher to go to hell?"

Again, he laughed. "I suppose it does. If I wanted to. But I don't. I was thinking about it last night. I'm going to finish that book, Ruth. Show the world that I'm not washed up as a writer."

"Honey, that's wonderful."

"But you can quit teaching now. If you want."

"I adore teaching."

"Yeah, I know. I have a feeling we won't be very successful at this being rich stuff." He thought of Alex and Elaine. He knew they wouldn't have the same problem.

The fog was starting to lift. Through the mist, Danny could see the outline of the sun. It looked flat, like a shiny silver dollar. A day that had begun in darkness was about to turn bright.

"Tell me more about Tracy," said Ruth. "I don't understand. Why did she run off?"

"Her boyfriend said she felt trapped here. Like she was in jail."

Danny heard a cell phone ring. When he looked up, he saw that Mick was standing by the garage, holding a phone to his ear. "It's a long story," said Danny. He wondered who might be calling Mick. "You know, sweetheart, I think I should probably get going. I'll call you later in the day, okay? I should have more information by then."

"Oh, honey, I love you. I'm so sorry this happened."

"I love you, too. More than you could ever know."

"You'll call if you need anything."

"I will."

"Be safe."

"You, too. Bye."

After clicking off, Danny returned his attention to

Mick. His head was bent as he talked. Danny tried to hear what he was saying, but he was too far away.

Suddenly, Mick stuffed the phone in his back pocket, hopped into his truck, and started the motor. An instinct told Danny that he should follow. He waited until Mick had backed out of the drive and was on his way to the service road, and then he rushed over to his rental car. Thankfully, he had his keys and wallet with him.

For the next forty minutes, Danny followed the truck at a reasonable distance. It wasn't likely that Danny would lose him in such open country. Instead of heading northeast toward the Twin Cities, Mick took County Road 8 west. Just this side of Maple Lake, as the speed limit dropped to twenty-five, he pulled into the parking lot of the Lake Breeze Motel. Danny kept driving, but turned around at a gas station about a block away and headed back. By the time he reached the motel, Mick's truck was empty. There were only three other cars in the lot and Danny didn't recognize any of them.

Parking close to the exit, Danny slipped out of the front seat and cut quickly to the far end of the building. The motel was old, the screens on the doors and windows rusted. Tufts of weeds sprouted from the cracks in the sidewalk. The truck was parked in front of room number five. Danny approached cautiously. As he neared an open window, he could hear Tracy's voice. Then Mick's. *Bingo.*

Now that he'd found Tracy, Danny wasn't about to let her get away. But there was no reason not to listen to the conversation—or, more accurately, their argument. Mick sounded pissed.

"I was worried sick about you, damn it."

"Don't blow a gasket," said Tracy. "I figured Mom was watching you."

"Well, she wasn't."

"But I couldn't take the chance. And anyway, I wasn't sure you'd go through with it. It seemed to me like you and Mom were getting a little too chummy."

"I like your mother. So shoot me. But I would never have betrayed you. You've gotta know that."

Danny bent down and looked inside. Tracy was sitting on the bed. Mick was standing over her, hands on his hips. Neither faced the windows, so Danny kept on watching.

"How did you get here?" demanded Mick.

"A friend."

"Who?"

"Just a friend, okay?"

"What are you going to do now?"

"I need money. I want you to take my cash card and go withdraw two thousand dollars. Bring it back here."

"Then what?"

"I haven't decided yet."

Mick sat down on the bed next to her. "You're not going to like this, but I know what happened to you, that you were molested when you were a kid. Your mom felt like she had to tell the family—since you took off like you did. I just happened to be there."

"She had no right!"

"And I've got some more bad news. I didn't want to spring it on you right away, but you gotta be told." He took her hand. "It's your grandma. She . . . died in her sleep last night."

Tracy just stared at him.

"I'm sorry. I know you loved her a lot."

"I didn't love her. I *hated* her." Her voice grew even more strident.

"But—"

"If anybody could have prevented me from being molested, she could've."

"You mean . . . she knew?"

"She had to know."

Danny wished he could see their faces more clearly. The rusted screens made it almost impossible.

Tracy whispered something to Mick. Mick whispered something back, then he slipped his arm around her shoulder. They sat silently for a few seconds. Danny guessed that Tracy was crying.

Finally, Mick said, "We're in this together, Trace."

"Then go get the money."

"I'm scared you won't be here when I get back."

"Where else would I be? This place is a freakin' pit. I want out of here before I catch some infectious disease."

Mick stood while Tracy searched through her backpack for the card.

"Trace?"

"Huh?"

"Why did you leave your overnight bag in the grove?"

She didn't immediately answer. Handing him the card, she finally said, "I was hiding behind some bushes until it was time for my ride to pick me up. Out of the blue, Alex walks past me—just a few yards away. He was on his way up to the main house."

"What time was that?"

"Around one. I got scared. And then when I saw Doc Holland's car pull into the driveway, I figured there were entirely too many people around, so I took off. I guess I forgot my bag. Good thing I had my backpack on."

"What was Holland doing there at that time of night?"

"Beats me."

Mick took the card and pocketed it, then kissed her. "I'll be back."

When he opened the door, Danny blocked his exit.

"Jesus, Trace, it's your uncle."

"You're an idiot!" screamed Tracy. "He followed you."

Behind Mick, Danny could hear a door slam. Pushing into the room, he saw that Tracy had disappeared into the bathroom with her backpack. "Tracy, you're coming home with me. I don't want to fight with you, but you nearly gave your mom a heart attack leaving like that."

From behind the bathroom door, a voice said, "Leave me the hell alone."

"I can't." Danny glanced at Mick, who didn't seem to know what to do. He ran the flat of his hands down the fronts of his jeans, looking confused.

"Look, Tracy, your mom deserves better. She needs to know you're okay. She's scared to death."

"I'll send her a postcard."

"Not good enough."

"Just leave, okay?"

"Not without you."

"I'm not going back there," she yelled. "And I'm not letting her put me in some padded room."

"That won't happen."

"How would you know?"

Suddenly, the door opened. Tracy stepped back into the room. But this time, she was holding a gun.

"God, Trace," said Mick, backing up. "Where did you get that?"

"My backpack." It was slung over her shoulder. "It belonged to my grandfather. It works just fine. And it's loaded, in case you were wondering."

"Tracy, put it down," said Danny.

"Toss your keys on the bed," demanded Tracy.

She had the gun pointed straight at Danny's stomach. Looking at the piece of cold, hard steel, so foreign, so menacing, and at the steady hand holding it, Danny realized anything he had to say would be a waste of breath. He dug in his pants pocket for his keys and threw them on the bedspread.

"Take the keys," said Tracy, nodding to Mick.

"Trace, this is crazy."

"Do it!"

"Okay, okay." He scooped them up.

"Do you have any cash on you?"

Danny pulled his wallet from his back pocket. Inside, he found three hundred-dollar bills and two twenties. He handed them to Mick.

Motioning with the gun, Tracy said, "Get in the bathroom."

"Where are you going? Will you at least call your mother and tell her you're okay?"

"Shut up and do it."

"You won't use that gun. You can't just shoot me."

"You don't think so?" She cocked the trigger.

Danny backed inside. The door slammed in his face. He heard what sounded like a chair being wedged against the door. A moment later, the screen door slammed. A motor started. Tires screeched. And they were gone.

18

Sophie carried a new round of coffee into the living room. Friends of the family had started arriving shortly after noon. News traveled fast out in the country. Thankfully, if there was one thing Millie Veelund had an abundance of, it was china cups and silver platters.

It was now three in the afternoon and Sophie still hadn't left. Once it became clear that she might need to stick around to help with the onrush of visitors, she'd called Bram to tell him that Millie had died and that she wouldn't be home until later—she couldn't say exactly when. She explained that one thing had led to another, and ultimately, she'd taken over the kitchen. It was her way of helping the family, who were up to their ears in visitors in the living room. The food dropped off by concerned neighbors became Sophie's responsibility.

The Veelunds' usual cook had come in for work around ten, discovered what had happened, and fainted dead away on the kitchen floor. After she was revived, Elaine had sent her home. And then, as other mourners started arriving, Sophie realized that Elaine couldn't handle it all alone. Elaine took center stage in the living room, like the good politician she so clearly was, explaining to visitors in quiet, earnest tones, what she knew about her mother's death. She mainly talked to the women. The people surrounding Alex were mostly men.

Zander had been put on phone duty. There had been a steady stream of calls since about one o'clock. Sitting at a desk in the kitchen, he wrote down messages from well-wishers and answered as many questions as he could. Sophie got the impression that most of the people who called wanted inside information. Zander appeared to know most of the callers personally. He used first names. He also deftly sidestepped the more prurient questions.

Danny had evaporated around noon, and so had Mick. Sophie wondered if they'd gone off together. She couldn't imagine why they would, but then she had very little time to imagine much of anything. It was all she could do to handle food donations and coffee and cookie detail. The people who came by merely to drop off a hot dish inevitably stayed for the better part of an hour. And they all seemed to expect some kind of refreshment. Sophie was glad to help. Neither Elaine nor Alex were thinking clearly. They were on autopilot, accepting the onslaught of compassion as graciously as they could.

Sophie felt the sorriest for Doc Holland. He'd arrived just as Millie's body was being removed to the coroner's van. He was so overwhelmed with grief that he'd demanded to see her. The paramedic helped him up into the van. Sophie and Elaine stood back, watching as he kissed her tenderly. The driver and one of the police officers had to help him out because he'd left his cane in the house. He batted at his eyes, but couldn't seem to stanch the flow of tears.

Sophie had first met Doc when he was in his early forties. She'd been thirteen at the time. When she visited the Veelunds' house—before they moved to the country—he was often around. Elaine told Sophie once that Doc Holland was her dad's best friend. After Carl's death, Doc had become a kind of surrogate father to the kids. He was an old man now, heavyset and arthritic. After the paramedics left, he sat down in the corner of the living room, his face puffy and red, saying very little, but dabbing at his eyes constantly with a white handkerchief. Nobody paid much attention to him.

After pouring more coffee, Sophie returned to the kitchen to make another pot. She heard the doorbell ring again, but when she glanced out into the foyer she saw that Elaine had gone to answer it. Sophie hadn't actually eaten a meal today, but had survived on a chocolate chip bar here, a slice of coffee cake there. Her stomach was beginning to feel queasy. She needed some protein, some fruit or vegetables. Searching through the refrigerator, she took out a tray of cheese and meat that someone had brought earlier in the day. She made herself a sandwich and sat at the kitchen table to eat it while the coffee brewed.

When she was finished, she offered to make a sandwich for Zander, but he shook his head. He was too busy on the phone. Her energy renewed, Sophie began assembling clean cups and saucers on a silver platter, leaving a space for the coffeepot.

On her way through the foyer, the doorbell chimed again. Since nobody came out of the living room to answer it, she set the tray down on a low table and opened the door. She expected more neighbors, but instead found a young man in a gray uniform standing on the front porch surrounded by half a dozen flower arrangements. Sophie had forgotten about that part of bereavement. She would need to find a place to put all the flowers that would be arriving. She asked the delivery man to bring them into the foyer. After signing his clipboard and closing the door behind him, she set off to find Elaine. The coffee would have to wait.

Sophie stood under the living room arch and searched the room, but Elaine was nowhere to be found. Crossing the dining room to Millie's study in the back of the house, she saw that the door was partially closed. Approaching quietly, she could hear a man's voice, then Elaine's. The man's voice was familiar. And then it struck her. She looked inside.

Nathan had his arms around Elaine. He touched her hair. He was saying, "I'm glad you called me. I wish I could have been here for you earlier." Then he kissed her.

Instantly, Sophie felt herself ceasing to be a woman of character. She wanted to yell *fire* in a crowded theater. Dropkick Elaine through the side window. Elaine had no business sucking Nathan into her chaotic life. Nathan had every right to date whomever he wanted, but not Elaine. *Not Elaine.* She made a good friend, but she made a lousy lover and an even worse wife.

But before Sophie could march in and break the two of them up, she was seized by a moment of great emotional clarity. *She* was the one who had her priorities out of whack. The better part of valor was to get the hell away from both of them.

Returning to the kitchen, Sophie stood by the sink and washed her hands. She didn't know why she needed to wash her hands, she just did. Perhaps she was absolving herself of any responsibility to protect Nathan from his fate. After Elaine chewed him up and spit him out, he might come crawling to her to commiserate, but she would remain stoic. It wasn't her place to save him—or to listen to him whine. Was she her ex-lover's keeper?

Damn straight she wasn't.

Just as Sophie was about to return to coffee detail, she heard a knock on the back door. She stood on her tiptoes and looked out the window. A police car had pulled up on the path that separated the main house from the pool house. When she opened the door, she found three officers standing outside. "Ms. Veelund?" asked the oldest of the three men.

"No, I'm a friend."

"I need to speak with a member of the family."

She wanted to ask what this was about but figured she would get an answer soon enough. As she was about to run and get Alex, he walked into the kitchen, introducing himself as Alexander Veelund.

"I saw the squad car pull up," he offered as an explanation. "Did you find my niece?"

"No, sir. This isn't about that. It's about your mother." The officer in charge removed his hat. "I'm sorry about your loss, Mr. Veelund, but I'm afraid I've got some bad news. We pushed your mother's autopsy through real fast, like we promised. We got the results about an hour ago."

"And?" said Alex.

Zander, who'd been talking nonstop on the phone, said a quick good-bye. He remained at the desk, but turned around so he could see what was happening.

"Your mother was a diabetic," stated the officer.

"For many years," said Alex.

"How did she receive her insulin?"

Zander stood up. "By injection."

"And you are?"

"Galen Zander. I was Mrs. Veelund's personal assistant."

"When was the last time she received an injection?"

"Last night before bed."

"Who gave it to her?"

"I did."

The officer studied him hard for a moment, then returned his gaze to Alex. "The doctor who did the autopsy found that your mother's glucose levels were extremely low, perilously low. I'm not a doctor, so I can't give you all the particulars, but the cause of death will be listed as an insulin overdose."

"I don't understand," said Alex.

"I'll give it to you plain and simple. Your mother didn't die of natural causes, Mr. Veelund. We believe her death was a homicide."

19

Holding a blindfold, Sophie met Bram in the Maxfield's lobby. She was wearing a raincoat to hide her clothes, and three-inch heels—her power shoes—to hide her short stature. Twelve-year-olds were taller than she was.

It was Tuesday, early evening, and Bram was just getting home from the station. He'd spent all last night with his daughter looking for rugs, but Sophie had other plans for him tonight.

"Put it on."

"Excuse me?" He took off his shades.

Sophie thought he looked incredibly suave in his white linen suit with a black shirt open at the collar. "The blindfold. I want you to put it on."

"Am I allowed to ask why?"

"It's a surprise." She surveyed the hotel lobby, figuring it was just her luck that Margie would dance out from behind a potted palm and whisk them off to spend the evening discussing "lighting options."

When she tried to slip the blindfold over Bram's head, he balked. "Come on, stop it. You can't actually expect me to walk through the lobby looking like Arlene Francis on *What's My Line?*"

"Shhh, sweetheart. Your age is showing."

He glowered, then gave up and tied on the blindfold himself.

"Can you see?"

"My entire life is flashing before my eyes."

"Imagine that." She led him to the elevators, careful that he didn't bump into any of the guests. They rode to the eleventh floor in silence. When they finally got off, Bram said, "Let's be philosophical. Why would one be asked to wear a blindfold? Are you about to make me walk the plank?"

"Guess again."

"You're going to line me up against a wall and throw knives at me, missing me by mere millimeters."

"That's a thought." She slipped a key card into suite 1139B and opened the door. Leading Bram inside, she told him to stand still and wait. She took off her raincoat and tossed it over a chair. Once the candles were lit and everything looked exactly the way she wanted it, she said, "You can take the blindfold off now."

"I'm not sure I want to."

"Okay, then I'll take you back downstairs and you can wander around the lobby looking like a reject from a magic show."

"How about you take it off for me." He bent down to make it easier.

As she slipped it free, he grabbed her around the waist and drew her close, kissing her like he hadn't kissed her in months.

"You're feeling frisky tonight."

Taking in the full suite, the bedsheets turned back in the bedroom, the pillows perfectly fluffed, and in the adjoining sitting room, a small round table set for a formal dinner—and Sophie standing before him in a sexy negligee—he grinned. "Looks like I'm not the only one."

"Should I ring for our dinner, or would you like—" She glanced into the bedroom.

"I want what's behind door number two."

"That would be me?"

"That would be you."

Several hours later, Bram and Sophie were just finishing their chocolate fondue—creamy dark chocolate with fresh strawberries and melon—when there was a knock on the door.

"Oh, God," said Sophie, wiping a smear of chocolate off her chin. "She found us."

"Who found us?" asked Bram, taking a sip of the Barsac, his favorite dessert wine.

"Margie."

He flicked his eyes to his wife, then down at his glass. "She has been a bit much."

"Why do you think I arranged this rendezvous in one of our guest suites? I thought it was Margie-proof."

The knocking grew louder.

"Maybe we better answer it."

"I will," said Sophie. "You keep your lips zipped." Tossing on her raincoat, she opened the door a crack. Sure enough, it was Margie.

"What are you doing down here?" she asked, trying to look into the room over Sophie's head.

"I'm, ah . . . meditating."

"Meditating? Do you do that a lot?"

"It's what keeps me centered, gives me inner peace." She could tell by the look on Margie's face that Margie didn't think the meditation was helping much. Suddenly,

Sophie heard the sound of water running. She glanced around and saw that Bram had left the table. The suite had a double Jacuzzi, and the sound probably meant he'd gone into the bathroom to start them a tub.

"What's that noise?" asked Margie.

"Running water. Helps me meditate. Makes me think I'm sitting by a peaceful stream."

"Do you know where my dad is?"

"He, ah, went to a lecture."

She folded her arms. "Funny. He never told me about that. I smell food."

"I always eat when I meditate. It helps concentrate my . . . my . . . my *essence*."

"You're weird."

"To each her own. Just out of curiosity, how did you find me?"

"I talked to someone at the front desk."

"Who?" Sophie would make sure they got fired.

"One of the staff. I don't know her name. Anyway, if you see Dad, will you tell him I'm looking for him?"

"Sure thing."

She hesitated, clearly in no hurry to go. "Hey, did you hear the news about old Mrs. Veelund? She's dead. The police think it was murder."

"Yes, I know all about it."

"Amazing, huh? To think we were just down there last weekend."

"Yeah, amazing."

Margie tucked a lock of hair behind her ear. "Listen, there's one more thing. I think my furniture will be delivered on Thursday. I'll be working that day, so I was hoping someone here could let the movers in. Is that a problem?"

"I'll take care of it," said Sophie.

"Thursday," repeated Margie. "All the boxes are labeled. All they have to do is put them in the right rooms."

"I've got it."

"Say, when you're done meditating, why don't you come up to my apartment? I've got some cool ideas for window treatments I'd like to run past you."

"You know, Margie, I think I'll have to pass on that tonight. I'm kind of tired."

"Oh. Sure, I understand. What time does Dad get home?"

"No idea."

"Okay. Well, thanks. See ya." Reluctantly, she turned and walked off down the hall.

Sophie shut the door. Turning around, she saw that Bram was back at the table. "You heard all that?"

"Every word. Coffee?" He held up the silver pot.

"Sure." She removed her raincoat and sat back down. "You're not mad, are you? You don't think I'm devious?"

"Of course you're devious. It's what I love about you. Look, sweetheart, I know my daughter can be a little difficult. I want you to know that I appreciate all the time and effort you've taken with her. Once she gets more established in town, makes some new friends, we'll have to schedule a date just to spend ten minutes with her."

Sophie's heart leapt with joy. "You're probably right." She stirred cream into her coffee.

Bram sat back and patted his stomach. "Great meal."

"I assume the Jacuzzi is next on the agenda."

"Any problems with that?"

"Are you kidding?"

"I poured in some of the stuff you had sitting next to

the tub, so it's going to be more on the order of a bubble bath."

"Excellent."

"I assume the suite is ours for the entire night."

"This is *not* the kind of hotel that rents rooms by the hour, dear."

He grinned.

Once they were comfortably ensconced in the bubbles, the candles lit, the champagne poured, Bram said, "Tell me more about Millie Veelund. You were asleep when I got home last night. And this morning you didn't mention anything about a homicide."

"I didn't want to get into it until we had more time."

"Thanks to my beautiful wife, I've got all the time in the world," he said, spreading his arms wide.

Sophie was eager to tell him what had happened after the police arrived yesterday. "Okay, I think you know everyone involved. First, Alex Veelund."

"I've played golf with Alex many times. I like him. He's a good man."

"And his brother, Danny. He's been home visiting his mother for the past few days."

"Daniel Reed Veelund. We've never met, but I admire his writing."

"Then there's Elaine, and Galen Zander—"

"Zander was Mrs. Veelund's assistant, right? I've only met him once. He struck me as a smart guy, but kind of brittle."

"Good description. And then, Tracy, Elaine's daughter; Mick Frye, Tracy's boyfriend; and finally, Doc Holland."

"The old guy who was always hanging around Millie?"

"He's been a friend of the family forever. In my opinion, every one of them is a suspect."

"I'm all ears."

One of the things Sophie appreciated most about Bram was that he loved a mystery as much as she did.

"Okay. The coroner pushed the autopsy of Millie Veelund through quickly as a favor to the family. I'm sure he thought it was just a formality. But the results showed that she'd died of an insulin overdose."

Bram whistled. "The klaus von Bülow weapon of choice."

"Except von Bülow was acquitted and his wife didn't die. In her case, the excess insulin caused an irreversible coma. But Millie Veelund was an old woman. Her immune system was compromised by asthma, years of diabetes, and heart disease."

"So who gave her the lethal dose?"

"That's the million-dollar question."

"How did she normally receive her insulin?"

"Zander would test her blood sugar and administer a shot before she went to bed. Doc Holland taught him how to do it. He'd done it for years, so it's unlikely he'd get the dosage wrong. Millie's medication was kept on a shelf in the downstairs pantry. Zander said that when he did the evening medication, he always brought her shot up on a small silver platter, along with a cup of sugar-free cocoa. The cocoa was kept in a tin in the kitchen."

"Was the medication cabinet locked?"

"No reason to. After the police arrived at the house yesterday, they asked all the visitors to leave. Then they executed the search warrant. The guy in charge gathered us all in the living room to ask a few questions. His name was Prentice. Sheriff Earl Prentice.

"Zander was adamant that he'd given Millie the proper dose, said he always gave it to her in her left arm. The doctor who did the autopsy found a second needle mark on her right arm. So the theory is that she was given a second shot, sometime in the night."

"Then Zander's off the hook?"

"If he's telling the truth."

Bram was silent for a few seconds, thinking it over. "How could Millie be given a second shot? She would have screamed bloody murder, tried to stop it."

"The autopsy also found a fairly high level of benzo-diazepines in her blood. Millie took Ativan for anxiety—and also for insomnia. Doc Holland had prescribed it years ago. He examined the bottle and said he thought it was about half gone. It should have been almost full."

"So she was drugged."

"That's the theory. The police took the tin of cocoa to test it. They think someone may have ground up the Ativan and dumped it into the cocoa. But here's a complication. The same night Millie died, Tracy ran away. The next day, Danny followed Mick to a sleazy motel in Maple Lake. That's where Tracy was staying. Danny listened through the screen door, so he got a real earful. When he finally confronted them, Tracy pulled a gun, took his wallet and his car keys, and locked him in the bathroom."

"Yikes," said Bram. "So she escaped again."

"That's right. Danny finally got out of the bathroom and called Alex to come pick him up. Anyway, according to what Danny learned, Tracy said she was sick of being trapped and treated like a mental patient, so she climbed out the window of her bedroom. In order to do that without being discovered, she had to drug the bodyguard. The police figure it was in the woman's Coke."

"Do the police think there's a connection between the bodyguard being drugged and Millie being drugged?"

Sophie shrugged. "The same medication was used. Beyond that, I don't know. Somehow Tracy managed to get off the property."

"I assume Mick helped her."

"He was supposed to wait for her in his truck on the service road about a mile from the house. But she never showed. She left her overnight bag behind in the grove next to the tennis court."

"Why?"

"Well, I guess Alex walked up to the pool house around one to take a swim. He must have come right past her without knowing it. She told Mick that she was so startled that she just rushed out of there and in the process forgot her bag. But whatever the case, she managed to get to that hotel somehow. Someone else must have picked her up and taken her there."

Sophie went on to explain that Tracy had been molested as a child. She told Bram everything she'd learned, and then said that Elaine believed one of four men was responsible.

Bram cringed when Sophie listed Elaine's two brothers, and then Doc Holland and Galen Zander. "How long has Elaine known about this?"

"Just a few months."

"But . . . I don't see that the molestation would give Tracy a motive to murder her grandmother."

"I agree with you, except she had means and opportunity, so the police can't count her out. Not until they find her and talk to her."

"Go on," said Bram, sipping his champagne.

"Well, it seems there was a lot of activity around the house on Sunday night—into the wee hours of Monday morning. Not only did Tracy fly the coop, but when

Mick came back to the house to find out why she hadn't met him like she'd promised, he decided he'd better search the house. That's when he bumped into Zander in the pantry."

"What time was that?"

"Around three in the morning."

"And what was Zander doing in the pantry?"

"He said he couldn't sleep so he'd gone downstairs to get himself a glass of milk."

Bram's eyes narrowed. "Sounds kind of fishy."

"But again, if Zander murdered his employer, why? The thing is, Zander said he saw Danny coming out of Millie's room. He wasn't positive about the time, but he thought it was around eleven-thirty."

"What was Danny doing there?"

"He admitted that he'd gone in to talk to her. Apparently, they'd had a rather heated discussion the day before."

"About what?"

"That was never clear to me. But he said he'd been thinking about some of her comments and he wanted one last opportunity to talk. He'd scheduled a flight out early the next morning, so he figured it was his last chance."

"She was still awake?"

"I guess her pattern was to read for a while before turning in. So, yes, Danny said she was awake."

Bram studied one of the candle flames. "In a family as rich as the Veelunds, money issues have to be huge. Who would benefit financially by Millie Veelund's death? Do you know what's in her will?"

"I believe Millie's estate is divided equally among her three children. If that's true, then inheritance has no bearing on her murder. But there are other motives."

"Like what?"

"Well, leaving the money angle aside for a moment, let's say Millie somehow stumbled onto the identity of Tracy's molester."

"But I thought you said her grandmother didn't know."

"But what if Tracy confided in her about it. It's possible. Let's say Millie learned of the abuse and confronted the molester. That person would have a great deal to lose if she went public with what she knew."

"Except why would Tracy tell her grandmother if she wouldn't even give the name to her therapist? Were Tracy and Millie close?"

"They were years ago. I'm not sure about now."

"What's your other theory?" asked Bram.

"Okay. On Friday night, Millie announced that she planned to sell Veelund Industries."

"Wow. That must have come as quite a shock."

"It was," said Sophie. "I know for a fact that Elaine was furious. She didn't give a damn about all the companies Alex has acquired, but the Log Lodges—"

"The company her dad started."

She nodded. "It's been her life's work. She loves that company, Bram. She built it into what it is today."

"Had her mother signed any papers yet?"

"No. She hadn't even decided who she was going to sell it to. Apparently, she had several good offers."

"What did Alex and Danny think about it?"

"Danny didn't appear to care one way or the other. But Alex did. Just before Millie dropped her bomb, Alex had proposed taking Veelund Industries public. Elaine was against the idea. But then Millie cut off all discussion by announcing that she was selling."

"Do you know why she wanted to sell?"

"Not really. I imagine she thought she was getting

older, that she wouldn't live forever, and she saw the company as a huge source of contention among her kids. By selling it, she could eliminate all of that. I know for a fact that she had a meeting with Alex on Saturday morning. I assume they talked it all through."

Bram nodded. "It was the morning you and Elaine drove over to his place so you could see it. That guy who runs Kitchen Visions was there."

"Roman Marchand. Elaine figured he was the one who was pushing Alex to take the company public. Actually"—she hesitated, but only for a moment—"Elaine told me something in confidence, but I don't think I have to keep it from you, as long as you promise to keep this under your hat."

"Do I *look* like I'm wearing a hat?"

When she turned around, he kissed her. "Clever."

"I thought so. But back to the story—"

"Well, Elaine has felt for a long time that Alex was gay. Turns out, she was right. When we walked into his house, it was obvious that Marchand had spent the night, and he didn't sleep on the couch."

"Ouch. If that's the case, Alex is pretty deep in the closet about it."

"Elaine confronted Roman. I mean, she has no problem with her brother being gay, but she's not very happy with his choice of partners. I imagine he stayed in the closet because his mother would have disapproved. Or worse."

"Meaning?"

"Elaine thinks she might have removed him as the head of Veelund Industries."

"And removed him from the will?"

"I can't imagine a parent would go that far."

"That's because you have a gay son, and you don't

have any religious or social opinions that tell you he's evil, sick, or sinful. What little I know about Millie tells me she wouldn't have come to the same conclusion."

"So, if Alex thought she was on the verge of finding out about his sexuality, you think he was capable of murder?"

"If he thought his whole life was about to go down the drain, who knows what he'd be capable of?"

Sophie nodded, thinking it over. "Not to mention that both Alex and Elaine have powerful feelings when it comes to Veelund Industries. Who knows what happened behind the scenes before Millie's death?"

Bram leaned forward and poured them each more champagne. "Do you think the police have a handle on all of this?"

"No."

"Are you going to talk to them? Give them the benefit of your vantage point?"

Sophie had considered it. "I don't think so. The police are smart. They'll figure it out on their own."

"You could save them some time."

"I could also get an otherwise innocent person in trouble. There's no witness to what happened, Bram. Whatever conclusions the police draw will be based on circumstantial evidence. And that always makes me uneasy."

"Unless someone confesses."

"Fat chance of that."

"Well," said Bram, raising his glass high, "all I can say is: Here's to fat chances."

"And fat people."

"Hear hear."

Sophie clicked her glass to his. "May the guilty party get nailed, and may the innocent—"

"Inherit," said Bram with a grin.

20

The next morning, Sophie spent a few hours at her office at the *Times Register* Tower in downtown Minneapolis. Wednesday was the day she needed to file her weekly restaurant review at the paper. She wanted to go over what she'd written about Chez Sophia one more time before she turned it in. Her intent was always to be scrupulously fair, but after the meal she realized that if she didn't say something critical, the review would be perceived as a whitewash. So she found a few unflattering comments to make about the waitstaff. She pointed out that, at times, the service was not only a little slow, but indifferent. Not that she wouldn't gladly wait for food as glorious as Nathan's. He'd truly lived up to his reputation.

Sophie wondered how he would perceive the review, if he would be pleased or annoyed. And, of course, thinking about Nathan reminded her of the private scene she'd witnessed at Prairie Lodge on Monday afternoon.

It had been such a chaotic day. Even though Sophie had never really liked Millie Veelund, her death had left her feeling both shocked and sad. Death always returned people to the essentials.

Unfortunately, what Sophie remembered most viscerally about Monday was watching Nathan and Elaine paw each other in Millie's study. It had seemed so irreverent. Then again, Sophie had lived long enough to know that people often had unrealistic expectations of the bereaved, as if losing someone important placed a person outside the normal range of emotion. It didn't. Elaine's mother might be dead and gone, but Elaine and Nathan had clearly formed some sort of attachment in the days since the two of them had been reintroduced. Sophie felt responsible for their meeting, so in a sense, she felt responsible for what happened afterward. But in truth, she couldn't control either of them, nor would she want to.

Ever since Monday afternoon, Sophie had been examining her feelings to determine if her negative reaction was based on jealousy. Was she the kind of woman who said, I don't want you, but nobody else can have you? It horrified her to think her love for Nathan had sunk to such a pathetic, teenage level. If Elaine made him happy, who was Sophie to say it was wrong? If there was ever a time Elaine needed a strong shoulder to lean on, it was now. Serendipity might have brought them together, but only true caring would keep them there. Still, in the deepest recesses of her soul, Sophie couldn't help but think the relationship was a bad idea. She told herself that it wasn't jealousy that made her want to tell Nathan to run, as fast and as far away from Elaine as he could get. It was concern. And yet where emotions were as conflicted and complex as hers, how could she ever be sure?

Sophie felt that she and Bram had connected last night in a way they hadn't in a very long time. They'd spent the entire night in the guest suite. She felt a tiny moment of triumph knowing she'd thwarted Margie. But then she felt guilty for the next hour because of that tiny moment. So much for glee.

By noon, Sophie had completed her work at the newspaper. She grabbed a quick sandwich at a deli on the Nicollet Mall, then returned to the Maxfield. As soon as she walked in the front door Brenda Swenson, the concierge on duty, waved her over.

"There's a moving van outside," said Brenda. "They just got here. They need to get into your daughter's apartment. I showed them where the service elevator was and told them to park around back."

"They're a day early," said Sophie. Last night, Margie had said they were coming on Thursday. "I don't suppose Margie is around."

"I called her apartment, but I got her voice mail. I can ask one of the bellmen to go unlock it."

"No, I'll take care of it," said Sophie. She headed over to the reception desk. After retrieving a duplicate key, she took the elevator up to the twelfth floor. The hallway was quiet, so she assumed the moving crew hadn't started bringing boxes up yet.

Sophie unlocked the door to the apartment, propping it open with a door stop. She picked up some discarded clothing in the foyer, thinking that Margie wouldn't want the delivery guys to know what color her bra was. As she entered the living room, she came to a complete stop. There on the couch was Mick Frye. He was lying on his stomach, snoring. An empty bag of corn chips and a half-filled liter of Coke sat on the floor next to him.

She walked over and nudged his foot. He snorted and flopped on his back. Not exactly the reaction she was looking for.

"Mick, wake up."

His eyes fluttered.

"Nap time's over."

As soon as he saw her staring down at him, he sat bolt upright. "Mrs. Baldric!"

"It's *Ms. Greenway*, but never mind. What's going on? Where's Tracy? What are you doing here?"

"I, ah—" He ran a hand over his prickly face. He had a heavy beard and it looked like he hadn't shaved in days. "I needed a place to crash last night."

"I thought you lived with your parents."

"I do. I mean, I did. They asked me to find an apartment last week. I was spending all of my time with Tracy, so it didn't matter. But now—"

"Where is she?"

He scratched his head. "She ditched me again."

"You don't have a lot of luck with her, do you."

He seemed embarrassed.

She sat down on the couch. He moved as far to the other side as he could get. There was nowhere else to sit in the room, so unless they wanted to stand, they were stuck.

"That wasn't very nice—what you did to Danny on Monday," said Sophie.

The corners of his mouth turned up. It wasn't a smile, but it was the beginnings of one. "No, I suppose not. Is he pissed?"

"I'd say that was a safe bet."

"Yeah. Well."

"When did Tracy ditch you?"

"We were having dinner at a cafe on Lake Street last night. I went to the bathroom. When I got back to the booth she was gone. So was my truck. I called Margie and she picked me up."

"And you spent the night here?"

"Margie's great. I'm glad she's back in town." He ran a hand over his buzz cut, looking uncomfortable.

Sophie had the sense that he was weighing his options. Did he want to talk to her, or didn't he? She had a feeling that he did.

"Look, Mick, you know Millie Veelund's dead. But have you heard—"

"Margie told me that the police think it was murder."

"They also think Tracy may have been involved."

His eyes grew round and frightened. "That's a lie!"

"Is it?"

"Sure. She wouldn't hurt her grandmother."

"Did she ever tell her grandmother she was molested?"

"She never told anyone. Not even me. The only reason I found out was because Elaine told everyone after Trace split. Tracy was pissed as hell when she found out."

"You told her?"

"Of course. I wanted to ask her about it."

"Did she tell you who molested her?"

"Do you think I'd be sitting here if I knew who'd done it? I'd make that guy pay. When I told Trace that, she just said it was a lot of macho crap. I don't think she likes men very much. That's the whole problem."

"What whole problem?"

He glanced at her, but didn't respond.

Sophie wondered if his silence was hostile. She was having a hard time reading him. "Do you have any idea who might want to hurt Millie Veelund?"

"No."

"Do you think Tracy is still thinking about suicide?"

"Hell no. She said it was a mistake. Thank God it wasn't my fault."

"You thought it was?"

"Partly."

"Why?"

He picked up the bottle of Coke and unscrewed the cap. "I should have watched her more carefully."

"That's it?"

"I should have checked the bathroom for razor blades."

He was giving her answers, but she knew he was reaching for them. Problem was, she didn't know how to make him tell the whole truth. "What did you two do after you left Danny at the motel?"

He took a sip of the Coke. Sitting back against the couch cushion, he seemed to relax a little. "We drove around for a while. Trace wanted to clean out her bank account, so we went to an automatic teller and got about two thousand dollars. We spent the night at another cheap motel. Trace said she didn't know how long she'd be on the road, so she had to be careful with her money. She had to make it last. She didn't even want to go out to breakfast yesterday. We got some fruit and cheese from a grocery store. Finally, last night we had some burgers. But then she took off. I don't have a dime right now. I couldn't even pay for the meal."

"She stuck you for the check?"

"Margie paid for it."

"And then you came here."

"Yeah. Most of yesterday, Tracy and I just hung out. Drove around. Tracy's definitely got something on her mind, but she wouldn't tell me what it was. Whenever I started a conversation, she told me she needed peace and quiet so she could think."

"You care about her, don't you?"

"Yeah, I do. A lot. Elaine doesn't think I could love her daughter because Tracy isn't the same kind of woman she is. But that's just a bunch of egomaniacal crap. Tracy is beautiful. She's sweet. Well, not all the time, but sometimes. Except she's real messed up. I wanted to help her. I thought I could. But now . . ." His voice drifted off.

"You have no idea where she is?"

He didn't answer immediately. "No," he said finally, but it wasn't a definite no.

Once again, Sophie had the sense that he wasn't being totally forthcoming.

"She's really mad at someone," he mumbled.

"You mean the man who molested her?"

"I guess so."

"But you're not sure?"

He rested the Coke bottle on his knee. "She's got a gun."

"Danny said that. It belonged to her grandfather."

"I think she intends to shoot someone with it."

Now he had her full attention. "Why do you say that?"

"We stopped at a gun shop so she could buy a bunch of ammunition. Then we drove to this field way out in the county. She practiced shooting cans off the same damn rock for nearly two hours. Why do that if you aren't going to, you know, use it?"

Good question, thought Sophie.

"It's like . . . last summer, she was so happy. But then, around August, she hit a bad patch. Except ever since the suicide attempt, something's changed. I don't know how to define it exactly."

"Try."

"Well, before it happened she was depressed. Now she's angry."

A loud noise from out in the hallway pulled Sophie's attention to the door.

"What's that?" asked Mick, shooting to his feet.

"It's the movers. Margie's furniture is being delivered today."

"Oh," he said, looking relieved.

"Since you're here, maybe you could make yourself useful—help with the boxes. When you're done, I'll buy you a steak dinner downstairs in the Fountain Room."

He slipped his hands into the back pockets of his jeans. "You're not going to call the police? Or Elaine?"

"I think you should have a good meal first. After that, we'll discuss it."

He smiled at her. "Thanks."

For the next hour, Sophie acted as straw boss. She directed boxes into the living room, the kitchen, and the bedroom. At one point, she stepped out into the hallway and saw Mick talking to one of the movers. Mick smiled at her and waved as he headed back to the service elevator for another load.

After signing the final papers, Sophie looked around for Mick but couldn't find him. She asked one of the movers if he knew where Mick had gone. "You know. The tall young man who's been helping you."

"Oh, he left a while ago."

She took off her reading glasses. "He did?"

"Yeah, he told me to tell you thanks for the dinner invitation, but he'd have to take a rain check."

The nerve of him, thought Sophie. Giving her the slip after she'd been nice to him. "Which way did he go?"

"Last time I saw him," said the mover, "he was getting on a bus."

Sophie sank down on a box. She'd let the chicken fly the coop. How could she ever tell Elaine?

21

As soon as Sophie got back to her apartment, the phone rang. She raced into the kitchen and grabbed the one on the counter. "Hello?"

"Sophie, hi," came her mother's voice.

"Hey, Mom! Where are you?"

"Tokyo. We're about to get on a plane. It's been delayed for one reason or another, but they've finally started boarding. I'm glad I caught you before we had to leave."

"Where's Dad?"

"He went to buy a copy of the *New York Times*."

Sophie's dad was a news junkie. She figured he channeled CNN in his sleep. After 9/11 he'd become even more obsessed with keeping his finger on what was happening in the world. Sophie's reaction to the devastation had been somewhat different. She wanted to hide her head under a pillow and forget the rest of the world existed. She assumed there was a happy medium somewhere in between those two extremes, but neither she nor her father had found it.

"We should be home soon," continued Pearl.

"Do you have a flight number yet?"

"We're spending a day or two in San Francisco, so I'll call you from there. Your father wanted to know if you found out any information on the log homes. He really wants to move on that when we get back. And you know your dad. When he gets an idea in his head—"

"I know," said Sophie.

"Have you talked to Elaine?"

"Yes, but . . . well, Millie Veelund died a few days ago."

Her mother was silent for a moment. "I'm sorry to hear that. She's been in bad health for years."

"It wasn't her health," said Sophie. "The police think she was given an overdose of insulin."

More silence. "Do they know who did it? Or why?"

"Not yet."

"Oh, there they go, calling our section," said Pearl, sounding distracted. "And here comes your father. I better get off. Give Millie's kids my love, okay?"

"I will," said Sophie. "And I'll see you soon."

Clicking off the phone, Sophie decided to run over to the south wing and check her parents' apartment one more time. She'd asked maintenance to put a fresh coat of paint in the bathroom. She wanted to make sure everything had been done. She also wanted to open a few windows to air the place out. On the day her parents would arrive home, she'd make sure fresh flowers were placed in the entryway and in the bedroom, and that the kitchen was stocked with a few essentials—milk, eggs, ketchup (in her father's mind, eggs and ketchup went together like Astaire and Rogers), fresh coffee beans, bread and butter. Her parents could handle the rest of the grocery shopping when they got home.

Sophie sniffed the air as she entered the apartment. The paint smell wasn't too strong. The carpet had been freshly cleaned and was still a bit damp. From the foyer, she could see into the living room and since the door to the balcony was open, she decided not to walk on the carpet until it was dry.

As she turned to leave, she spied the rusted metal box, the one that had belonged to her great uncle. The broken lock dangled enticingly from the front hinge. She paused, fighting an inward battle. She fingered the lock, flipping it back and forth. She was so frustrated by Mick disappearing on her. Here was another mystery. But this one she could solve. Right now. This minute, if she had the nerve.

She was a bad person. She had no scruples. On the other hand, if she could come up with a reasonable rationalization, she'd be okay. But that would take time. She made a quick decision. She'd open the box now and figure out the rationalization later.

Tucking the box under her arm, she walked the quiet hallway from the south tower back to the north and returned to her apartment. After pouring herself a glass of iced tea, she sat down on the living room couch. There was probably nothing important inside the box, nothing of particular interest. Her mother had pack-rat tendencies, just like Bram. Sophie slipped off the lock and pulled back the top.

Inside she found a bunch of letters written to her mother, all tied together with a gold satin ribbon. They looked ancient. Checking them over, Sophie concluded that they spanned the years from 1950 to 1952. There were several different return addresses, but the writing all looked the same. The sender hadn't written his or her name on the outside. The postmark was from Minneapolis. Thinking back, Sophie calculated that her mother was still living at her parents' home in Bovey at the time. In

1950, she would have been eighteen. Sophie's mother and father had married in 1954, and moved the next year to the Twin Cities.

Underneath the letters was a notebook. Black cover. Nondescript. The kind you could buy in any drugstore. The year 1972 had been taped to the front. Sophie would have been fifteen that year. She set the letters down and opened the notebook. Only the first twenty or so pages had been used. The rest was blank. But there was no mistaking her mother's handwriting.

Before she realized it, Sophie had read the first page, and then the next . . . and then. . . .

Pearl's Notebook
March 29, 1972

I should have waited for Henry and Sophie to come out of the house. I knew Henry would worry when he found that I'd taken the car and driven off without him, but time was running out. Carl had been drinking heavily all evening, and besides that, he was terribly upset. He had no business getting behind the wheel of a car, especially on a night when the roads were growing more slick by the minute. He was a car wreck waiting to happen. I had to get to him, make him pull over and listen to reason. Whatever had transpired between Carl and his wife wasn't the point any longer. When I caught up with them, I planned to drive the two of them back to the house. If Carl wanted to leave, Henry and I could take him wherever he wanted.

The service road was two lanes, but only one was being used as the guests fled the party. Everyone was driving so slowly that I knew if I stayed behind them I'd never catch up to Carl's Cadillac. I swerved into the left lane and sped ahead, all the while watching for Carl's car. I made it all the way out to the county road without spotting it.

Everyone in the long line of cars leading from the house was turning right, on their way to County Road 31 and the long drive back to the Cities. Something told me that instead of following the crowd, I should turn left, and that's what I did. I drove along with the windows open because the rain was starting to stick to the glass. Even with the defrost fan turned up as high as it would go, I still had trouble seeing. Whatever was coming out of the sky— sleet, snow, freezing rain—was turning the world into one huge skating rink.

Less than a mile from the turn, I saw it. The Cadillac had skidded off the road and landed in a ditch about a hundred yards in front of me. Skid marks had dug into the shoulder. As I got closer I could see that the car had torn away great clumps of earth from the field as it hurtled toward a section of woods.

I rolled to a stop behind the car but left the headlights on. It was the only light I had. The front of Carl's Cadillac was wrapped around a tree. My heart was beating so hard I thought it would fly out of my chest. The passenger door was wide open and the seat was empty. I heard a groaning sound coming from behind me, and when I turned around I saw that Millie was lying in the field about fifteen feet away. If she hadn't made the sound, I never would have seen her. In the red glow of the rear headlights, I knelt down next to her. I said her name and touched her shoulder, asked her if she was all right. She was barely conscious, and soaked to the skin. But she was alive. I could tell her right arm was broken, and I assumed there might be some internal injuries. Covering her with my coat, which seemed pointless but nevertheless necessary, I told her I'd go get help. But I had to check on Carl first.

When I finally reached the Cadillac, I found that the driver's door was so twisted I couldn't open it. Running around to the other side, I climbed into the passenger's seat. Carl's eyes were closed, and he was incredibly still. I checked and found that he was barely breathing. His body had been pinned between the steering wheel and the seat and he was bleeding from his mouth and from a wound in his chest. I knew I should try to stop the bleeding but I didn't know how. When I touched his arm, he opened his eyes.

"Carl, I'm here," I said. "I'll drive back to the house and call for an ambulance. Millie was thrown from the car. We've got to get you both some help."

"No," he whispered. He didn't move his head, only his eyes. His hand found mine. And then he said my name. Softly. Tenderly. It broke my heart.

"I love you, Pearl," he said. "I always have."

I told him that I had to go get help.

"Don't leave me," he said. It was horrible. With every word, more blood leaked from his mouth. I brought up a fold of my dress to wipe it away.

"Why did you have to leave the house?" I said. I tried not to sound angry, but I don't think I succeeded. "Why did you drive off in a storm when you've had so much to drink?"

And that's when he told me. In a few broken sentences, he explained what had happened when he'd asked Millie for a divorce. She'd finally told him the truth. In the car, his life being crushed out of him, he said he wanted to kill her. If he'd stayed in the house, he would have. He had to get away, but she forced herself into the front seat. She needed to make him understand. He said he never would.

I told him that none of it mattered. What did matter was that he get some medical help.

He said he was dying. He didn't want to die alone.

What could I do?

And then he asked me for one last favor. He said that, after he was gone, I should go back to the house, to his study. There was a sealed envelope in the bottom drawer of his desk. On the outside he'd written "Agreement." The drawer was locked so he told me where to find the key. He wanted me to take the letter and tear it up. I was confused. I didn't understand. I asked him to explain it, but he didn't respond. He just looked at me. He seemed to be trying to memorize my face. There were tears in his eyes.

"I've made a terrible mess of my life," he said.

I told him that wasn't true. That he was a good man, a successful man.

"Do you love me?" he asked.

I squeezed his hand. "Always," I said.

He closed his eyes and, a few moments later, he was gone.

22

By Thursday afternoon, Sophie had given a lot of thought to what she'd read yesterday—her mother's note-book, Carl Veelund's love letters. She had so many questions, but they would all have to wait until her mother returned home. Whether or not she would ever be willing to admit to her relationship with Carl, it was clear that she'd been in love with him. The irony of the situation wasn't lost on Sophie. Her mother had been in love with two men.

As she picked up the letters and slipped the golden ribbon back around them, she heard a knock on her office door. Swiveling her chair around, she saw Nathan standing there.

As a reflex, she stood up. Nathan hadn't visited her at the hotel since he'd been released from prison a year ago. She thought she'd made it clear to him that he wasn't to come to the Maxfield. For her own peace of mind she needed to keep him as far away from Bram as possible, and she thought that he not only understood her ground rules, but that he'd agreed to them.

Glancing quickly at her watch, Sophie saw that it was going on three. Bram would be on the air for another hour, so she relaxed a bit, thinking she had some time. She had to admit that she was curious to know why he'd come. She wished she had a better poker face because he could probably read everything she was thinking.

"Do you have a minute?" he asked, stepping hesitantly into the room.

"You could have phoned, Nathan."

"I could have." Without being invited, he lowered himself into a chair on the other side of the desk. He was wearing jeans, work boots, and a chambray shirt—his *uniform* as he laughingly used to call it. He looked rough and handsome, so different from Bram's sophisticated elegance.

"Can I get you something?" asked Sophie. She might as well be civil. He wasn't her enemy. "A cup of coffee?"

"Nothing, thanks. Look, Soph, I need to talk to you about Elaine."

The last thing she needed was for her ex-boyfriend to ask her advice about his new girlfriend.

"You know her better than I do," said Nathan.

Sitting down, she said, "I know her in a different way than you do."

"Did she tell you we were dating?"

"I'm aware of it, yes."

"I assume you know about the murder investigation."

"I know it's ongoing."

He met her eyes, then looked down. "I'm worried about her, Soph. With her daughter on the run, and now the suspicion she's under—"

"Are you saying the police think she had something to do with her mother's death?"

"They've been interrogating the entire family, Elaine included."

"They're just doing their job."

"Yeah, I know. But it's taking a toll. On everyone."

Running a hand through his hair, he added, "I feel especially sorry for that old guy . . ."

"Doc Holland?"

"He's been staying at the house, sleeping in one of the upstairs bedrooms. Nobody's got the heart to kick him out. That other man . . . the butler—"

"You mean Zander? He's not a butler, Nathan. He was Millie's personal assistant."

"If he looks like a butler and acts like a butler, he's a butler. Anyway, he's taking care of Holland—bringing him his meals, making sure he eats. Elaine told me that Holland was totally devastated by her mother's death, not that I couldn't see it with my own two eyes." He paused, then leaned forward. "You don't think Elaine had anything to do with her mother's murder, do you? She seems so . . . decent. So . . ."

"Spare me the details."

He narrowed his eyes at her. "Don't tell me you're jealous."

"Let me repeat to you what I said the other night. Elaine has a terrible track record when it comes to men. Marriage is more or less a hobby with her. *And* she's on the rebound from husband number three. Catch my drift?"

"I'm not planning to pop the question, Sophie. We're just dating. Having some fun."

"Fine. Whatever."

"So answer my question. Is she the kind of woman who could commit a murder?"

Sophie didn't answer immediately. It was her opinion that, given the right set of circumstances, almost anyone was capable of murder. But if she answered Nathan's question in the affirmative, he might take it the wrong way. He might think she actually *was* jealous. Sinking to a bit of character assassination was just the proof he needed. "I don't know," she said finally. "I don't think so, but I suppose anything is possible."

"I have a theory about this whole mess." He folded his arms over his chest, thinking about it for a moment. "Last night, Elaine told me that her daughter had been molested when she was a kid. I assume you know about it."

"I know it happened, but that's about all."

"What if Millie Veelund knew who the guy was, or simply had a strong hunch? And what if she confronted him about it? I think there's a good chance he was the one who murdered her."

"Two birds with one stone. The molester is also the murderer."

"Exactly."

"I've had the same thoughts. Only problem is, it's just a theory. There are other motivations involved, some that are every bit as strong."

"Like what?"

Sophie leaned back in her chair. "Did you know that Millie was planning to sell Veelund Industries?"

Nathan whistled, opening his eyes wide. "No way."

"She announced it just two nights before she died."

"Geez, I can imagine how that went over. Elaine's whole life is that company. And Alex, too, from what I can tell."

"Alex and Roman Marchand wanted to take the company public."

"Elaine thinks Marchand is a parasite."

"He's Alex's right-hand man."

"I know. I guess Tracy worked for him last summer, in the Kitchen Visions office."

That was the first Sophie had heard of it. "As what?"

"Oh, a secretary, or a file clerk. Something menial. Elaine told Tracy that if she refused to work on her degree, she should do something productive. So she ran some job openings past her and they finally settled on the one at KitchenVisions. Apparently Tracy got sick of it after a few months and quit. With what she's about to inherit, she won't be taking any more dead-head jobs for a while."

Sophie's ears pricked up. "Did Millie leave her some money?"

"A substantial trust fund, from what I understand. I don't know how much, but I do know she'll be a rich young woman. If she ever comes out of hiding."

"I wonder if Tracy knew about the trust?"

Nathan raised an eyebrow. "You think she offed her grandmother for the money?"

"Stranger things have happened."

Sophie was about to tell him that she'd had a long talk with Tracy's boyfriend, Mick, but the sound of Bram's voice in the hallway stopped her. She checked her watch again. It was too early for him to be home, but here he was. Her first instinct was to hide Nathan, stuff him in a closet or behind a plant, but there was nowhere for him to go.

An instant later, Bram appeared in the door. His smile faded as he saw that Sophie had a visitor. "I'm interrupting," he said stiffly.

Sophie jumped up. "No, no, not at all. Nathan was in the neighborhood so he stopped by."

Nathan stood and turned to Bram. "Hi," he said, hooking his thumbs around his belt. "I, ah . . . I was just wondering what kind of review Soph was going to give my restaurant in next Sunday's *Times Register*."

Bram's eyes moved from Sophie to Nathan, then back again to Sophie.

"I was just about to leave," added Nathan. "I've got to get back to the restaurant."

"Nice to see you again," said Sophie, knowing her voice sounded fake.

Bram didn't move out of the doorway, so Nathan had to flatten himself against the door frame to get out.

"You're home early," chirped Sophie, silently berating herself for sounding so damn guilty. Bram had hardly caught them in flagrante delicto. They were just talking.

"I was feeling tired, so the station manager decided to air a *Best of Baldric* for the last hour."

"Oh," said Sophie. "Just tired? But . . . you're okay, right?"

"Does he come here often?" asked Bram, still not moving from the door.

"Nathan? No, of course not. He's dating Elaine."

He loosened his tie and unbuttoned the top button of his shirt. "Lucky Elaine."

"Bram . . ."

"I think I'll go for a swim."

She followed him out of the room, past the reception desk, and into the lobby. Once they were in the elevator, they couldn't continue their conversation because several hotel guests were riding up at the same time. When they reached the sixteenth floor, Bram got off and headed for their apartment.

They were alone now, but Sophie didn't know what to say. She wasn't sure if he was angry or hurt, or just miffed.

Ethel met them at the door as they entered. Bram picked her up, carried her into the bedroom, and deposited her in the center of their bed, then stripped off his clothes and pulled on his sweats. He wasn't talking, always an ominous sign. Sophie sat down on a chair in the corner. She felt as if she were the little mouse in a children's story. If she just got small enough, maybe he wouldn't be mad anymore.

"Why did you review his restaurant?" asked Bram.

Sophie was a bit taken aback. "It's my job. I waited too long as it was. I usually review new restaurants within the first two months."

"But why did *you* have to do it? Your son could have."

"Sure, Rudy does occasional reviews, but never new restaurants. Rudy's learned a lot. He's a great assistant, but he's not ready for the big reviews yet."

"Says you."

"It's true."

"The truth is, you wanted to see Nathan and this gave you just the opportunity you were looking for."

"Bram, I asked you to come along, but you had something else going on that night."

"Yeah, that would have been a fun evening, watching him drool over you."

"I'm a middle-aged woman. Nobody drools over me."

"*He* does. It's revolting." Bram leaned over to tie his shoelaces. "I wish that guy would just disappear."

"Why are you getting so upset?"

"You mean he doesn't call all the time? You don't get together when I'm not around?"

"Of course not."

"You've never been able to put him behind you, Soph.

After my heart surgery, I thought you had. But I see I was wrong."

"That's not true."

"Have you slept with him?"

She felt instantly light-headed. "Bram!"

"Since the day he walked back into your life, I haven't had a moment's peace. Who do you want, Sophie? Me or him?"

"I want *you*."

"But you want him, too."

"No."

"You love him. I'm not blind."

"Don't do this."

"I thought that if I gave you some time, if I just kept looking straight ahead, if I ignored him, he'd go away. But it doesn't work like that. By the way, Margie thinks you've still got a thing for him, too."

"Margie? What's she got to do with this?"

"She's not stupid, you know."

"I never said she was. But how could she possibly know how I feel?"

"You can't be friends with an old boyfriend. It doesn't work."

"Says who?"

"Says everyone in the goddamned world except you." He got up and grabbed his gym bag from the floor of the closet.

She stared at his shoelaces, trying not to cry. Tears were the last thing this discussion needed. "But we're not friends, Bram. Not in any real way. I hardly ever see him."

"I'm supposed to believe that? You take every chance you get to be with him. I'm sure I don't even know about all the times you get together. Maybe you haven't slept with him yet, but how long before you do?"

"Stop it!"

Without looking at her, he stomped out of the room.

"Bram, you can't leave. We've got to talk this through."

But before she could get up, she heard him slam out of the apartment.

23

Since his mother's sudden death, Danny had spent a great deal of time wandering through the house alone, sitting in various chairs, opening books he was unable to read. If anyone had cared to observe him, they wouldn't have been able to tell he was crying, except that his shoulders were shaking. In his mind's eye he saw his distant past—a boy, thin-chested and bright-faced, blond buzz cut because that's what his mother liked, gentle to a fault. How that boy had evolved into the middle-aged man he saw in the mirror now was a mystery, one he didn't want to concentrate on too carefully.

Danny realized that, without his mother around, without the kind of commotion caring for an old woman created, the rooms of the old house seemed profoundly still. Within that stillness he could hear his life echoing. His mother's death had made him sentimental. He hated sentimentality.

In Manhattan, Danny's world was rarely quiet. He couldn't help but wonder what kind of novels he would have written if he'd stayed in Minnesota, married a good Lutheran girl and remained close to the old homestead. Would he have written at all? Or would he have moved in some different direction? Maybe he would have become a petty politician. Perhaps he would have spent his days sleepwalking through the boredom of an office job. New York had kept Danny's senses on edge. For that, he was grateful.

Standing now in the living room, looking up at the geometry of light his father had created with towering, cathedral-like windows, he felt a wave of grief so strong that he had to tense all his muscles just to keep upright. Whether the grief was for his mother or for himself, he couldn't tell. All he knew was that his life would have been altered beyond recognition if he hadn't met and married Ruth.

People often asked Danny what he wrote about. His stock answer was that he explored the necessity of the uneasy compromise. If pushed further, he would explain that he was fascinated by the decisions human beings made that were born out of the struggle between ideals and practicality. He was rarely pressed for a more lengthy response.

As twilight settled on the prairie, Danny walked out on the front porch to get some air. He found Doc Holland sitting in one of the wicker chairs, staring at a smear of orange just above the horizon. It was a picture perfect evening.

"Have you had dinner?" asked Danny.

Doc shook his head. "Not hungry."

"I'm sure Zander would make us a sandwich."

Nodding to a chair, Doc said, "Zander's not here."

"Where is he?"

"Canterbury Downs. He likes the ponies, in case you didn't know."

"Since when?" asked Danny.

"Since they built the racetrack. He tried to keep it quiet

so your mother wouldn't find out, but that's where he spends his free time. With the money Millie left him burning a hole in his pocket, I figure he couldn't wait to get out of here."

"Well then, maybe I should fix us some dinner."

"Just sit. Keep me company."

Danny didn't exactly have anything pressing, so he relaxed into a chair and propped his feet up on the wood railing. The police had made it clear he wasn't to leave town. Spending a few days at the house fit his current mood, so he didn't resist, but if his enforced stay went on too much longer, he'd be on the horn to his lawyer in Manhattan.

In the past few days, Danny had fallen into a kind of routine, calling Ruth every evening at ten. They'd talk for an hour or so. Her first question was always about the police investigation—had they discovered anything new. So far his answer was always the same. They hadn't. One of these nights maybe he'd have news of a breakthrough in the case. His mother's will had been officially read this morning, so he'd have that information to give her tonight. Not that anything was a surprise, with one exception. His mother had rewarded Zander's nearly thirty years of service with a cool million.

"Nice evening," said Doc, brushing a fly away from his face. A newspaper rested in his lap, a pair of half glasses on his nose. In the evening light, his face looked lacy with freckles.

Doc had a certain gentleness about him that always put people at ease. Danny liked him. He knew that Doc had tried hard to be a father figure after Danny's dad had died, but nobody took him seriously. Alex was too old to want another man telling him what to do. Elaine adored Doc, but she made it clear that nobody could replace her father. And Danny, well, he tried to be kind and accept the old guy's overtures, lame as they were. At thirteen, Danny hardly found it a highlight of his week to be taken into Maple Lake for an ice cream cone.

"I've been sitting out here all afternoon," said Doc, folding one leg over the other. "I just don't know what to do with myself now that your mother's gone." He looked away. Gazing up at the sky, he added, "I loved her, you know. It wasn't just friendship on my part."

"I always thought the two of you would get married after my dad died."

"No, that was never in the cards." He shifted in his chair. "I knew your mother before she married your dad. Did you know that?"

Danny shook his head.

"She was working as a secretary at the university when I was a medical student. Your mother was the strongest, smartest girl I ever met. She had such confidence, such ambition. A couple months before she met your dad, I asked her to marry me. But she turned me down."

"I'm sorry. I didn't know."

He shrugged. "I made peace with that a long time ago. Millie knew she'd never want for anything if she married me, but it wasn't enough. My ambition didn't stretch as far as hers. I was content to be a family practitioner. It was a fine living, but nothing grand. When she met your dad, she had stars in her eyes. She knew immediately that he was a guy who was going places. Like they used to say, she wanted to hitch her wagon to a star, and that's exactly what she did."

"But you stayed friends." Danny recalled how many times in the last thirty years his mother had called Doc "hopelessly needy." Not a very flattering assessment coming from such a dear old friend.

"Yeah, through thick and thin we always stuck together. Actually, it was probably for the best that I never settled down with any one person. I mean, I enjoyed playing the field. I certainly never wanted for female companionship, though trust me, it's harder to find these days." He winked at Danny. "I always liked my girls frisky. Still do, except they run too fast now and I have a hard time catching them." He laughed, then sighed. "But I miss your mom something fierce. We were well past our romantic feelings, but I loved talking to her. We'd argue about anything and everything. She had strong opinions, but that was all right with me. She valued ideas. Not many people do."

"That's one way to look at it."

Doc glanced over at him.

Danny figured he was in for a lecture. Doc had a tendency to grow didactic when he thought someone had judged Millie too harshly.

"The truth is, son, I'm not as sharp as I used to be. Things get past me now that never would have in my younger years. I'm . . . forgetful. Sometimes I'm even a little confused. I'm still as strong as an ox, knock on wood, but I get lost in the past. You probably don't know what the hell I'm talking about."

"Actually," said Danny, "I do."

"There are times when I don't just get *lost* in the past, I feel like I get *stuck* there. It's frightening because . . . what if I can't get back? That's one reason I stayed on here at the house. Going home, being alone, scares the bejeebers out of me."

"You can stay here as long as you like," said Danny.

"Thanks. But I can't. Not really. I'll have to make some hard decisions soon." Folding his hands in his lap, he asked, "Have you had any word from Tracy?"

Danny shook his head. "Nothing. I hope she turns up soon. Say, Doc, speaking of Tracy. When I caught up with her the other day at that hotel in Maple Lake, she said she saw your car the night she took off. Must have been around one in the morning."

"Really," said Doc, scratching his shoulder.

"Was it you?"

"Yes, it was me."

"How come you came back here? I saw you leave around ten."

He shrugged. "Couldn't sleep, so I went out for a drive. I do that sometimes. Being in the country always calms me down. Seems that when my brain switches off, I always end up here."

"It's happened before?"

"Once or twice."

"You just turned around and went home?"

"Yup, that's about it." He looked over at Danny. "How come you didn't tell the police Tracy saw my car that night?"

"I didn't want to get you in trouble. I know you didn't murder my mother."

"I suppose I should thank you for that vote of confidence."

"No thanks necessary."

Doc returned his gaze to the sunset. "What's going to happen to this house now that your mother's gone?"

"Oh, I don't know. I suppose Alex or Elaine will move in. Or maybe they'll sell it. We own it jointly now."

"What about you and your wife?"

"Our home is in New York."

"How about Zander? What are his plans?"

"I don't know," said Danny, noticing a pair of head-lights on the service road heading their way. "I doubt he'll want to stick around here much longer."

As the car came closer Danny could see that it was Alex's Mercedes. After swinging in behind Danny's rental, he got out.

Doc waved. "Come on up and have a seat," he called amiably.

Alex trotted up the steps. "Evening."

"Heard anything more about that sniper in the grove?" asked Doc.

"Actually, yes," said Alex, loosening his tie. "They found the rifle the guy used. It was pushed under a part of the wood lattice on the south side of the house. It belonged to my dad, but whoever used it wiped it clean of fingerprints."

"Tough break," said Doc.

"Yeah."

Danny assumed he was just getting home from a day at the office.

"I need a drink," said Alex. Without further comment, he headed into the house.

Danny could tell by the look on his brother's face that something was wrong. "I better go talk to him," he said, getting up.

"You kids need to stick together," said Doc. "That's what your mother would have wanted."

Danny found Alex in the rec room in the basement, standing behind the bar. He'd taken off his suit coat and tossed it over a chair. A bottle of wine had been placed on the counter, but he appeared to have thought better of it and pushed it aside. An open bottle of bourbon and an empty shot glass sat directly in front of him.

Danny sat down on one of the bar stools.

"Want one?" asked Alex. He nodded to the bourbon.

"Sure, why not."

Alex looked as if he'd aged ten years in the last few days.

"Are you okay?" asked Danny.

"No."

"Want to talk about it?"

Alex poured them each a stiff shot. "Down the hatch," he said, lifting his glass to his lips, then tossing it back.

Danny sipped his. "What's up?"

"Roman."

"Oh." Danny had guessed a long time ago, as far back as high school, that Alex was gay, though Alex wasn't honest with him about it until several years after he'd graduated from college. He figured that others suspected, but that's all it was. Speculation.

It was the night before Alex's wedding. He'd gotten royally plastered on Russian vodka and ended up sleeping on the couch in Danny's hotel room. Before he sank into his alcohol-induced oblivion, he'd told Danny the truth. Danny could have cared less, which Alex knew. That was why he trusted him with such a sensitive piece of information.

The next morning Danny encouraged Alex to fess up, ditch his fiancée, and go sell shoes or work at Kmart. Live an honest life. But Alex couldn't give up his dream. He felt it was his birthright to head his father's company, to take it to the next level, whatever that meant. Danny hoped that Alex would tell Elaine. She was in engineering school at the time. But Alex said no, there was too much competition between them. There always had been. He loved her, but he didn't trust her.

That made Danny sad. Of course, the person who would have blown a gasket if she'd found out was their mother. The fewer people who knew the truth, said Alex, the better. Danny respected his wishes. But keeping up the charade now—what was the point?

"Look, Alex, you probably don't want to hear what I've got to say."

"You're right. I don't." He downed another shot.

"Why don't you dump Marchand? Elaine thinks the guy's bad news and I'm inclined to agree."

"You're wrong."

"Sometimes the truth is hard to hear, but it doesn't make hearing it any less necessary."

Leaning across the bar, Alex grabbed Danny by his shirt and said, "You keep this up, pal, and I might have to wipe the floor up with you."

"Oh, that's just great. Macho shit coming from my gay brother."

"Gays are macho," said Alex indignantly. "At least, some of us are."

They both started to laugh at the same time.

Alex let go of Danny's shirt and poured himself another drink.

"Okay, so maybe Marchand isn't such a bad fellow," continued Danny. "Maybe he does love you, but he loves your money, too. Can you ever trust a guy like that? And think about this. If he was never honest with his wife about his extracurricular activities, what makes you think he's honest with you?"

"He loves me, Danny. That's not the issue. But he's been so depressed, ever since Mom announced she wanted to sell the company. Honestly, I feel like, if I go through with it, it will kill him. I don't know what to do. No matter what decision I make, I feel like a traitor."

"But I figured you would lobby to take the company public now that Mom's not around to stop you."

He shook his head. "I changed my mind."

"Oh, right. I remember now. You had that heart-to-heart with her before she died. Did she convince you that selling Veelund Industries was the right thing to do?"

Stiffening his shoulders, Alex said, "I need to do what she asked. It was her last request and I take it seriously."

What a load of crap, thought Danny. There had to be another reason. "Does Elaine know about your change of mind?"

"We haven't had a chance to talk about it." He hoisted another shot.

"So you're in the middle. Elaine wants you to do one thing, and your lover wants another. And you, being a good son, are still trying to please Mama."

"Don't be an ass. It's not that simple."

"I figured that, not that I understand all the ins and outs." Danny swirled the liquid in his shot glass, but didn't take a sip. "You realize, don't you, that controlling you is Marchand's ticket to fame and fortune. His *only* ticket."

"Just can that talk, okay? Roman fell in love with *me*. Not my bank account. And also . . . because I'm such a dynamic businessman."

"He told you that?"

"Many times. He's drawn to power and money. So what? He wants to be a player, Danny. He freely admits that. He also says he's given up everything to be with me.

His wife. His company. If I let him down now, he'll have lost everything."

"What bullshit. That's nothing but emotional blackmail. You *saved* his company by buying it and then hiring him to run it. And if his wife was that important to him, he wouldn't have left her. If he really loved you, he wouldn't force you to do something you're dead set against."

"He says I'm afraid of success, that in some twisted part of my psyche I don't want to outshine my father."

"Oh, *pullease*."

Alex laughed. "That's exactly what I think." Tossing back another shot, he continued, "If I want to sell the company, will you back me? Elaine will be against it, but the two of us could outvote her."

Danny was torn. "I . . . I don't know. I guess I'd have to think about it."

"She'll say I just want to take the money and run. That I talked a good game but my heart was never in it."

"Is that true?"

"What if it is?" He set the shot glass down, then stared at it.

Danny had barely touched his drink. Before his bout with cancer, he'd been a much heavier drinker. But in the past few years, his desire for alcohol had diminished. He didn't need artificial stimulants to get him high. Just being alive did it now.

"Listen," said Alex, bending closer to Danny. "If I tell you a secret, you've got to promise to keep quiet. Okay?"

"Okay," said Danny. He could tell his brother was getting a little tight.

"Mom . . . well, see . . . she told me something before

she died. It's the reason why she wanted to sell the company."

"Give."

"She said she should have sold it a long time ago, but it meant so much to Elaine and me."

"Then why sell at all?"

"Because . . . legally, it was never hers."

Danny narrowed his eyes. "Excuse me?"

"Dad made her sign a legal document before they were married. I don't know if you'd call it a prenuptial agreement, but that's what it was in effect. In it, she signed away all rights to his company. If they got divorced, or if he died, the company would be held in trust for his children. Mom would have been taken care of financially, but she would never have inherited the business."

"You mean that old dragon scammed us? The company was *always* ours?"

Alex nodded.

Danny was stunned into silence.

"Except, after Dad's death, the document couldn't be found."

"Yeah, right. She probably destroyed it."

"It's possible, I suppose, but I think she was telling me the truth. She said there was only one copy and that Dad kept it in his bottom desk drawer—a locked drawer. After he died, it was missing. Actually, I remember her searching through the house for weeks after his death. She seemed frantic. At the time, she didn't tell me what she was looking for. But she finally did a few days ago, when we had that meeting. She maintains she never found it."

"It's moot now."

"Actually, it isn't," said Alex. He topped off Danny's drink, then poured himself another. "There's a clause in the document that could have major bearing on our inheritance—if the thing ever showed up. That's why Mom wanted to sell the company. She told me we needed to liquidate and get the money offshore as fast as possible. Just in case."

"In case this document ever surfaces."

"Exactly."

"Did she have some reason to think it would?"

"No, but she wanted her children to have clear title to the money before she died. If we inherited through her will, it wouldn't be a problem."

"I don't understand. What's the clause in the prenup that had negative bearing on our inheritance?"

Downing the drink, he said, "It was the sentence that talks about Dad's business being held in trust for his children, the 'issue of his body.' "

"Yeah? Where's the problem with that?"

"Mom told me that she had an affair while they were married."

Danny closed his eyes. He knew what was coming next.

"One of us isn't his kid."

24

Sophie had been sleeping fiftfully when a knock on the front door woke her. She glanced at the clock on the nightstand and saw that it was two-twenty in the morning. Across from the foot of the bed, the TV was still on, the sound off, the picture so bright it hurt her eyes.

For a moment, she felt disoriented. She reached out her hand to touch Bram, but his side of the bed was empty. And then she remembered the fight they'd had. Bram had come back from swimming, changed his clothes, and left to get some dinner on his own. He hadn't returned until nearly eleven. He walked into the living room and said that he knew they needed to talk things through, but that he was too tired to get into it again tonight. He grabbed his pillow and went to sleep in the spare bedroom.

Sophie sat up in bed for the next few hours, worrying and eating potato chips while she watched TV. She finally fell asleep. She wasn't sure when, but it felt like about five minutes ago.

By the time she'd slipped into her robe, Bram was already in the hallway.

"Who the hell do you suppose is out there?" he asked, rubbing the sleep out of his eyes.

"If they don't stop that banging," said Sophie, "they're going to wake the entire sixteenth floor."

Bram reached the door first. Swinging it open, Margie nearly jumped into his arms.

"Dad, you've got to come. Hurry!" She grabbed his hand and pulled him out the door.

"What's going on?" asked Sophie, switching on a light.

"It's Tracy," said Margie. "She's in my apartment. Come on! There's no time to talk."

They took the service elevator down because it was closer to Margie's apartment. When they reached the twelfth floor, Margie led them through the front door and into her bedroom.

"Oh, my God," said Sophie, covering her mouth with her hand. The scene that met her eyes was one of destruction. Two of Margie's floor lamps were shattered and bent. An empty sack of cheese curls lay crushed beneath an overturned chair, the contents of the bag strewn about like confetti. The bedspread was half on the bed, half on the floor. Drawers were pulled out and dumped. The room was in shambles.

Tracy lay across the bed, flat on her back, arms at her sides, her eyes closed.

"Is she—" Sophie couldn't finish the sentence.

Bram bent over her, feeling for a pulse in her neck. "She's alive, but just barely." He pointed to the marks on her throat. "Looks like someone tried to strangle her. We better call nine-one-one."

"I already did," said Margie. She looked terrified.

"What happened?" asked Bram, turning around. "Who did this to her?"

Margie took a step backward. "I don't know. Honestly.

I just got home a few minutes ago and I found her like that. I called the paramedics and then I came up to get you."

"How did Tracy get in here?" asked Sophie.

Margie eyed her furtively. "Well, she . . . ah, called me this afternoon. Asked if she could crash at my place tonight. I told her sure. No problem. But I wouldn't be home until late. I left a key for her at the concierge desk."

First Mick spends the night, thought Sophie, and now Tracy. Margie had to know more than she was letting on.

"Honey," said Bram, not even trying to hide his exasperation, "Tracy's mother has been going crazy looking for her. The poor woman is beside herself with worry. You should have told me you knew where she was."

"I realize that now," said Margie, her voice turning to a whine. "I'm sorry, Dad. But she made me promise I wouldn't tell. She said she needed a base of operations—just for the night."

"What did *that* mean?" said Bram.

"How should I know?"

"Is there anything we can do for her?" asked Sophie, moving a bit closer to the bed. Only one lamp remained in the room, and it didn't give off much light. "I suppose I should alert the front desk that the paramedics are on their way."

"I don't think we should touch her or anything else in this room, for that matter," said Bram. "This is a crime scene now. You better use the house phone in the hall."

"Where are those paramedics?" said Margie, glancing toward the door. She was a bouncing ball of nerves.

"I should call Elaine, too," said Sophie. "She's got a long drive ahead of her if she's going to meet us at the emergency room."

Sophie was on her way out when Bram said, "Hey, what's this?" He stepped over to the dresser and crouched down. On the floor next to a couple of cheese curls was a man's tie clasp. "Is this yours?" he asked, looking up at his daughter.

Margie walked over. "No, I've never seen it before."

"I have," said Sophie. It was a simple gold bar with a bucking horse attached at the center. "It belongs to Zander. I saw it on him the other day when I was at Prairie Lodge."

"Do you think he's the one who did this to Tracy?" asked Margie.

"There's no sign of forced entry," said Bram. "I checked the lock on the way in. If Zander attacked her, she must have opened the door to him. I assume that means she wasn't afraid of him."

"Margie?" Sophie waited until she had the young woman's full attention before continuing. "One question before I go. When I let the movers in here yesterday, I found Mick Frye asleep on the couch. He said he'd spent the night. That was two nights ago. Was Tracy with him?"

Margie looked startled. Facing her dad, she said, "No, it was just Mick. Really. He doesn't have a dime, Dad. I told him he could stay if he slept on the floor. But when I got home, he was gone. He was looking for Tracy, too. We all were. I thought, if I had a chance to talk to her tonight, maybe I could convince her to contact Mick."

"But not her mom," said Sophie.

"No, her mom, too. But when I got here"—she glanced over at the bed—"I never thought this would happen."

"Do you know if she planned to meet someone here?" asked Bram. The sternness in his voice made it clear he wasn't happy with his daughter's actions.

"Not that I know of."

"She didn't say anything about Zander coming by?"

"Not a word."

Just then, something else caught Bram's attention. Getting down on his hands and knees, he crawled toward the bed.

"What is it?" said Sophie, almost afraid to ask.

"Jesus. It's a gun." The barrel was poking out about half an inch.

Bram looked up at his daughter. "Did you know she was armed when you told her she could stay here?"

"No!"

Sophie didn't buy it. If Mick had been willing to give Sophie that piece of information without being pressed, he undoubtedly told Margie about it, too—and probably much more. Sophie had the sense that Margie was the repository of a great deal of information she wasn't willing to share. It left Sophie wondering why. Margie had been Mick's friend in high school, but how on earth had she grown so fond of Tracy so fast? What was the connection? And if Mick was so penniless yesterday, maybe he was still around. He insisted that he loved Tracy, but when money was involved, was it ever that simple?

"All she told me was that she needed to hide," said Margie. "She didn't figure anybody would look for her here."

"Well, Zander knew where to find her."

"Maybe she thought she was safe because she had a gun," said Sophie.

"God, I wish those paramedics would get here." Margie walked over to the window and looked down at the street. "Hey, there they are!"

Hurrying out of the apartment, Sophie ran into four men pushing a gurney around the bend in the hallway. She pointed them toward Margie's door, then continued on to the end of the hall where the courtesy phone was located. All the while she kept wondering how she would break the news to Elaine.

25

The lights in the emergency room blazed. Sophie and Bram sat in the waiting room close to the sliding front doors in order to catch Elaine as soon as she arrived. The paramedics confirmed Bram's suspicion that Tracy had been strangled. They called it a "ligature assault." The loss of oxygen to her brain and the condition of the air passages in her neck seemed to be their most immediate concern. Tracy didn't appear to have any broken bones, but they weren't sure about internal injuries, and they couldn't wake her. Her blood pressure was unusually low, and her heartbeat rapid, neither of which were good signs. Until she was checked over by a doctor, nothing further could be determined.

But Tracy was alive, thought Sophie. For now, everyone needed to hold on to that.

Margie was off finding a soda. She promised to bring coffee back for Bram, but she'd been gone so long, Sophie figured she'd forgotten. Bram had taken hold of Sophie's hand when they'd entered the hospital, and he'd kept on holding it. Sophie was grateful. She knew he was still angry at her, but he had the maturity to know that this wasn't her fault. At a time like this, they both needed the comfort of human connection.

Forty-five minutes to the dot after Sophie had placed the call to Elaine, Elaine walked through the doors into the emergency room. She held herself tightly, as if movement itself were the enemy.

Sophie and Bram stood.

"Where is she?" asked Elaine. Her voice belied her physical composure. She was barely holding it together.

"The doctors are working on her," said Sophie.

"I need to speak to whoever's in charge."

"There was a nurse here just a moment ago," said Bram. "Maybe she could give you more information."

While they talked, the doors opened again. This time Nathan walked in. He looked rumpled and unshaven, as if he'd just gotten out of bed.

Bram let go of Sophie's hand.

"He drove me," said Elaine, looking around until she spotted the nursing desk. "I couldn't drive myself. I would have ended up in a ditch."

"Nice of you," muttered Bram.

Nathan nodded. "Least I could do."

"He was at my place," said Elaine, offhandedly. "If you'll excuse me." She hurried over to the desk and spoke briefly with the man sitting behind it. He pulled out a chart and glanced at it, then buzzed Elaine back into the main part of the emergency room.

Bram, Sophie, and Nathan sat down.

If Sophie had tried, she couldn't have come up with a more awkward situation. She supposed she could take the bull by the horns, take responsibility for the conversation and introduce a subject, but nobody wanted to talk, so she just sat and looked around.

Finally, being the one who was the least ill-at-ease, Nathan said, "Elaine told me that Tracy was strangled."

Sophie nodded.

"She also said you found one of Zander's tie clasps in the bedroom. I always figured that guy was kind of hinkey." He shook his head. "Wouldn't it be ironic if it turned out the butler did it?"

"He's *not* a butler," said Sophie.

"The police are over at the hotel right now," said Bram, stretching his arms to release some tension. "Searching the apartment. Maybe they'll find something more."

"I hope so," said Sophie. "I imagine they'll pick Zander up for questioning first thing in the morning."

"They'll pick him up before that," said Bram.

"You bet they will," said Nathan.

They were ganging up on her now.

"I wonder where Margie is," said Sophie.

Bram checked his watch. "It's going on four. Want me to go find her?"

Before Sophie could answer, Elaine reappeared. She looked unsteady on her feet as she walked toward them.

"What is it?" said Sophie, rising to meet her.

Elaine swallowed before speaking. "Tracy's . . . in a coma. And she's got several fractured ribs. One of them punctured her right lung."

"Oh, God," said Sophie. "Is a punctured lung serious?"

"Yes," said Elaine. "But they think they've got it under control. They did a procedure with a syringe, took out some fluid, and they've got her on oxygen. She'll be restricted to bed. That won't be a problem because she's not awake yet. If she were, the doctor said she'd most likely be in a lot of pain."

"Then I'm glad she can sleep through this part of it," said Sophie.

Elaine closed her eyes. "Yeah, me, too. The doctor said

her breathing is okay, but they're worried about complications. He explained a whole range of potential problems they have to watch for. My mind just shut off. I couldn't take it all in." She started to cry.

"Just take it as it comes," said Nathan, putting his hands on her shoulders. "I know this is hard, but you're doing great." He folded his arms around her.

"I've got to stay strong . . . be there for my daughter when she needs me."

"And you will be," said Nathan. "You will be."

She sniffed a couple of times, then backed up. "They're doing a neck X ray right now. When they're done, they're moving her to intensive care."

"I want to see her," said a voice from behind them.

When Sophie looked up, she saw Mick standing with Margie. So that's where she'd been. Had she called him, or had Mick been lurking in the shadows all along?

"Get out of here," said Elaine. She was angry and he was a safe target.

"No." He stood up to her, glaring at her defiantly.

"You have no business bothering my daughter anymore. You're out of her life."

"You might have fired me, Elaine, but it doesn't change how I feel."

"That's right," said Margie. She moved closer to him.

"Do you think I give a rat's ass how you feel?" said Elaine. "If you'd cared about her, you wouldn't have let her leave my mother's house. She was safe there."

"No, she wasn't," said Mick. "You, of all people, should know that."

"That's why I installed that bodyguard on her door."

"Not enough."

"After you drugged her!" shouted Elaine.

"He has a right to see her," said Margie.

"This isn't your problem." Bram stepped between Elaine and Mick.

"Tell them," insisted Margie. "Tell them the truth."

"Nobody gets in to see my daughter unless I say so," barked Elaine.

"Afraid that's not the way it works." Mick seemed to be enjoying the moment. "See, Tracy and I . . . we're married. She's my wife. Nobody's going to keep me from seeing my wife, Elaine. Not even you."

26

Elaine sat on one side of the hospital bed, Mick on the other. In between lay Tracy's comatose form—a kind of no-man's-land, full of deep secrets and wells of misunderstanding. Out of reverence, or perhaps a certain sense of humiliation, neither had said a word to the other. They'd both insisted that they loved her, and yet they'd both failed her—failed to protect her, and even worse, failed to understand her.

Elaine had sent Nathan home around six A.M. Tracy had been moved to the ICU by then and only family members were allowed in. Elaine kissed Nathan on the cheek and thanked him. He was sweet to stick around. She could tell he and Bram had some sort of staring match going and that it made Sophie uncomfortable. Sophie and Bram had left shortly after Nathan. Sophie's parents were arriving home later in the day and Sophie needed to be there to welcome them. Elaine was so grateful for Sophie's friendship. She promised that she'd call later with an update on Tracy's condition.

Margie had left with Bram and Sophie, for which Elaine was grateful. It was just Mick and her now, sitting watch at Tracy's bedside, waiting for her to wake up. The doctors hadn't made any promises. Elaine knew her daughter was fighting for her life. In a way, she was glad for Mick's company. They'd been partners in crime, and now they were partners in misery.

Mick did look miserable. So miserable that Elaine was starting to believe he really did love her daughter. Either that or he was an awfully good actor. When the nurse came in to check on Tracy, Elaine took the chance to move her chair closer to his. Once the nurse had left, Elaine caught his eye.

"When did you and my daughter get married?" she asked, keeping her voice low. She needed to know.

He leaned forward, resting his arms on his thighs. "Well, it was a week ago—the same day she tried to commit suicide. Don't be angry, Elaine. She didn't do it because of me. She told me that a million times. See, we'd gone down to get the marriage license the week before. It was all her idea. You know Tracy. If it wasn't, I never could have convinced her. She never actually said she loved me, but in time, I thought she would. We got married late Friday afternoon. We planned to keep it a secret, but then she got this idea in her head that she wanted to tell you, so we drove down to your place. You weren't home, so we waited. Tracy opened a bottle of wine. I didn't want any. Once she started drinking, she just got quieter and quieter, you know? She just kind of stopped talking to me. She was always moody. I guess I thought she was just having another one of her moods. But then she started crying, almost hysterically, and I couldn't get her to stop." He began wringing his hands.

"She finally calmed down a little, said maybe she'd take a bath. I wanted to order a pizza because we hadn't eaten since breakfast, and she said to go ahead. There was a place in Coralville that would deliver. She apologized for falling apart, said that when it came right down to it, she was a little nervous about telling you we got married. She figured taking a bath would help calm her nerves. Somewhere in there I called you. I thought maybe you should come home. Trace and I talked for a while through the door, but then she said she needed to think. I could tell she was still crying a little, but it wasn't as bad as before. She told me to go watch TV. The pizza arrived maybe a half hour later. I hollered at her that she better hurry up or it would all be gone by the time she got out. She called back that she wasn't hungry. I didn't like the sound of that, but I also didn't want to upset her. So I gave her some time alone."

He lowered his head. "I should have known something was wrong, but she's pulled her silent treatment on me so many times before, I just thought it was more of the same."

"You should have told me you were married," said Elaine.

"I wanted to. I almost did a couple of times. But after Tracy got out of the hospital, she insisted that we keep it a secret. I was her ace in the hole. If you tried to commit her, I would ride in on my white horse and save her. At the very least, I could delay you and her shrink long enough for her to escape."

"You didn't think she *needed* help?"

"Sure I did, but she was terrified of being locked up. Except . . ."

"Except what?"

He hesitated. "I don't know quite how to put this."

"Just say it."

"I didn't push her, Elaine. I never pushed her. She was the one who wanted to get married."

"Why would she marry you if she didn't love you?"

He rubbed his jaw. "I don't know. But, after the suicide attempt, after she got to your mother's house, she seemed . . . changed. I told you that before. She was more sure of herself. Almost cocky, like she wasn't afraid of anyone. I mean, she had no trouble telling me what to do, but around everyone else, she always seemed so timid. But that was all gone. She ordered Zander around like he was her personal servant. And she even sassed that old guy."

"Doc Holland?"

"Holland, right. She told him to go piss up a tree. The old guy's face turned beet red. I thought it was pretty disrespectful, but Tracy thought it was hilarious."

"I had no idea."

"All she talked about was getting even."

"With whom?"

"She wouldn't say. But then, when I found out she'd been molested as a child, and that's why she was in therapy, I figured she was going to get the guy who did it. She sure had it in for someone. God, it was killing me to see her like that. I wanted her to be happy that we were married, but it wasn't even a blip on her radar screen."

Elaine would have been delighted to think her daughter had found someone to love her, if Tracy had returned that love. But before her disappearance, it seemed that her daughter had been consumed with revenge, not the joys of young married life. Tracy didn't even trust Mick enough to give him the name of the man she was after. Elaine had no doubt that the man who had molested her when she was a girl was the same one who had just attacked her in Margie's apartment and nearly killed her. According to the evidence at the scene, that man was Galen Zander.

If there was a God, Zander was already in custody, on his way to lower hell.

"Can you ever accept me as your son-in-law?" asked Mick.

Elaine had lost all patience with him. He seemed so sappy and sincere. His youth and naïveté gave her a headache. Under other circumstances she might have felt sorry for him, but every ounce of sorrow she had was directed toward her daughter. For Mick, she felt only pity. The curse of her life was to be surrounded by weak men.

Before she could answer Mick's question, a doctor walked in. He checked Tracy's IV, then spent a few moments talking to the nurse who sat at a computer terminal just inside the door. When he was done, he stepped over to where Elaine and Mick were seated.

Elaine stood. "Did you get the X ray of her neck back?"

"It didn't tell us anything new. We still don't know how long her brain was deprived of oxygen. That's critical."

"You're concerned about brain damage," said Elaine, feeling her stomach tighten.

"Yes. We're watching her very carefully. The next twenty-four hours should tell us a lot." He glanced at Mick. "I understand you're her husband."

Mick rose from his chair. "That's right."

"I'm sure you've got questions about the pregnancy."

Elaine's eyes opened wide. "The what?"

The doctor glanced down at the chart. "According to this, your daughter is ten weeks along."

Elaine's unblinking eyes turned to Mick.

"That's impossible," said Mick. "She never said anything to me about a baby."

"You bastard!" cried Elaine.

Mick whirled around to look at Tracy.

"You're not *that* big an idiot. You know how babies happen."

"But . . . we never slept together. Not once. If she's pregnant—" He turned back to Elaine. "I'm not the father."

"Then who is?" demanded Elaine. Even as she said the words, a thin, small voice in the back of her mind offered an answer. "Who is?" she whispered, feeling suddenly sick to her stomach.

27

"Bram, they're beautiful! You shouldn't have."

"I shouldn't have?"

"No, no. You should have. You should have!"

Per her husband's instructions, Sophie had opened the door to their apartment at exactly three o'clock. Outside, on the floor in the hall right in front of the door, she found a dozen, long-stemmed roses in a beautiful crystal vase.

"They're pink," said Bram.

"I can see that." It was her favorite color. She knew it was trite for a grown woman to adore pink, but there it was.

Sophie held the phone in one hand and picked up the vase with the other. "I'll put them in the center of the dining room table where we can both enjoy them. Bram, they're just gorgeous." She noticed a card. "You are *such* a sweetheart."

"I agree. I am one in a million. Guys like me don't come along every day, you know. We don't grow on trees—or, or . . . all the other clichés I can't think of at the moment."

"And *I* don't take clichés with a grain of salt."

He laughed. "God, but we're amusing."

"We are."

"You are what you eat."

"Beauty is only skin deep."

Bram paused. "You're not speaking of *my* beauty, are you? Mine goes clear to the bone."

"You have a glamorous soul."

"Well, if not glamorous, at least it's pretty. Look, Soph, I'm sorry I got so angry at you yesterday. It's just . . . seeing Nathan in your office like that, I went a little berserk. I've never been the jealous type. I mean, I didn't think I was."

"It was totally innocent, Bram. He just stopped by."

"I realize now that he's dating Elaine. I'm thrilled. I wish them years of happiness. Maybe they'll move somewhere far far away. Like the tip of South America. Or better yet, the wilds of Mongolia. He can open a restaurant featuring sautéed moose or boiled yak. She can build igloos." Another pause. "So you forgive me?"

"Oh, Bram, let's just forget about Nathan."

"Good plan. Listen, I've only got four minutes and ten seconds left. It's top of the hour news and weather time. Have your parents arrived yet?"

"No," said Sophie, glancing at the grandfather clock in the living room. "Their plane gets in at three-fifteen. They didn't want me to pick them up. They're taking a cab. I expect them around four, four-thirty."

"Tell them I'll see them tonight. We're still doing the welcome-home party, right? We're killing the fatted lamb chop?"

"We'll have dinner in the Zephyr Club."

"Excellent choice. By the way, speaking of lamb chops, I talked to my buddy Al at the St. Paul P.D. a while ago. I asked him if he knew anything about Galen Zander—if they'd picked him up yet."

"And?"

"They brought him in for questioning around four this morning. Talked to him for several hours. He insisted he was innocent, that he had nothing to do with Tracy's attack. He even produced a witness who said he was nowhere near the Maxfield last night. I guess the witness checked out, so they had to let him go."

Sophie hadn't expected that. "Do you think someone was trying to frame him?"

"That's what Zander thinks. The police aren't so sure, but unless they can break his alibi, he's off the hook. Keep this next part under wraps, okay? Seems he's the key suspect in Millie Veelund's murder, too. He was the one who administered her insulin shots, so he had access. Mick said that when he climbed in Tracy's bedroom window the night she disappeared—the same night Millie was murdered—that he found Zander downstairs in the pantry, where the insulin was kept. Zander said that he was having trouble sleeping, but the police don't buy it."

"If he did murder Millie, what do they think his motive was?"

"Money. Millie left him a million dollars in her will— his reward for years of loyal service. It would be pretty ironic if he offed the old girl just to get his hands on it and then went to jail for her murder. He was at Canterbury Downs yesterday celebrating, and later at a bar where he picked up some girl. She was his alibi for last night."

"A prostitute?"

"I don't know if she had sex with him for money, but I do know she was awfully young—and looked even younger."

"Did the police ask him about Tracy? If he'd molested her?"

"They did," said Bram. "But obviously he wasn't going to admit it and they don't have any proof. He said he had nothing to do with Tracy's problems, then or now."

"And the only one who knows the name of the pedophile is lying in a hospital bed in a coma. How convenient."

"Have you heard from Elaine?" asked Bram.

"No. I called the hospital a little while ago, but there's been no change."

"What an incredible mess."

"You know," said Sophie, musing out loud, "if Zander is off the hook, that means someone else attacked Tracy last night. Who would do that, Bram? What kind of monster are we dealing with?"

"Like you said, the suspects are fairly limited."

"The police need to concentrate on the molestation. That's the key."

"For Millie's murder, too?"

"Oh, geez, I don't know. Maybe."

"Ten seconds to airtime. Gotta run, sweetheart. We'll talk more later. Bye."

28

A shadow fell across Tracy's bed.

"It's only me," said Doc Holland, smiling down at Elaine. He patted her shoulder. "I'm sorry if I startled you. I played my usual trump card. They only want family in the ICU, but I told them I was your family doctor. I hope you don't mind. I had to come see how Tracy was doing."

"How did you know she was here?" Elaine stood and gave him a hug.

"Danny."

Danny and Alex had come down to the hospital around noon. Roman was with them, bearing flowers. Elaine didn't care if she made a scene. She refused to let him in the room. Alex walked him back to the ICU waiting room, where he and his flowers could rot, for all she cared. Danny and Alex stayed only a few minutes, but in that time, Elaine saw her own shock reflected on her brothers' faces.

Mick had left a few minutes before to grab something to eat, so Elaine was alone in the room—as alone as one can be with a nurse sitting ten feet from the hospital bed. The nurse wasn't in the room at the moment. She split her time between Tracy and another patient across the hall.

"Would you like to sit down?" asked Elaine, nodding for Doc to take Mick's chair.

He hesitated, stepped closer to Tracy and looked closely at her, then checked out the swelling in her neck. "Has there been any change in her condition?"

"Not that I'm aware of."

"No breathing problems?"

"Should there be?"

"Well, that's always an issue after an injury like this. But she's holding her own. That's a good sign." He touched the skin on Tracy's arm, making a low, indecipherable noise in the back of his throat.

"What is it?" asked Elaine, jumping up. "Is something wrong?"

"Her skin is clammy."

"What's that mean?"

He turned to her, holding a finger to his lips. "I've always believed that a person in a coma is far more in touch with what's happening around them than we realize." Bending close, he said softly into Tracy's ear, "I'm here for you, kiddo. It's Doc Holland. I'm here to help take care of you." He brushed her hair tenderly. "You've got yourself into a bit of a fix, honey, but you're strong. Just remember that. Your mother and I are going to sit and talk for a while, so you rest. When you wake up, maybe I'll be here. That would be nice, wouldn't it? I'd dearly love to see your eyes open right now." He waited for a few seconds, watching her closely, then shook his head and sat down, muttering, "You never know."

"I'm glad you came by," said Elaine, resuming her own seat. She was so completely at her wit's end, and Doc was the closest thing to a father she'd known since she was a child.

He leaned over to pat her knee. "The world calls us to be a part of it. It's a fierce pull, this being alive stuff. Problem is, life doesn't come with an instruction book, unless you believe in the Bible. I've lived too long, seen too much, to rely on something so essentially confusing. Now, your mother, she was different. She found comfort in religion. I believe in God, mind you, but not the way she did. Millie was so certain about her ideas and values. Me, well, I figure there's always somebody out there trying to tell you what to do, what's right, what's wrong. It's a damn nuisance."

When Elaine smiled, it felt as if the muscles in her face were made of concrete. "You're quite a philosopher."

"Not really, but age makes you one even if you weren't when you were younger." He narrowed his eyes at Tracy. "I don't like her color."

"Should we call someone?" asked Elaine, feeling her anxiety zoom into the stratosphere.

"They've got her well monitored." He looked around at all the equipment. "Besides, it's probably just an old man's eyesight. Now, Danny, on the other hand. I haven't wanted to pry, but he's lost some weight. How's his health?"

"Fine, as far as I know. The cancer is gone, but he's still careful about what he eats. I think he's even started exercising, which is very unlike him."

"That could account for it," said Doc. He used his cane to help him shift back in his chair. "I couldn't believe your mother didn't leave a specific bequest to Danny's two kids in her will. I suppose it was that old Jewish animus again."

"Mom was a bigot."

"Must have hurt Danny."

"It did."

"When Tracy gets back on her feet, are you planning to go ahead with your mother's idea of turning the house into a bed-and-breakfast? Millie thought it would be good for Tracy. Get her interested in something besides her problems. Your friend Sophie said she'd help."

"I haven't even given it a moment's thought," said Elaine, rubbing her eyes.

"Funny how life works."

"What do you mean?"

"It makes for some strange bedfellows."

She still didn't understand.

"Pearl, Sophie's mother, was engaged to your father once upon a time. Did you know that?"

"They were?"

"Sure. They were high school sweethearts. I guess I figured your mother told you."

"She didn't."

"The night your dad died, he and Pearl spent some time alone in his car. I saw them drive away from the house. I was standing at the living room window."

"What are you saying?"

He shrugged. "Just that I always wondered what they talked about that night."

"Are you suggesting they were having an affair?"

"No idea. All I know is, your mother jumped through a lot of hoops to please your dad. I'm not sure Millie ever felt loved. I hated Carl for that. He was one of my dearest friends, but he didn't treat your mom the way she deserved."

It didn't come as a shock to Elaine that her parents weren't happy. In some part of her psyche she'd always known it, though she'd successfully hidden that knowledge away inside herself where she didn't need to think about it. But an affair? She couldn't imagine her father, the original straight arrow, cheating. "Why are you bringing this up now?"

Doc sighed and folded his hands in his lap. "Since

your mother's death, I guess I've been revisiting the past a lot. Just because I was there, lived through it, doesn't mean I understood it. And"—he glanced over at Elaine, a rueful look on his face—"you're old enough to realize that *everlasting love* and *knights in white armor* are fairy tales. They have nothing to do with real life."

She wasn't quite sure where he was going. She waited for him to continue.

"Well, if you do make your parents' home into a bed-and-breakfast, you won't have to kick Zander out. You knew that the police brought him in for questioning this morning."

"Danny told me."

"When I left a few hours ago, he was upstairs packing."

"You mean . . . the police let him go?"

"He had an alibi. They didn't have a choice. He said he was moving to that new Savoy Millennium in downtown Minneapolis for the time being. He also said that he had nothing to do with what happened to Tracy."

"Right." As if Elaine would believe a word he said.

Suddenly, Doc stood up. "Get the nurse!"

"Why?"

"She's starting to seizure."

Before Elaine reached the door, the nurse rushed into the room.

Everything was a blur after that. Elaine heard strange words being shouted—crash cart, intubate. Nobody explained what was happening, but they didn't need to. She knew something dire was happening to her daughter. She backed into a corner and stayed there until a young man told her she had to leave. She resisted, saying she'd keep out of the way if he'd just let her stay, but she was finally escorted out of the room as other hospital personnel charged past her.

29

Alex spent the afternoon talking to a representative from Pike Bay Construction, a company in Vermont that had made the most impressive buyout offer for Veelund Industries. It was a solid deal at a fair price. What it required now was two signatures, and that was the rub. Elaine might agree to it if she knew the full story, but the timing had never been right for him to sit down and break the news to her. He'd made a date to have breakfast with her this morning, but when Tracy was attacked and sent to the hospital, his opportunity was lost in the shuffle.

The problem was, the iron was hot now. If they were going to strike a deal, it had to be soon. So that meant convincing Danny. Alex felt certain that he could talk him into signing the contract. Unlike Alex and Elaine, Danny didn't have a cushy income. Being a writer was an iffy financial situation at best. And he hadn't published a book in years. Elaine would hit the ceiling when she found out what they were up to, but Alex felt confident that he was making the right decision. He was protecting his family, even though Elaine didn't realize it yet.

Alex's first reaction, after his mother had dropped the bomb about her affair, was to insist that everyone get a DNA test right away. But the more he thought about it, the less the idea appealed to him. What if it turned out that *he* was the child of another man? As long as the prenup stayed lost, the question was moot, but if it ever did turn up, Alex wasn't sure if he could trust Elaine. He knew she loved him, but she also loved her career. If he wasn't a legitimate heir, it would put her in the driver's seat at Veelund Industries and Danny would probably do what she told him to do. That left Alex uncertain about his financial future. Still, no matter who their fathers were, the three of them were family. On the off chance that the prenup did resurface, Alex felt he had no choice but to act fast to sell the company.

Not that Alex wasn't deeply invested in knowing who his father was. If he had to guess, he'd say that Danny was the least like Carl Veelund. Elaine was the most like him, in terms of her business sense and personal drive. And Alex, well, he looked the most like Carl. He was big, blond, and athletic. As far as he could see, it was a crapshoot. Any conclusions he came to were nothing but speculation. Perhaps a simple blood test could settle the issue, but that would have to wait until the company was sold. Once the money was safely in the bank, they'd have plenty of time to figure out their parentage.

Arriving home just after five, Alex found Roman's car in the drive. Roman had refused to stay at the cabin after the shooting incident. When the rifle was found in a crawl space under the main house, he went ballistic, accusing everyone in Alex's family of trying to kill him. Alex wasn't sure who was actually being targeted, but he did agree with Roman about one thing: There were a limited number of people who had access to his father's gun cabinet. The shooter had to be someone he knew.

Grabbing his briefcase, Alex headed up the walk to the

front door. He'd spent several nights at Roman's town house in St. Paul, but the last two nights, by mutual agreement, they'd slept apart.

One fact Alex had learned about Roman in the past few years was that he had no particular talent for happiness. He was constantly annoyed, upset, or angry. He was a possessive man with a hair-trigger temper, one who wanted to control his world. And yet, Alex didn't judge him. Roman had had some bad luck, but Alex wanted to change all that—if Roman would only let him.

Once inside the cabin, Alex found Roman in the bedroom, bent over two suitcases.

"What's going on?" asked Alex, coming to an abrupt stop in the doorway.

Lifting a pack of cigarettes from the nightstand, Roman shook one out and lit it. After taking a deep drag, he said, "What happened with your meeting today? Will you sell my company out from under me?" His hand shook slightly as he held the cigarette to his lips.

"We've been all through this. Again and again. Don't turn this into high tragedy, okay? This is something I have to do."

"Ah, yes. Because of your mother." With the cigarette dangling from his lips, he returned to his packing. "Once I thought we had the same goals, you and me, but I see now that we don't. You are a frightened man. That much I know. You do not care for me, not the way I thought." He moved over to the dresser and opened one of the drawers.

"How can you say that? I want to spend the rest of my life with you. Selling the company is . . . necessary . . . to that future."

"But you won't tell me why. Not the real reason."

"I can't."

Roman grunted, removing the cigarette from his lips and tapping ash into an ashtray. "You do not trust me."

"I do," insisted Alex. "But it's . . . complicated. A family matter."

"And I am not family."

Alex's voice grew tender. "You're *my* family."

"Then sell Veelund Industries without including Kitchen Visions in the deal. Give it back to me. Give my life back to me. We can return to Canada together. I promise you, we will be happy then. I will make you the happiest man in the world." His eyes pleaded.

"I can't. There's a deal on the table and I have to take it." Alex sat down on the edge of the bed, his uncomfortable gaze moving to the suitcases. Virtually every scrap of clothing Roman had brought to the cabin in the past two years was there, ready to be hauled out. Alex saw it for what it was—a last-ditch effort to exert the only pressure he could. In the end, Roman would give in. He would stay with Alex and they would start a new business together. But between now and then, the road would be tricky.

Taking another drag from his cigarette, Roman said, "I'm leaving town. Returning to Toronto."

"When?"

"At the end of next week. There is nothing left for me here."

"You're trying to punish me."

"If I thought it would get my company back, I would torture you, Alex."

"You *are* torturing me."

"Now who makes this into a Shakespeare tragedy?" A harsh smile touched his lips. "Do you think we are Romeo and Juliet? That love rules the world? Love is a whore, my friend. The kind of relationship you offer me is exactly like a marriage—being locked away forever by the aims of another. I will not be used that way. Not by you, not by anyone."

For a moment, Alex's certainty wavered. Roman knew how to play the game. "You're willing to turn your back on me, on our future together, just because of a business deal?"

"You think my life's work is a small thing?"

"No, of course not. But—"

"You are happy to be rid of your father's company. I am not blind."

Alex watched him scoop up his socks.

"Your mind is like a block of wood. You do not examine the world. You do not truly comprehend other people. You see only what you want to see."

The phone on the nightstand gave a jarring ring.

"Let it go," said Alex.

Roman glanced down at the caller ID box. "It is the hospital."

Taking a deep breath Alex said, "Then I better answer it." He reached over and picked up the receiver. "Hello?"

"Son, this is Doc Holland. I'm here in ICU with your sister. I'm afraid I've got some bad news."

Alex closed his eyes. "Yes?"

"It's Tracy. She died a few minutes ago. I'm truly sorry."

He bowed his head. "Where's Elaine?"

"She's still in the room. She asked me to call you and Danny. She would have done it herself, but . . ."

Giving himself a moment to steady his nerves, he said, "It's okay." He felt an ominous thundering in his ears. "Is Elaine . . . all right?"

"She's pretty torn up. We both are."

"What happened?"

"Well, it's not unusual to have breathing problems after the kind of injury your niece sustained. The doctors did everything they could to save her, but it wasn't in the cards."

"I see." He cleared his throat. "Will you tell Elaine that I'll be there as soon as I can? I'm leaving right now."

"I'll do that."

Alex put the phone down, then looked over at Roman. "Tracy died. I have to go to the hospital. Will you be here when I get back?"

After taking a last drag on his cigarette, Roman crushed it out. "No," he said, returning his attention to the dresser drawer.

30

The plane carrying Sophie's parents back to Minnesota on Friday afternoon was almost two hours late. When they finally arrived at the Maxfield it was close to five-thirty. Sophie and Bram met them in the lobby with balloons and flowers. The staff had all lined up to greet them, welcoming the world travelers home. Sophie was so glad to have them back that she started to cry. Seeing Sophie's tears, her mother started to cry. All the crying made Bram and Henry laugh, which in turn started everyone else laughing and crying. So much for emotional reticence in Minnesota.

Henry gave specific directions to the bell captain about what to do with the extensive array of luggage.

Removing the unlit cigar from his mouth, Henry said, "We just kept buying more luggage when we needed it. Your mother went wild in Italy, Soph. Loves that Italian leather. She thought the Italian men were pretty okay, too. But she still prefers old Finlanders." He winked at Bram.

After dinner at the Zephyr Club, the gourmet restaurant on the top floor of the south tower, Henry wanted to call it a night. "I'm jet-lagged," he said on the way back to their apartment.

"I'm not the least bit tired," said Pearl, adjusting her turquoise necklace.

They both looked so wonderful, thought Sophie. Tanned. Healthy. Her father's hair was a tad more salt-and-pepper. Her mother's hair was no longer gray, but had been dyed blond. Other than that, they seemed unchanged. Not a pound heavier. Not a day older.

"I don't want to even look at that luggage until tomorrow morning," added Henry, chewing on his unlit cigar as he entered the living room. "I just want to climb into a pair of my old pajamas and hit the sack."

"Aunt Ida, Uncle Harry, and cousin Sulo are planning to drive down from Bovey to see you this weekend," said Sophie. She opened up the balcony door to let in some fresh air.

"Agh," said Henry, elbowing Bram in the ribs. "Family. Can't wait to see what presents we brought them."

"We've got suitcases filled with gifts," said Pearl, smiling broadly. "In addition to what we've already sent home."

Removing his sport jacket, Henry hung it up in the front closet. Slapping Bram on the back, he kissed Sophie and Pearl good night, then headed into the bedroom. "Nighty night," he called over his shoulder.

"The place looks wonderful," said Pearl, sighing contentedly as she touched a doily here, a vase there. She sniffed the air. "You've had the carpet cleaned."

"The entire place, from top to bottom," said Sophie.

Bram glanced at his reflection in the mirror over the couch, adjusting his tie. "Since you're not tired, Pearl, what do you say we all go for a walk?"

Pearl shook her head. "After that big meal, I just want to sit."

"Me, too," said Sophie, patting her stomach.

"Quiet down out there!" called Sophie's dad. "There's an exhausted old man in here trying to get to sleep."

Pearl pressed a finger to her lips. "You go, Bram. Sophie and I've got a lot to catch up on."

"I can still hear you," called Henry.

"Mom, why don't you come over to our apartment? That way, Dad can have some peace and quiet."

"Good idea," called Henry.

"We're leaving, Dad," whispered Sophie. She grinned at her mother.

"Lock the door on your way out," he said in response.

"He must be able to hear a pin drop," said Bram, stepping out into the hallway.

"From twenty yards away," called Henry. "And my sight's still pretty fair. But if I don't keep shoveling in the bran flakes, I'm in deep trouble."

"Sweet dreams, Dad." Sophie was happy to close the door on his last comment.

Once Bram and Ethel had left for their after-dinner stroll, Sophie and her mother made themselves comfortable on the couch, each with a mug of coffee.

"I'm sorry Margie couldn't join us for dinner," said Pearl. "But it's really wonderful that she's come back to stay."

"Yes, wonderful," repeated Sophie, hoping her mother didn't hear the lack of enthusiasm in her voice.

After the attack on Tracy in Margie's apartment, Margie had moved into Bram and Sophie's spare bedroom while the police did their forensic search of the crime scene.

"How's Bram's health?" asked Pearl, taking a sip of coffee. "He looks wonderful."

"He had a small episode the other day that gave me a scare. Ended up in the emergency room. But the doctor gave him a clean bill of heath. He's eating well, and exercising, so I just keep my fingers crossed and hope for the best. There's so much heart disease in his family."

"Biology isn't destiny," said Pearl. "Or it doesn't have to be." She set her mug of coffee on the end table.

Before her mother could launch into a new section of her travelogue, Sophie had a couple of burning questions she had to ask. "Mom?"

"Yes, dear? Is something wrong? All of a sudden, you look so serious."

"Actually, a week ago, a pipe broke in the subbasement. It flooded one of the storage rooms."

"Oh, my," said Pearl.

"One of the maintenance men found this." Sophie rose and walked over to a cabinet next to the TV set. She opened a low cupboard and took out the rusted metal box. When she turned around, she could see that her mother's eyes had locked on it with a look of discomfort.

"Do you remember hiding this in the storage room?" asked Sophie, sitting back down.

Pearl fidgeted with her necklace. "I, ah, well, yes. I put it down there. Years ago. I'd forgotten about it. Wasn't there a lock on it?"

"It broke," said Sophie. "It was badly rusted."

"Oh, sure, well," said Pearl, fussing with one of her earrings.

Sophie opened the top, revealing the contents.

"Oh, my." Pearl gave a nervous laugh. "Will you look at that. Did you . . . I mean, have you . . ."

"I couldn't help myself, Mom."

"No, I suppose not. I suppose you want to talk about all this. After all, Elaine is your good friend. And Millie just died. Oh, my," she said again. Her face had flushed a deep red.

"Look, Mom, if you don't—"

"No, you deserve an explanation. It's just . . . your father doesn't know about any of this."

"That's why you hid the box in the storage room."

She looked down at it, lifting out the notebook. "Will you keep my confidence, Sophie? It would only hurt your father if he found out."

"Did he know you were in love with Carl Veelund?"

She opened the book to the first page. "He knew we were engaged when I was eighteen, and that Carl broke it off to marry someone else. Her name was Catherine Isley. He met her when he was a junior at the U of M. They married when he graduated, but she died about a year later."

"That must have hurt you terribly," said Sophie.

"It did. I never stopped loving him. But then I met your father. We were married the year Catherine died. I didn't know she was gone until I ran into Carl at a Minneapolis Library Guild function two years later. He told me what had happened. He was still reeling from the shock. I'd just had a miscarriage so we were both in pretty bad shape emotionally. One thing led to another and we started getting together for coffee. Your father is a good man, Sophie, but he didn't understand how broken up I was about losing the baby. He had his work, but I was home alone. I don't think I'd ever felt that lonely before. Carl seemed to understand. He'd always wanted children, so he and I talked about it. I talked about the miscarriage, and he

talked about losing Catherine. It brought us close again.
It didn't take long before we realized that we were still in
love."

"Did he want you to leave Dad?"

She nodded. "I was deeply torn. You may not understand this, but I loved them both."

"I do understand," whispered Sophie. Nathan had
come back into her life while her parents had been on
their round-the-world tour. Sophie hadn't brought the
subject up because it seemed too complicated for a letter
or a brief phone call. "But you decided to stay with Dad.
Why?"

"I guess it's pretty simple, although it took me years to
figure it out. I had to look inside myself, sweetheart. I had
to find what I suppose was my moral center. I'm not religious, but I do believe in the sanctity of vows, and I'd
made a vow to your father. I took that seriously. It wasn't
as if I didn't love him. I did. The problem was I loved
Carl, too. But in this world, you can't love two men."

"So you told Carl that you couldn't marry him."

"I had to."

Sophie wanted to ask if her mother had ever been unfaithful, but she didn't have the nerve. "Did you ever
wonder what your life would have been like if you'd divorced Dad and married Carl?"

"In the early days, all the time. I still think about it occasionally, because if I'd married him, he wouldn't have
died in that horrible car accident. But then, I would never
have had you. You get to a point in your life, if you've been
lucky, if you're happy, where you can't imagine it any
other way. I love your father. I've never regretted spending
my life with him. But I did regret what happened to Carl.
Marrying Millie was a disaster from the very beginning."

"He must have loved her."

"She was pregnant, so he felt he had no choice but to marry her. And he adored Alex, their firstborn, so I guess he felt it was worth it. He adored all his kids. They were the best part of his life."

Sophie had so many questions. "The night that Carl died, you wrote that one of the staff brought him an envelope. He took it to his office and opened it, then got really upset and stormed out. You went in and retrieved the note from the wastebasket. Once you'd read it, you put it in your purse. What did it say, Mom?"

Pearl just stared at her.

Sophie felt she needed some coaxing. "You wrote that Carl said there was a certain solace in finally knowing what the worst thing was that life could throw at him. Had Millie been cheating on him? Was that it?"

Pearl closed the cover of the notebook. "Yes, she'd cheated on him."

"Who with? Do you know?"

"I do."

"That's why he wanted the divorce."

"I imagine so."

"What did he say to you when he was dying? He told you to go back to the house and find some agreement he'd signed. Did you do it?"

She nodded.

"Do you still have it? The agreement?"

Again, she nodded. "It's in a safety-deposit box."

"Did you read it?"

"I didn't have to. Carl told me what was in it."

"What about that note, Mom? The one that started it all. The one Carl received on the silver platter."

"I threw it away."

"But what did it say?"

She hesitated. "Do you have a pen?"

"A pen?" Sophie grabbed one off the coffee table and handed it to her.

Opening the cover of the notebook, Pearl said, "To the best of my recollection, this is what it said."

> *Carl—*
> *It's A +.*
> *Sorry, man.*
> *Stanley*

"What's it mean?" said Sophie. "A plus? Is it a grade?"

"A blood type."

Sophie's eyes opened wide. "A blood type for one of his kids?"

"Yes."

"Are you saying that he wasn't the father of one of his children? Is that what he told you when he was dying?"

"That, and much more," said Pearl.

31

On Saturday evening, Danny stood at the window in his bedroom, cell phone in hand, talking to his wife back in New York. It was an hour later on the East Coast, which meant it was a little after eleven in Manhattan. Ruth never turned in before midnight. She was a night owl, a late-night reader, just as he was.

"Tracy's funeral is set for Monday," he said, sitting down on the bed. He kicked off his shoes, then lay back, his head propped up by a stack of old feather pillows. "We'll do Mom's memorial service back at the house later in the afternoon."

"Danny, this is such a shock. How's Elaine doing?"

"She's devastated. We all are. I told you Tracy was pregnant, didn't I?"

"But no one knows who the father is."

"Mick insists he never slept with her. On their wedding night, she tried to kill herself. Not a very auspicious beginning to a marriage. The thing is, Elaine is convinced that the man who molested Tracy all those years ago molested her again last summer. She thinks that's who the father is. She's rounding up everyone who's been around Tracy, demanding that they take a blood test."

"Surely she's not including you in that."

"Me *and* Alex."

"My God, she thinks you or your brother could have molested her daughter?"

"It's killing her, but yes, that's exactly what she's afraid of. Alex and I went down this morning and had the test."

"How humiliating."

"If it will set her mind at rest, it's fine with me. The police will need to get a court order to force Zander to give blood."

"Can they do that?"

"I suppose. He's still the prime suspect in both murders. What kind of surprised me was that Doc Holland was supposed to meet us at the hospital this afternoon, but he never showed. Elaine wants him to have the same test."

"Do you think he has something to hide?"

"A sickening thought."

"You must hate being there, sweetheart . . . with all that suspicion in the air."

"I'll be home soon."

"Not soon enough for me. You haven't—"

"No. And I'm not going to. There's no point."

Danny reached over and switched off the light. In the dark, he could imagine that Ruth was lying next to him. He curled himself around her voice. "Look, honey, I've booked a flight out of here on Tuesday morning."

"Is Alex still determined to sell the company?"

"Yes." He sighed. "Elaine is against it, of course. I guess I'm the tiebreaker."

"What will you do?"

"I haven't decided. But . . . there's something I haven't told you. Something that will probably have no bearing on what happens to Veelund Industries, but . . ."

"What is it? You're scaring me."

"Alex had a long talk with Mom before she died. Seems that she had an affair while she and my dad were married. She told him that one of us was fathered by another man."

Ruth was silent. After a long moment, she said, "How . . . incredibly . . . awful. Danny, I'm so sorry."

"Yeah."

"Who is it? Which one of you?"

"She wouldn't say."

"Oh, God. That's so like her. Who'd she have the affair with?"

"I don't know. Frankly, I'm not even sure I believe the story. Mom wanted to sell the company. Apparently she told Alex that she'd signed a prenup before she married my father—if he was my father. If he died, or if they got divorced, she signed away all claim to his business. She would be taken care of financially, but of course, we all know the cash cow in the family was Veelund Log Lodges. Except, after they were in that car accident, after Dad was gone, she couldn't find the agreement."

"Oh, right. We all believe that."

"She told Alex that she wanted to sell the company just in case the prenup ever resurfaced. That way, the money would be legally in her name and she could pass it on. If we inherit through her will, we're all legitimate children. See, Dad's will left the company to his children—I believe the term was his 'issue'."

"Kind of an old-fashioned way to put it."

"But it's clear. And if Mom wasn't lying, then one of us, according to that agreement, would be cut out of any inheritance." Danny rolled over on his side, cupping the phone between the pillows and his ear. "Alex finally told

Elaine about it at dinner tonight. I thought he might wait until after the funeral, but she started talking about what a bad idea it was to sell the company, so he probably felt he didn't have a choice."

Ruth hesitated. "How did Elaine take it?"

"Hard to say. She drank a lot of wine; by the end of the meal, she'd pretty much stopped talking. We all had. There's so much tension in the air around here that we're walking on tiptoes. One offhanded comment at the wrong time could create a spark that would blow the roof off. So many subjects are off limits, it's hard to carry on a normal conversation."

"And I thought *my* family was the last word on neurosis."

Danny laughed.

"Thankfully, our kids are sane," said Ruth.

"Speaking of kids, is Zoe coming home anytime soon?"

"She's here right now. Took the train down this morning. She isn't going back until Tuesday evening."

"What about her classes?"

"She doesn't have anything on Mondays this quarter. One of her Tuesday classes got canceled, and she moved a meeting with a professor—"

"The independent study?"

"Right. She moved the meeting to next Friday. So if you get home early on Tuesday, you can spend part of the day with her."

Danny had been thinking of calling Zoe. "Is she there right now?"

"She's watching a movie in the study."

"Honey, I'd like to talk to her for a minute."

"Sure. I'll go get her."

Danny flipped on his back. He could imagine his wife padding down the carpeted hallway in her bedroom slippers. The light in the den would be off. Zoe would be lying on the couch with all the windows open. She was just like him. She liked fresh air, even if it seemed too hot or too cold. Central Park was just a few blocks away. If he were home by Tuesday afternoon, they could all take a walk together. Maybe stop and have coffee. Danny wanted his normal life back. Staying in Minnesota even another day seemed like too much to ask. And yet he had to stay. He had to play this through to the end, wherever it led.

A second later, Zoe came on the line. "Hey, Dad."

"Hi, sweetheart. How's your love life?" It was his standard opening, and it never failed to illicit a groan.

"Oh, Dad. Nothing's new. I told you. I don't have a boyfriend right now. I'm too busy."

"Too busy for love?"

"You're such a sap."

"Maybe. But trust your old man. Loving well is the best part of life."

"Maybe you should crochet me a pillow with that message on it."

"Maybe I should."

They both laughed.

"Look, honey, there's something I've been wanting to ask you. It's serious, so I expect you to take a minute to think about it before you answer."

"What?"

"Okay. When you've come here to Minnesota, to my mother's place, has anyone ever . . . acted inappropriately with you?"

"You mean sexually?"

"Yeah. Sexually."

"You mean, as in . . . a perv?"

"Well—"

"Tried to drag me into the bushes?" She laughed.

"I'm not joking."

"No, Dad. Nobody ever tried that."

"How about with your sister?"

"No. And she would have told me. She can't keep a secret."

"Okay."

"You're asking me because of Tracy, right?"

"Did Mom tell you?"

"I never knew, Dad, but then, Tracy and I were never very close. But . . ."

"But what?" He felt the muscles in his neck tighten.

"Well, there was this one thing. Abbie and I were riding dirt bikes around the property one afternoon. I was maybe, oh, eleven. Abbie would have been eight. It was right after Aunt Elaine had the smaller log houses built. Anyway, we stashed our bikes in the tall grass near Wisteria Cottage. We didn't think anybody was around, so we walked up to the front door. It was locked, of course. Abbie spotted a rabbit and took off after it, but I stayed. I walked around looking at the house for a while and that's when I saw that one of the back windows was open. The screen pushed up real easily, so I hoisted myself up and climbed through. I'd never seen the inside. I remember thinking I'd like to live there. And then I thought, hey, this would make a great secret fort. I mean, Elaine was hardly ever around. The place had lots of furniture, so it was comfortable. There was even a TV. And I found some Coke in the refrigerator. You never let us drink Coke, so I felt totally cool—you know, *bad*—when I opened one of the cans. Like it was heroin or something." She laughed. "I kind of drifted around, imagining what Abbie and I could do with the place, and I ended up in the living room. I knew I couldn't make a mess, or people would find out that it was our new hideout. At some point, Abbie started banging on the front door, calling my name. She was scared because I'd disappeared. As soon as I let her in, she demanded that I share the Coke. So to keep her happy, I let her drink it. I told her that this was going to be our new secret place. We both got really into it. She sat under the kitchen table for a while. I scoped out the bedroom—I was looking for hiding places—and that's when I found it."

"What did you find?"

"A floorboard was loose in one of the closets. I ran to the kitchen and got a fork, and Abbie and I pried it up. It wasn't hard. Actually, it was two boards. And underneath we found all these pictures of girls, probably around Abbie's age. They were all naked. Some of the pictures had adults in them. I'd never seen anything like it before. I know now that it was child porn, but at the time, Abbie and I just thought it was weird. We sat there on the floor in the closet for maybe ten minutes, just flipping through them."

"I wish you'd told me."

"God, we would have been *so* embarrassed."

"Did you recognize any of the children?"

"No. But while we were sitting there we heard the front door open. I was so scared I almost wet my pants. Abbie and I scrambled out the bedroom window so fast we didn't even look back. Needless to say, we never went back."

"Did you see who came in?"

"No."

"Did you put the pictures back?"

"We didn't have time."

"So, whoever came in must have known you were looking at them."

"I imagine."

"Nobody ever said anything to you? Looked at you funny?"

"Not that I remember."

"Did you see a car when you were running from the house?"

"There were no cars around. I'm sure of that."

"So whoever came in must have walked. And they must have had a key."

"I suppose. Who had keys to the place?"

"Elaine. And she kept a set of keys to the model homes on a hook in the kitchen at the main house. Anyone could have taken them—or made copies."

"Do you think the person who hid the porn was the same perv who molested Tracy?"

"I think it's a good guess."

"God, I hope they nail that guy's knees to the floor."

"Me, too," said Danny, taking a deep breath. "Guys like that don't deserve to live."

32

An ample woman with a sweet, reedy voice delivered the graveside address at Tracy's funeral. Sophie stood with Bram and her mom and dad, looking around at the crowd of mourners who'd come to pay their last respects. Most of the faces were middle-aged or old, suggesting that Tracy hadn't had many close friends.

It was a lovely, cloudless fall morning, temperatures in the low sixties, but Sophie felt chilled to the bone. She gathered her coat more closely around her body, folded her arms over her chest, and gazed sadly at the casket. We love our children so much, partly because they exist outside the realm of cynicism. She'd been greedy for that innocence when her own son was a boy. What struck her most about this young woman's loss was that Tracy's innocence had been stolen from her, and now someone had ended her chances of a happier future—of any future at all.

On the other side of the raised platform holding the casket, Margie and Mick stood together, hand in hand. Mick was crying silently, scraping tears away from his face. Sophie hadn't seen much of Margie since she'd moved into the spare bedroom, though she knew that Margie and Mick had become almost inseparable. Mick was a millionaire now, slated to inherit his dead wife's money in a matter of days, but he didn't seem to be thinking about that at the moment. He appeared to be truly grieving Tracy's loss. Sophie's heart went out to him.

Next to Margie and Mick were Alex and Roman. They weren't holding hands, but they stood with their shoulders pressed together. As the minister continued talking, Roman removed his sunglasses and nodded to her. Sophie glanced around to see if there was anyone else he might be looking at. But no, he appeared to be looking straight at her. Alex turned to Roman, then followed his gaze. He nodded to Sophie, too, but immediately returned his attention to the minister. Roman replaced his sunglasses, but Sophie had a feeling he was still watching her.

Elaine stood at the head of the casket, next to the minister. Nathan was right behind her, his head bowed. Elaine's face was strained but controlled. No tears escaped her eyes. A handkerchief was balled in her right fist, but she didn't use it. To her direct left was Doc Holland. He leaned heavily on his cane, his face red with perspiration. Danny stood on the same side as Sophie, so all she could see of him was the back of his blond head. She was a little surprised that his wife and kids hadn't come out for the funeral.

Finally, the minister was done talking. Before the casket was lowered into the ground, she asked everyone to say the Lord's Prayer with her. People bowed their heads. Sophie felt Bram's hand slip around her own.

By noon, the crowd was starting to disperse. Everyone was supposed to head back to the church for a lunch provided by the First Lutheran Women's Circle. Sophie approached Elaine as she was walking back to her car. Nathan was already sitting in the driver's seat.

"Can I talk to you for a second?" asked Sophie.

Elaine turned to her, giving her a hug. "Thanks for coming."

"You know how sorry I am."

"It's a horror, Sophie. An absolute horror. I think I'm still in shock."

"This is probably a bad time, but . . . I'd like to bring my mother out to talk to you and your family."

"You're right, this isn't—"

"It's important. Very important. Look, to make a long story short, I found a notebook of my mother's while she was out of the country. Actually, I came across it just last week. She wrote about the night your dad died. I think . . . I mean . . . she's got some information you and your family need to hear."

"If it's about the affair my mother had, we already know. She told Alex before she died. One of us was fathered by another man."

Sophie held her eyes. "It's more than that, Elaine. I think you need to hear what my mom's got to say." She looked over at the car. Nathan was watching them.

"Okay," said Elaine reluctantly. "Might as well do it today. My life can't get any worse than it is right now. We're doing Mom's memorial service—spreading her ashes by the creek—at three. Why don't you and your mother come out around four? Danny and Alex will still be around."

"I think you'll want this to be a private conversation."

Elaine glanced at Nathan. "He won't be there for Mom's memorial. It's just family."

"Then we'll see you at four."

Danny led Sophie and her mother into the living room. Alex was seated on one of the couches, still wearing his dark gray suit. As a sop to comfort, if there was such a thing on a day like this, he'd taken off his tie. Elaine sat next to him. They both had martini glasses in their hands. As soon as Sophie and her mom entered, they stopped talking.

"Would either of you like something to drink?" asked Danny.

Sophie shook her head.

"No thanks," said Pearl.

With her nerves doing a number on her stomach, Sophie lowered herself onto an ottoman. Her mother chose a chair facing the couch. Danny stepped over to the cold fireplace and rested his back against the stones.

No one spoke.

Finally, twisting her wedding ring back and forth on her finger, Pearl said, "Thank you for letting me come. This isn't easy for me. I never expected to have this conversation with any of you." She kept her eyes on the ring. "I care about all of you, you know that."

"You loved our father," said Alex, setting his glass down on a log coffee table in front of him. "My sister told me that the two of you had been engaged once."

"A long time ago. That's right."

Studying Elaine, Sophie could tell that the martini she held in her hand wasn't her first—or even her third. She might not be drunk, but she wasn't far from it.

"Get to the point," said Elaine. "Save us the trouble of a blood test. Which one of us isn't his kid?"

Pearl looked up. "If you'll all allow me a couple of minutes, I'd like to tell you about the night your father died. There are some things you need to understand. I was the last person to talk to him. We spoke for quite a while that last night. We took a drive together before the weather turned bad. And later, when I found him pinned behind the wheel of his car after the crash, I stayed with him until he died."

"Just get on with it," said Elaine, motioning for Alex to refill her glass.

"I think you've had enough," said Alex. "I'm sorry, Mrs. Tahtinen. Elaine's . . . not herself today. She's usually more polite."

Lurching off the couch, Elaine grunted. "You don't have to make excuses for me. I just lost my daughter—and my mother. And now, maybe I've lost my father. I'd have to be made of iron not to want to anesthetize myself after the last few days." She poured another drink from the martini shaker, added a handful of olives, then stumbled back to the couch. "Go on. Don't let my enormously appropriate self-pity stop you."

Pearl waited until she'd resumed her seat before continuing. "The night your dad died, he received a note from a private investigator, a man he'd hired to find some information for him. Midway through the evening, I saw one of the hired staff walk up to your father. The man carried a silver platter with an envelope on it. Your dad took the envelope and went immediately to his study. I'd been watching Carl all night because he seemed upset. He was drinking heavily, which wasn't like him. I thought he should be happy—he'd just built the house of his dreams. That night was a celebration, a party, a time when he should have been glowing with pride and satisfaction. I followed him and, from a crack in the doorway, watched him open the note. Whatever it said left him looking desolate. He crumpled up the paper and tossed it in the wastebasket next to his desk, then left the room. Maybe you'll think this was completely out of line, but I went into the study and read the note. You're right. I did love your father and I couldn't stand to see him in pain. I didn't understand the information he'd been given, didn't understand what was written on the note, so I went to find him."

"What did the note say?" said Alex, leaning slightly forward.

"A plus," said Sophie. "When Mom told me, I thought it must be a grade."

"But it was a blood type," said Elaine.

Pearl nodded.

"Whose?" she demanded.

"I'll get to that in a minute," said Pearl.

"No, *now,*" said Elaine, spilling part of her drink down the front of her dress. "We've waited long enough."

Pearl glanced at Sophie for support, but all Sophie could do was shrug. She felt Elaine had a right to know.

"Do you understand blood typing?" asked Pearl. "It's fairly complex."

"Just tell us!" shouted Elaine.

Pearl looked from face to face. "Okay," she said finally. "Your mother was pregnant when she married your father. In the back of his mind, your dad always wondered if it was his child."

"You mean *me,*" said Alex. "I'm the one?"

Sadly, Pearl nodded. "He thought the sun rose and set on all of you. He'd always wanted children, and your mother knew that. That was how she hooked him—how she drew him into the marriage. And that's what he found out that night. Carl's blood type was B—or BB. Your mother's was BO. There's no way he could have fathered a child with an A blood type."

Alex stared at her, then bent his head.

"I'm so sorry," said Sophie.

"I've always known. In my gut, I've always *always* known."

"Let me continue," said Pearl.

"There's more?" asked Elaine, clearly impatient with her slowness.

"There are things you need to understand."

Without speaking, Danny sat down on the arm of the couch next to Alex.

"First, that Carl told me it didn't matter. That Alex was his son, no matter what any blood test said. I won't lie to you. I won't tell you that the news didn't devastate him. But it didn't change the way he felt."

"Right," muttered Alex.

"You have to believe that," said Pearl. "You knew, in your heart, how utterly devoted your dad was to you. To all of you."

"Cut to the chase," said Elaine, finishing her drink in one gulp.

"When I went looking for your father, I found him outside in his car, ready to drive away. I knew he was too drunk to drive, so I made him move over and I took the wheel. We were gone, oh, maybe an hour. In that time, he didn't talk much, but on the way back to the house, he said that he was going to ask your mother for a divorce."

"That night?" asked Alex.

"Yes. As soon as we got home, he dragged her off to have a talk. The weather had turned so nasty that I found Henry and Sophie and told them that I thought we should leave. But we got sidetracked, and then, when I went outside to look for Henry, I was told that Carl and Millie had just left in their car. According to what the valet told me, Carl was driving. The roads were getting worse by the minute. I panicked. I knew Carl was in no shape to drive. And I wondered why he'd left with Millie."

"Why had he?" asked Alex.

"They'd had a terrible fight. Your father said that he was afraid that if he didn't get out of the house, that . . . he might hurt her. So he took off. But she followed him. He'd asked her for a divorce, but she wanted to talk him out of it. She begged for his forgiveness. He just kept driving faster and faster. When they skidded into that field, your mom jumped out of the car. It's what saved her life. I arrived a few minutes after the car had hit the tree. I wanted to go for help, but Carl knew he was dying and he didn't want to die alone. So I stayed. We talked, or rather he did. There were some things he wanted me to know—and something he wanted me to do."

"What?" said Elaine. She was mesmerized now, no longer impatient.

"He said that Millie had been unfaithful more than once. That Alex wasn't the only one who wasn't his biological child."

The silence in the room pressed on them all.

"Who?" said Alex.

Pearl drew her purse into her lap. "I'm sorry, Elaine, but—"

Elaine gasped. "No! I don't believe you."

"It's true," said a voice from the front foyer.

Turning around, Sophie saw Doc Holland walk slowly, painfully into the room.

"You!" said Elaine, throwing her empty glass at him. It missed him by yards, smashing into a painting hanging on the wall.

"*You're* our father?" said Alex, clearly dumbfounded.

"I wanted to tell you. So many times. But Millie . . .

she wouldn't even consider it. And I was afraid of what you'd all think of me when you found out, and afraid that I'd lose Millie forever. I'm a coward. I admit it. But I never meant to hurt your father. He was my friend. My dear friend. That's why it was so painful. I was put in this position . . . I mean, I was only trying to help—trying to comfort the only woman I ever loved. I never meant—" He sank into a chair, looking ravaged. Ashamed. Ashen.

"Did Dad . . . I mean Carl . . . know that you'd fathered us?" asked Alex.

"No," said Pearl. She looked a little dazed. "Carl had no idea who the man was."

Doc Holland wiped his face with a handkerchief. "It was . . . complicated. I loved Millie, but she loved Carl. Millie was pregnant when she married him. She said the baby was his, and I believed her—until little Alex went to the hospital with a bad fever. You were just two years old. I wasn't your physician, but I happened to glance over your chart one day and noticed your blood type. I knew what Millie's was, and I knew what Carl's was. And I knew you couldn't be his son. That's when I confronted her. My blood type is AA. I demanded to know if you were my son, Alex. Your mother said she didn't know. That she didn't want to know. But she told me she was desperate. Carl wanted more children. She'd been trying to get pregnant again ever since you were born. Nothing was happening. She was so sad, so distraught. Carl was gone a lot and I was angry at him for that, so we started getting together in the evenings, just for a drink. I was just trying to help her through a bad patch, but one thing led to another and we began an affair that lasted about six months. I really thought she'd leave Carl. It would have been for the best. But when she got pregnant again she ended the affair. I saw then that she was just using me."

"Did you know Elaine was your child?"

"Not until after she was born. Again, Millie said she didn't want to know, but I had blood tests run."

"Carl was your *dear* friend," said Elaine, her voice oozing sarcasm. "Right."

"What about me?" asked Danny. He'd said so little, it was as if the sofa had spoken. "I assume my father was sterile. That's why Mom couldn't conceive. Am I your third child? Did you have another affair?"

Doc Holland looked at Danny with a joyless smile, one that didn't part his lips. "No, son. You were Millie's miracle."

"What's that supposed to mean?" asked Elaine.

"Millie was getting worried again about two years after Elaine was born. She came to me one night, said Carl wanted another child, but again, she couldn't seem to get pregnant. She acted the seductress, but this time I was disgusted by it. I told her so. I didn't want to hurt her, but I wouldn't be used like that again. Turns out, a few weeks later, she told me she was pregnant. It was Carl's child."

"You're sure?" said Elaine.

"Yes," said Doc, giving her a hard look. "I am. I have the tests to prove it."

"My God," whispered Danny. "I'm the only legitimate heir. She knew it all along. She *knew* it."

"I doubt your father ever had his sperm count checked, but I assume it wasn't nonexistent, just low. I think Millie had made some kind of pact with God. If He gave her a child with Carl, she promised to devote her life to His service. She couldn't fulfill that promise right away because she had to take over the reins of the company until you kids were old enough to assume the leadership."

"But . . . there was some kind of prenup," said Alex. "Dad forced Mom to sign it before they were married."

Doc Holland seemed confused. "I think you're wrong about that, son. Millie never said anything to me about it."

"There *was* a signed agreement," said Pearl.

Everyone turned to look at her.

"That's the last part I need to talk to you about."

"I don't know why we should believe any of this," said Elaine. She got up and wobbled over to the table that served as a small bar. She splashed straight gin into a martini glass and tossed it back.

"You can have DNA tests done," said Doc. "I encourage you to do so. I hope, when you find out the truth, that you won't hate me—that you'll allow me into your lives. I love you all, ever since I first set eyes on you. In my own, self-pitying sort of way, I feel like the family I should have had was stolen from me. But I have no one to blame but myself."

"I think we'll need some time to think about *that*," said Elaine.

"Of course," said Doc. He seemed deflated now, thinner, smaller, like a ball that had been leaking air and was slowly turning into a rumpled shell.

"Tell us about the prenup," said Alex.

Glancing down at her purse, Pearl removed a thick envelope, a contract with a blue cover, and smoothed it open. "This is it. When Carl was dying, he told me to go get it, take it from his office and burn it. He knew that if it was ever executed, that Alex and Elaine would be cut out of his will. He didn't want that. He wanted all three of you to inherit his company. He had great faith in the business and in all of you. He knew the company would make a lot of money one day. If getting rid of the agreement meant that Millie would inherit, too, it was the way it had to be."

"But you didn't burn it," said Danny.

"No," said Pearl. "I didn't."

"Why?"

"I wanted to see what Millie would do. If it looked like she was going to run the company into the ground, if she refused to take the advice of the men your father trusted, then . . . I was going to use it to take the business away from her." She handed the contract across to Danny. "You see, Carl had made me the executor of his estate. Until you three reached your majority, he put me in charge of seeing that the company stayed on the right course. I watched Millie for many years. When Alex and Elaine were old enough, when they'd finally taken their places in the company, I put the agreement in a safety-deposit box and forgot about it."

"So . . . it was never Mom's company to give us," said Danny.

"You mean, she made us sweat and grovel, and it was always ours?" said Elaine.

"Yes," said Pearl. "But, I suppose, if Danny wants to take you and your brother to court, he could use this contract to have your mother's will invalidated. *Danny* is the sole, legal owner of Veelund Industries, although Carl wanted you to own it jointly."

Danny thought about it for a second, then burst out laughing.

Alex and Elaine just stared at him.

"Come on," he said, slapping Alex on the back. "Don't you see how ridiculous this is?"

"What are you going to do with that?" said Elaine, nodding to the contract.

"What do you think?"

"Toss us out on our ass?" said Alex.

Still laughing, Danny got up and poured himself a shot of bourbon. "This calls for something stiffer than iced tea." Holding up the shot glass, he said, "To us."

"Us?" said Alex.

"To my brother and sister and me. Titans of industry. You guys run the store and I'll go back to New York and be a writer."

"What about the people who offered to buy it?" asked Alex.

"Tell them to take a flying leap."

"What about taking it public?" asked Elaine.

"Let's just leave things the way they are for now. Okay?"

"Okay," said Alex. "But . . . there's the matter of Roman."

"Make him walk the plank," said Elaine, a wicked smile on her face.

"We'll discuss it. At our next board meeting," said Danny. He looked flushed with excitement.

Sophie couldn't help but smile. At this moment, they all seemed so happy. After everything they'd all gone through, they deserved it. And yet, with all the questions still swirling around them, that happiness hung by the thinnest of threads.

33

Elaine was in a savage mood. She'd been hurt and she wanted to hurt back. On Tuesday morning, she entered the lobby of the new Savoy Millennium in downtown Minneapolis. Her eyes darted furtively as she clutched a shoulder purse to her side, heading straight for the elevators that would take her to the twenty-third floor. The penthouse suites. Zander was already flaunting the inheritance he'd received from her mother. It made Elaine sick to think about it. She'd called him less than ten minutes ago, so she knew he was in. When he answered, she'd hung up. She didn't tell him it was time for a little "come to Jesus" meeting. When she left the hotel, she'd have her answers or Zander would be dead.

As she walked toward the room, she saw a hotel employee approaching from the other direction. He was pushing a room service cart, complete with white tablecloth, a fresh yellow rose in a thin glass vase, a silver coffeepot, a basket of rolls, and a silver-domed plate. There were only three other suites in this section, so Elaine waited, hoping the food was meant for 2416. She needed a way to get into the room, and it looked as though fate had provided her with one. She figured that, even without the ruse, Zander might let her in. But she didn't want to take any chances.

The man pushing the cart looked up at her as he got to the door. Elaine smiled warmly. Lowering her voice, she said, "Is this for Mr. Zander?"

"Yes," said the man. He was about to knock when Elaine slipped a fifty-dollar bill out of her purse. Her smile turned seductive. "Why don't you let me deliver the food? It would be so much more fun that way." She nodded to the door. "He's a . . . friend."

The hotel employee looked at the fifty. "It's against hotel policy."

"Yes, but it can be our little secret. What do you say?" She plucked another fifty from her purse.

"Well, I'm all for friendship." He took the money and stuffed it into his back pocket. "Have fun," he whispered.

She waited until he was gone, then knocked. "Room service," she called. She felt for the gun in her purse, needing to make sure it was there. When Zander opened the door, he had the usual supercilious look on his face. She'd seen it many times before, but today it made her want to gag.

Finding Elaine standing outside, Zander's look soured. "What do you want?"

"You better bring your breakfast in before it gets cold. Here, I'll help." She pushed the cart at him so fast and hard that he had to move or get run over. The door shut automatically behind her.

"I have nothing to say to you," said Zander.

"Nice suite." She glanced around at the furnishings. "Must have cost you some big bucks."

"I don't think that's any of your concern." He was

wearing a crisp yellow Oxford cloth shirt, a gray silk tie, and dark dress slacks.

Elaine had on sweatpants and a Planet Hollywood T-shirt.

"I'm going to have to ask you to leave."

She pulled the revolver out of her purse.

His eyes turned as round as saucers. "What—"

"Shut up. Turn around."

"Why?"

"Do it!"

He turned his back to her.

"Put your hands behind your back. Do it!" Pushing the gun into the side of his neck, she clamped a pair of handcuffs onto his wrists. Big purses came in handy.

"Elaine, I don't know what you think you're doing. I didn't hurt your mother or your daughter. And I don't know who did."

"Shut up." She shoved him toward a chair by the window, then backed up.

He sat down slowly, his eyes fixed on the gun.

She'd been planning this for days, ever since her daughter's death. Maybe she'd gone over the edge. She had a hard time believing that a normal, middle-aged woman could become so consumed by hate. But she was. Her old life seemed dead and gone. And she didn't care. That's what made her truly dangerous. "Recognize the gun?" she said, looking down at him. He was such a small man. He looked so pedantic, so clean, so harmless.

"No," he said, his expression turning defiant.

"It belonged to my father." As soon as she said it, she felt an odd emptiness in the pit of her stomach. Maybe Carl Veelund wasn't her real dad, but it still felt like he was. "I'm told it's a thirty-eight in perfect working order.

The cylinder has six chambers, but only one bullet in it. And now we're going to play a little game."

"You'd . . . you'd never use that gun on me. Come on, Elaine. Stop this. I'm happy to talk to you, but not at the point of a gun."

"Because you're such a reasonable man."

"I *am* a reasonable man. Yes."

"Good, then our game shouldn't take us long at all."

He breathed out slowly. He was starting to sweat. "The police have already talked to me. I know they found my tie clasp in that apartment at the Maxfield, but someone must have planted it. I have an alibi, Elaine. I was never there and I can prove it."

"Can you?" She cocked the trigger.

"Stop it! This is ridiculous. I was your mother's trusted assistant for years!"

"You helped her."

"What? Yes. Of course."

"You organized her life."

"Yes."

"And when you thought your inheritance was threatened, you ended it."

"You're wrong."

Elaine had formed a theory. She'd come here today to prove it. Maybe she could. Maybe she couldn't. But as far as she could tell, the police weren't making any progress in figuring out who'd killed either her mother or her daughter. Elaine was sick of waiting.

"You've been under a great deal of stress lately, Elaine. A great deal. You need to calm down, step back, and see that I'm your friend. I've always been your friend."

"You're right about one thing. I am close to snapping."

Zander looked as if he'd just been shocked by a jolt of electricity.

"That snap could come at any moment, Zander. Let's start." She uncocked the trigger, spun the cylinder, then cocked it again. "I'm going to ask you a question. If I don't get an answer, or if the answer feels like a lie, then I pull the trigger. You've got a one in six chance of, well"—she walked closer and pressed the gun to his forehead—"of having your brains explode all over that wall. I think you're a very bad man, Galen, so if that happens, frankly, I don't much care."

"How can you be like this? How can you be so cruel, so . . . cold?"

She shrugged. "One too many Lehane novels?"

"What? Elaine, think! You'll go to jail."

"Maybe. Maybe not. I can always say it was self-defense." She glanced over at her purse. "Actually, I've got some other stuff in there that I can use to set the scene for the police. I've thought about this very carefully, Galen." She knew he hated his first name, so she decided to use it exclusively. "I really don't think I'll go to jail for your murder."

"But—"

She pressed the barrel into his ear. "First question. Did you molest my daughter?"

"No."

She pulled the trigger.

"God!" he screamed, ducked down and cringed. "God, stop it!"

"Let's try that again." She spun the barrel and cocked the trigger. "Did you molest my daughter, Galen? Think a little harder this time."

"I—"

"Come on. Just get it off your chest. You'll feel better."

"I . . . I—"

"The *truth*, Galen." She could feel herself quaking inside.

"I . . . didn't mean to. It was . . . I'm—"

"You're what?"

"Sorry."

"You're a stinking, slimy, goddamned *pedophile,* that's what you are."

"Yes. Okay, yes."

She wanted to kill him. But slowly. She wanted to watch him suffer. "What about the baby she was carrying. Is it yours?"

"Baby? What baby?" His eyes grew wild. "I don't know anything about a baby."

"Did you rape her? Again? Recently?"

"No. God, no. She's much too—"

"Old? Do you know what you did to my daughter's life? Do you even care?"

"I told her how sorry I was."

"You terrified her!"

"I had to. Nobody could know. But I tried to make it up to her. I helped her, just like she asked."

"What are you talking about?"

"It was when she came to your mother's house to stay, after the suicide attempt—I mean, I don't know. She was different. You're right, she used to be scared of me, but she wasn't anymore. *She* threatened *me*. If I didn't do what she wanted, she was going to tell your mother what I'd done to her."

"So you killed her."

"No! I didn't kill anyone."

Elaine pulled the trigger.

"Help me!" he pleaded, falling off the chair, curling into a ball.

When Elaine looked down, she saw that he'd wet his pants. "Get up," she said, yanking him back into the chair. She cocked the trigger.

"You didn't spin the cylinder," he said, sweat beading on his forehead.

"No, I didn't. That's right. You're a gambler. You must be calculating your odds. Well, asshole, I just reduced your chances to one in five. Tell me what Tracy said to you."

"That . . . that she wanted to get back at someone."

"Who?"

"She didn't say. I asked her, but she told me it was none of my business."

"Was it a man?"

"Yes, I think so. But I don't know for sure."

"You're such a liar. You lied to me about molesting my child. You lied—"

"But I'm telling you the truth this time, Elaine. I swear I am! Tracy told me to go get one of your dad's rifles out of the rec room in the basement and leave it in the grove—by that big oak just south of the creek. I did it. I did just what she asked. She told me to make sure I left some shells with it. A full box."

"Are you saying that she was the sniper, the one who shot at Alex and Roman?"

"She must have climbed out her bedroom window and down the trellis, just the way she did the night she took off."

Elaine had to think fast. She doubted that Tracy was shooting at Alex. That left Roman. Had he been the one she'd slept with? Had he gotten her pregnant? Had he raped her? Elaine couldn't imagine her daughter sleeping with a man like Roman.

Sweat poured off Zander's face. "The guard was instructed not to go into Tracy's bedroom while she was sleeping."

"I know that."

"But . . . that wasn't all. There were other things Tracy asked me to do for her."

"Like what?"

"Put the gun down, Elaine. Please!"

"Answer the question."

Taking a deep breath, he said, "She told me to go get her a handgun from her grandfather's gun cabinet. And then, later, after she'd taken off, she called. Told me she needed a video camera and a tripod. That I should go buy them—and that I should learn how to use the camera and make sure the battery was charged."

"Did you?"

"Yes."

"And then what?"

"She said she'd call me. Tell me how I could get it to her."

"Did she call you?"

"I was at the track. She said she planned to spend the night at the Maxfield Plaza in St. Paul. Gave me directions. I was supposed to meet her there at ten."

"In Margie Baldric's apartment?"

"Right."

"So you went. You *were* there. Another lie, Galen."

He ducked his head. "I thought that if the police found out, they'd think I was the one who strangled Tracy. But I didn't. I just showed her how to use the camera, and then

I left. But I lost the damn tie clasp. I thought I lost it later that night, in the hotel room with that bimbo I picked up."

"The girl who gave you the alibi. I hear she was eighteen. That's a little old for you, isn't it?"

He looked away. "I didn't kill your daughter, Elaine. I swear it."

"Why did she want the camera?"

"Don't shoot again, okay? Please? I don't know why she wanted it. She never told me. But she set the tripod up in the bedroom closet with the camera pointing out through the crack between the door and the doorjamb."

"She obviously wanted to film someone without them knowing it."

"That's what I figured, too."

"But the police didn't find a video camera, Galen. So if you're telling the truth, what happened to it? You must have some thoughts on the subject."

"I don't know," he said. "Maybe the guy who killed her took it with him."

Maybe that guy was Roman Marchand, thought Elaine. She wondered how carefully the police had checked him out. "What time did you leave the Maxfield?"

"I was only there for a few minutes. I left around ten-fifteen. Tracy said she needed more money. I was supposed to bring her ten thousand dollars the next morning. But . . . it never happened because—" He closed his eyes.

Elaine removed the gun from his forehead. Sitting down on the couch, she studied him. He was pathetic. A pathetic pervert, sweating though his Oxford cloth shirt like a pig. But was he a murderer? "Did you know about the money Mom left you in her will?"

"Of course I knew. How could I not know? I was there

with her every time she went to see her lawyer. I drove her. I kept all her notes."

"So you had a lot to lose if Tracy decided to tell my mom what you'd done to her. As I see it, it would have been easy enough for you to give my mother an extra injection of insulin. You could have told her that the first one only had half of what she needed. She would have trusted you. Or you could have done it once the sleeping pill had sent her to dreamland." She thought for a minute. "Or maybe Tracy didn't need to tell my mother. Maybe she figured it out all by herself. Did she confront you, Galen? You would have denied it, of course, and she had no proof. But all she had to do was talk to Tracy the next day. You couldn't trust that Tracy *wouldn't* tell her the truth. And you didn't know that she'd picked that night to run away. You didn't have much time, and you needed to make it look like a natural death. Except the medical examiner was too smart for you. They realized the death wasn't natural. Mick discovered you downstairs that night, Galen. If memory serves, he said he ran into you in the pantry at three in the morning. You told him you couldn't sleep, so you'd come down for some milk."

"That's right."

"Milk, Galen? *Milk?*"

"Warm milk. It helps put me to sleep."

After what he'd done in his life, Elaine was amazed that he could sleep at all. But milk? It was beyond absurd. "There was no mention of a dirty pan, or even a dirty mug. How did you heat it? What did you drink it from?"

"I already told this to the police. I heated the milk in a mug in the microwave. And I washed the mug and put it away when I was done. I always leave a kitchen neat whenever I make myself something."

That she could believe.

Zander pulled his head into his shoulders, like a turtle trying to suck its head back into its shell. "Why doesn't anybody think it was odd that Danny went in to talk to your mother that night? It was late—midnight, maybe. What was he doing in her room at that hour?"

"They'd had a fight the day before. He felt he'd left some important things unsaid."

"Okay, okay. Maybe it was that simple. But there's still Alex. He came up to the pool for a late swim."

"But he never went into the house."

"That's what he *says*. But did you ever think that maybe *he* lied?"

There was a sudden knock on the door.

"Police," said a deep male voice. "Open up."

Elaine was off the couch in a flash. Still holding the gun on Zander, she found the key for the handcuffs and unlocked them. "Answer it," she said, not that it was necessary. Zander was already flying across the room.

"Lord in heaven, I'm so glad you're here. That woman was trying to kill me." He pointed at Elaine.

After setting the safety, Elaine dropped the gun and the cuffs out a narrow window behind the chair, a window only wide enough to get her arm through. This high up, there wasn't any need for screens. Below them was the back side of the building, mainly Dumpsters, a loading dock, and space for trucks to pull in. She hoped it landed somewhere safe.

"Are you Galen Zander?" asked one of two police officers.

"Didn't you hear me?" said Zander, rubbing his wrists. "That woman over there threatened my life!"

Elaine shook her head, spreading her arms and raising her palms.

"Your name?" asked the officer.

"Elaine Veelund. I'm Millie Veelund's daughter. I came here to talk to Mr. Zander about my mother. He used to work for her. But after he let me in, I realized he was in this terribly agitated state."

"She threatened to kill me!" sputtered Zander. "She has a gun."

"Is that true?" asked the officer.

"No, of course not." She held her arms wide and looked around. "You can check if you want."

The office sized her up for a few seconds, then looked back at Zander. "Mr. Zander, I'm arresting you for the murder of Mildred Veelund. You have the right to remain silent."

Thank God, thought Elaine. The marines had finally landed.

"I want my lawyer," snapped Zander.

"You have the right to an attorney. Anything—"

"I won't say a single word without my lawyer present."

"I understand that, sir, but I have to read you your rights."

"What happened to all your protestations of innocence?" said Elaine.

Zander shot her a withering look.

Innocent and *Zander* didn't even belong in the same sentence, thought Elaine.

"We'll need you to leave, ma'am," said the younger officer. "We have to secure this suite."

"Of course," she said.

The older of the two cops kept on with the Miranda

rights as the younger officer cuffed Zander's hands behind his back. As soon as the legalities were accomplished, Zander was ushered out the door.

Elaine followed, her thoughts now turning to Roman. *One down*, she whispered to herself. *And one to go.*

34

On the way past the reservation desk, Sophie was stopped by one of the staff. It was nearly six. She'd been away from the hotel most of the day—first shopping at Target with her mother, and then getting some newspaper work done at the *Times Register* Tower in downtown Minneapolis. She knew her father would be checking out the hotel today, making sure she hadn't sent it into receivership while he was gone. He was upset when he'd found that there'd been an attempted murder in one of the apartments, though he couldn't exactly blame Sophie for that. Still, while he was doing his inspection, she wanted to stay out of his way. But by the look on the reservationist's face, she'd probably made the wrong decision.

"What is it?" asked Sophie, sensing worry in the woman's expression.

"I'm sorry, Ms. Greenway . . . but it's your dog."

"Ethel?"

"We can't find her. When one of the bellmen went to take her out for her afternoon walk, she wasn't on her pillow in the lobby."

"Did you check my apartment?"

"We did. She wasn't there."

"Maybe Bram came home and took her out."

The woman slipped on her reading glasses. "No, he left you a note." She picked it up and looked at it. "He said he's taking his daughter to that blues festival down by the river tonight. He planned to leave straight from the station and wouldn't be back here until late."

Sophie was running out of options. "Maybe my dad took her. Or my mom."

The woman shook her head. "We checked with them."

Sophie rested a hand on her hip. "Well, she didn't just *walk* out of here. She barely moves her eyes, let alone her body—unless someone drags her."

"I'm really sorry, Ms. Greenway. We've looked everywhere. One of the bellmen said that, well, maybe she smelled the ribs roasting down by the river. That blues festival includes a huge rib fest this year, too. And it's only three blocks away. If you step outside, your mouth starts to water."

"Are you suggesting she just lurched her way out the door?"

"It's possible. She's not a big dog. And we've been insanely busy all day."

Sophie couldn't believe Ethel would just leave. She'd never done anything like that before. If you led her outside, she might walk over to a small patch of grass, if she could find one, and relieve herself. But then she'd just stand there, or find a comfortable piece of cement and lie down. Actually, she'd lie down anywhere, comfortable or not. *Unless* someone took her green tennis ball. Over the past year, Ethel had become fiercely protective of one particular ball. It was usually either inches from her nose, or in her mouth. When she slept, she curled around it. When she ate, it rested next to her dog dish. Sometimes she dropped it in the toilet. Bram loved that move. Sophie assumed she was trying to wash it. If someone had attempted to steal the ball, Ethel would undoubtedly have followed them. But nobody in their right mind would touch something covered in so much dog drool. It looked as if it had lived in a rain forest for several hundred years.

Instead of returning to her office, Sophie headed up to her apartment. Maybe Ethel was hiding under the dining room table or under the bed. She did things like that. Sophie had so much on her mind right now, she didn't want to add Ethel to the list.

Entering her apartment, she checked everywhere. She looked out on the patio, thinking that Ethel might have gotten locked out. She checked every room, looked under the beds and every piece of furniture, but Ethel was nowhere to be found.

Hearing her cell phone ring, Sophie followed the sound. "There you are," she said, picking it up off the side of the bathtub. She'd been looking for it for days. "Hello?" she said. "This is Sophie."

The line clicked.

"Charming," she said, stuffing the phone in the back pocket of her jeans.

As she returned to the living room, she noticed that the light was blinking on the caller ID box for her home line. Checking the name, she saw that Elaine had called, so she punched in her voice mail number to get the message.

"Sophie, hi. It's Elaine. It's about noon. Guess what? They just arrested Zander for my mother's murder! Finally, some action. I talked to the detective on the case and he said they think he was responsible for both deaths, but that they feel like they've got a stronger case against him for Mom's murder. And, actually, I talked to Zander this morning. I got him to admit that he *did* molest Tracy when she was a child—don't ask me how. All I can say is, this lady has learned a few tricks in her old age. But Zander also told me a bunch of other stuff. I believe now that the child Tracy was carrying was Roman's. I don't know how it happened, or why, mainly because I can't find him. I've called his office, his town house, Alex's place, everywhere I can think of, but he's not around. If you see him, not that you would, but if you do, will you call me? Between you and me, I think he's the one who murdered Tracy. I'll fill you in on all the details later. But I feel so stoked right now. I'll put that bastard behind bars if it's the last thing I do. Later, Soph."

Sophie sat down on the couch, attempting to make sense of what Elaine had just told her. It didn't surprise her that Zander had been arrested for Millie's murder, but Roman? Sophie remembered that Tracy had worked for him for a couple of months last summer. Maybe they'd formed a friendship. Tracy tried to hide her body under big shirts and loose pants, but anybody with eyes—and hormones—could see that she was built. If Roman had been married once upon a time, maybe he was bisexual, not gay. But sleeping with his lover's niece wasn't exactly smart. Neither was fathering a child with her. Lord, if Alex found out, there would be hell to pay. Sophie couldn't help but wonder where Mick fit into all of this. If Tracy had willingly slept with Roman, why did she go and marry Mick? Of course, there was always the possibility that if Roman was the father, he'd forced Tracy to have sex with him. God, thought Sophie. That poor girl. No matter what the truth really turned out to be, her life had been hellish. And Elaine was right. Roman's involvement did answer a lot of questions—if it turned out to be true.

On her way out the door, Sophie grabbed a leash. She had to find Ethel before she could calm down and concentrate on anything else. She was in the elevator on her way down to the lobby when her cell phone rang again. Fishing it out of her back pocket, she said hello.

"Ah, hi," said a young man's voice. "I, ah, I think I found your dog."

Sophie felt instantly relieved.

"Is she black? Kind of slow moving?" asked the guy.

"That's her," said Sophie.

"I got your number off the tag."

"Where are you?"

"I'm down at the blues fest on the riverfront. You know where that is? It's along Kellogg, right—"

"I know where it is," said Sophie. How on earth had Ethel gotten herself down there? "Just give me a couple of minutes. I'm not far away."

"Sure thing. I'm standing by the mini-doughnut booth across from a hotel. I don't know the name of it."

"I do. I'll find you," said Sophie. "I can't tell you how happy I am that you found my dog."

"No problem."

"It says 'reward' on her tag. How does a hundred dollars sound?"

"Great."

"Don't let her out of your sight. She means the world to me."

"I won't. See ya." The line clicked.

Sophie was thrilled. A quick walk down to the river and one problem would be solved. As the elevator doors opened and she stepped off, she glanced over at the reception desk and saw long lines of people waiting to check in. She felt guilty charging off after Ethel when there was so much work to do here. That's when an idea occurred to her. If Bram was at the blues fest, maybe he could go get her. That way, Sophie could stay and help out at the front desk.

She tapped #1 on the cell phone and hit the call button. Number one was programmed to call Bram's cell. When she raised the phone to her ear, nothing happened. She looked down at the readout. No number had been dialed. "Screw that," she said, punching in the numbers manually. Bram picked up right away.

"Baldric," he said gruffly.

"Bram, it's me."

"Hey. What's up?"

"Ethel got out."

"Define 'out.' "

"Out of the hotel. She was lost for a good portion of the afternoon."

"You're kidding. *Our* Ethel? Her ball roll out the door?"

"I don't know," said Sophie. "But she's down at the blues fest. You're there with Margie, right?"

Bram laughed. "That's quite an image. Ethel at a blues fest. Yes, I'm here. Margie and Mick just pulled up in his new silver Maserati 3200."

"That means nothing to me."

"It's a car. An expensive Italian car. He's already spending Tracy's inheritance."

Sophie found the idea nauseating. "I guess money corrupts everyone."

"Guess so."

"So, here's the deal," said Sophie. "Can you go over and pick Ethel up? Some guy's got her. He called me on my cell phone after getting the number off the collar." She explained where he was waiting. "So . . . can you be a prince and go get her?"

"Ah, Soph. This is the worst possible timing."

"Why?"

"I've been waiting in a line to get some Lincoln Dobbs ribs for the last half hour. There're only three people in front of me now. If I give up my place in line, it will take me another half hour to get the food. And Mick and Margie are waiting at the bandstand, holding the seats. Could you do it, honey? It wouldn't take you long. Ten minutes down, ten minutes back."

Sophie sighed. "Oh, I suppose. I don't want to be responsible for people starving."

"I thank you . . . from the bottom of my stomach. And I'm sure Ethel will, too."

She blew a lock of hair away from her forehead.

"See you later tonight, sweetheart."

"Right. Bye." She pocketed the phone, then took off out the front door, refusing to even look at the reception desk. Ethel came first.

The night had grown chilly now that the sun was setting. She wished she'd brought along a jacket, but there wasn't time to run back upstairs. She cut down Vermillion to Duluth Street and turned left. With her favorite walking shoes on, she made good time. As she crossed an alley in the middle of the block, she heard a sort of muffled bark. It was the same sound Ethel made when she tried to bark with the tennis ball in her mouth. Uff. Uff. Uff, uff. Glancing into the alley, she saw Ethel standing about twenty feet away.

"Ethel?" Had she run away from the young man down by the river? "Is that you?"

She started toward her. Moving deeper into the dim-ness, she could see now that Ethel was tugging against something. And then she saw it. A thin black cord had been tied to her collar. What the hell was going on? Sensing danger, Sophie stopped. She started to back up.

That's when a man stepped into her line of sight, a gun in his hand.

Sophie froze. "Roman?"

He motioned for her to move toward him.

Every instinct told her to run, but with a gun pointed at her chest, she wouldn't get two feet if he really intended to use it. "What . . . what's going on?"

"As you see, I have your little doggie," he said, grabbing her by the arm and slamming her against a black van.

Staring at the gun, Sophie said, "What are you going to do?"

"I am a businessman. I must take care of business," said Roman. He yanked her face first over to a brick wall, then pressed his full weight against her as he tied her hands behind her back with duct tape. When he yanked her to the front again, he slapped a piece of tape over her mouth.

She panicked, tried to scream, bucked as hard as she could to get away, but he held her fast with the weight of his body.

His breath stank of liquor. "You should never have called me back that night."

Her eyes opened wide. She had no idea what he was talking about.

"You should never have told me you knew who I was and what I had done. How could I let you get away when you are the only witness, the only person who stands between me and my future?" He yanked her away from the wall, then slammed her back against it hard. "Tracy got in my way, too. I never thought I could kill someone. But when I walked out of that room, I knew I could do it again—if I had to." He gripped Sophie's throat. "*You* made that necessary. You should have kept your mouth shut. But then, if you had, I would never have known the danger I was in. You are a stupid woman."

He's crazy, thought Sophie. He's going to kill me. Again, she tried to scream, but he slapped her hard across the face.

"Shut up," he whispered.

He shoved her down on the ground, then tied her ankles together with more duct tape. His strength amazed her. The next second she was up again, being dragged over to the back of the van. He hoisted her in like a sack of flour, then unhooked Ethel from her leash and tossed her in.

Sophie knew she had mere seconds before the door of the van was shut. Nobody could hear her then. She bellowed as loud as she could through her taped mouth. Bellowed and bellowed, and then bellowed some more.

Roman whacked her legs with a piece of rebar to make her stop.

Ethel didn't seem to like what he was doing. She dropped her ball and started barking. Suddenly, she lunged at him, clamping her teeth onto his ear. He tried to yank her off, but roared in pain as she hung on.

Sophie pulled herself into a sitting position. When she looked down, she saw that he'd dropped the gun.

"Goddamn you," he snarled, trying to pry Ethel's teeth loose.

At the same moment, a dark form whizzed past Sophie. An instant later, Roman was sprawled on the ground. Ethel let go and landed on a bunch of plastic garbage sacks.

"Get the gun," shouted Bram's voice.

The two men struggled as Ethel barked.

Margie suddenly appeared. She leaned down. When she straightened up, she held the gun in her hand. "Okay, asshole. You're busted."

Roman raised his hands.

Next thing Sophie knew, Bram was by her side. He ripped the tape off her mouth. "Are you okay?"

She gulped air. Her heart was pounding.

"Just take it easy, Soph. You're going to be fine." He removed the tape from her hands and feet. By the time he was done, Sophie could hear sirens.

"Mick stayed behind to call the police," said Bram. He took the gun from Margie's hand, but kept it trained on Roman.

In the darkness of the alley, Sophie could see that Roman was still on the ground, his head leaning against a Dumpster. The right side of his face was covered in blood. Score one for Ethel.

Sophie felt like she'd gone ten rounds with a jackhammer. Not even a minute passed before the police stormed in. Lights flashed. Guns were drawn. People shouted. A paramedic came and checked her over, pronouncing her bruised but otherwise sound. Questions were asked. Roman refused to talk, but Sophie tried to answer as best she could. She said that Roman was the one who'd strangled Tracy. He'd admitted it to her. For some reason, he thought she'd called him, accused him of the murder. Sophie explained that it wasn't true. She had no idea where he got that idea, but that was apparently why he attempted to stuff her in the back of the van and do whatever he planned to do with her. Ethel had been the bait.

Sophie leaned against Bram as Roman was finally

handcuffed and led away. The alley had been lit up like a stage set. Police photographers were taking photos. Forensic examiners were checking out the van.

"Come on, Ethel," said Bram. "Time to go home."

Ethel had been sitting in the van during most of the interrogation, the tennis ball clamped tightly in her mouth, but she hopped out as soon as everyone began leaving.

Mick and Margie were walking ahead of Sophie and Bram toward Mick's new car.

"How did you know I was in danger," asked Sophie, "when I didn't even know myself?"

Bram had his arm around her shoulder. Squeezing her tight, he said, "The phone number. We didn't put your cell phone number on Ethel's tag. We put our home number on it. As soon as I remembered that, I knew something was screwy. I found Margie and Mick and we followed the path I assumed you'd take from the hotel. When I heard all the commotion in the alley, we—"

"Rushed in."

"Well, we didn't rush. We tiptoed until we could scout out what was going on. But we tiptoed *fast.*"

Sophie leaned her head against him as they came out of the alley and started for the home. "Are you saying you didn't get your ribs?"

"Nope. When I ducked out, there were still two people in front of me. I don't think I was meant to eat those greasy, fabulously unhealthy ribs, Soph."

"So, you're saying you believe in fate?"

He kissed the top of her head. "When it comes to you, yes, I most certainly do."

35

On Wednesday morning, Sophie stayed in bed until after nine. Her run-in with Roman Marchand had left her feeling bruised and battered. The right side of her face was swollen and red from being slapped, and she'd received a gash in her thigh when he'd dumped her into the van. Every muscle in her body screamed from being stretched in the wrong direction. The police had requested that she come down to the station around eleven to give her statement. If she had to arrive on a gurney, she'd do it. She had to make sure that Marchand was put away for a long, long time. It was the only way she'd ever feel safe again.

Sophie had tossed and turned all night, thinking about what she'd say, reliving the event in order to describe it in detail. When she'd landed inside that van, inside the clanging metal hole, she felt as if she'd been dropped into a void, a place from which nobody ever returned. She was still a bit shaky, but she'd recover. Tracy, on the other hand, never would.

"I think I'm going to relive last night a thousand times," said Sophie.

She and Margie were sitting at the breakfast table, the

dregs of their breakfast spread out in front of them. Bram had gone into the kitchen to get more coffee.

"It was actually pretty clever," said Margie, nibbling on a piece of toast. "Marchand kidnapped Ethel so that he could get to you."

"Clever. Right." Sophie shivered.

Bram returned to the dining room and poured everyone more coffee. "I talked to my buddy, Al Lundquist, this morning. He said the police found the kid Marchand paid to call you, Soph. He was sixteen. Marchand gave him fifty bucks to tell you he'd found your dog. The kid didn't see anything wrong with it. He had no idea what Marchand was up to."

"I still don't understand why he was after me," said Sophie, twisting her coffee mug in her hand. "I saw him staring at me at Tracy's funeral, but I didn't figure it meant anything—well, anything other than that he was rude. It's just . . . I can't get over what he said to me before he tossed me into that van. He said that I'd called him, told him I knew he'd strangled Tracy."

Margie stopped nibbling her toast. "He did?"

Bram gave her a hard look. "Do you know something?"

"Well . . ." She tried to smile but it died on her face. "Actually . . ."

"'Actually' what?" said Sophie.

Margie jumped up from the table and padded back to her bedroom.

Bram and Sophie exchanged confused glances.

A minute later, she was back, a cell phone in her hand. She set it on the table and pushed it across to Sophie. "I was going to tell you about this yesterday morning, but you'd already left to go shopping with your mother. That's your cell phone. You've got mine." She tittered. "Just so happens, they're the same model. They must have gotten switched sometime in the last couple of days, while I was staying with you and Dad."

"I found this one on the side of the tub," said Sophie.

"Hmm, well, yeah, I was using it in there. I must have taken yours then because I couldn't find it. Oops. Stupid me." She shrugged and giggled.

"But what's your point?" said Sophie. And then it hit her. "Marchand called *your* number to tell me about Ethel. Why would he do that?"

"I didn't realize it until just this second, but now I get it."

"Then share it with us, Margie, please," said Bram. His politeness covered his anger.

"Well," said Margie, looking distinctly uncomfortable as she fiddled with her toast. "I called him. That night. The night Tracy was strangled."

Bram's eyebrows dipped ominously. "Explain."

"Well, when I got back to my apartment, my cell phone was lying next to her on the nightstand. I picked it up and put it in my purse. It was mine. I usually keep it with me, but I'd left it in the apartment that night. I didn't think it had anything to do with anything. And I needed it. Anyway, then I came upstairs to get you. But later that night, after we all got back from the hospital, when I was in bed trying to get to sleep, it occurred to me that maybe Tracy had called someone with my phone. I checked the calls I'd made recently, and the last number wasn't one I recognized."

"So you called it," said Sophie. A great yawning pit opened in the center of her stomach.

Margie nodded. "A man's voice answered. I didn't

recognize it. I asked who I was talking to, but all I got was silence. That's when I said, 'I know who you are and I know what you did.' "

"My God," said Bram, nearly spilling his coffee. "Whatever possessed you to say that?"

She shrugged. "It was just an impulse."

"How did the man respond?"

"He hung up. I figured he thought I was some stupid prank caller bugging him in the middle of the night. I mean, just because I didn't recognize the number didn't exactly mean much. I make a lot of calls, especially now because Carrie and I've started setting up our business."

Sophie had an irresistible urge to bounce the cell phone off Margie's forehead.

"So you must have reached Marchand," said Bram. "What's your caller ID say?"

"M. Baldric."

"Roman thought *my* last name was Baldric," said Sophie, remembering the day she and Elaine had talked to him at Alex's house.

"So he assumed you'd called him that night," said Bram, turning to Sophie. "That's how this whole chain of events got started."

"Do you realize you nearly got me killed!" Sophie's eyes shot daggers at Margie.

"Geez, chill, okay? How was I supposed to know I hit the jackpot? Got the real killer on the line. And hey, maybe someone should give me a little credit. I mean, without that call, he might have gotten away with murder. Nobody was looking at him as a suspect, *were they*?" She bugged out her eyes. "I mean, come on. Rub a few brain cells together. I did everyone a favor. It was a brilliant piece of work."

"You're nuts if you think I'm going to thank you for making that call," said Sophie.

"Margie has a point," said Bram.

Sophie whirled to look at him. She was aghast. She couldn't believe her ears. She'd been beaten up and forced into the back of a van, minutes from death, and he was taking his daughter's side?

"I knew Tracy had been madly in love with some guy last summer," continued Margie, pulling the toast apart and dunking half of it in a pool of grape jelly.

"How did you know that?" asked Bram.

"She needed someone to confide in and I'm a good listener. We spent a bunch of time together. I'm the one who gave her a lift the night she ran away from her grandmother's place."

"You drove her to that motel?" said Bram.

Again, she shrugged. "She asked for my help and I figured, what the hell."

"Go on," said Sophie, trying to keep the coldness out of her voice.

"Well, Tracy never gave me the guy's name, although I knew it wasn't Mick. She said the relationship had gone south and now she hated him. She was going to make him pay for what he'd done to her."

"What did he do—other than get her pregnant?"

"I didn't know about the pregnancy part. But he told her he loved her. That she was the most beautiful woman he'd ever known and he couldn't get enough of her. She assumed that meant they'd get married. It was only a matter of time. But when she pressed him about it, he blew up. Told her to back off, that nobody was going to tie him down again. I inferred from that that he'd been married once."

"Why did she marry Mick?" asked Bram.

"She didn't entirely clarify that point. I guess she was a lot like me. Kind of impulsive. And frankly, I think she wanted to be able to tell Marchand that somebody loved her enough to marry her. That she was a married woman now and he could take his dick and stuff it in the nearest mailbox for all she cared."

"Honey," said Bram.

"It's true. It's the way she felt. Maybe it had something to do with the pregnancy, too. Maybe she figured she could convince Mick that the child was his. Except, she didn't feel romantic about him. The idea of sleeping with him made her nauseous. Now me, on the other hand, I think he's pretty cute. And really sweet. A lot better catch than Marchand, but then everyone's got different tastes."

"Why didn't you tell us any of this?" asked Bram.

"I promised Tracy I'd keep her stuff a secret. I couldn't break a promise. Personal integrity is everything to me, Dad."

Sophie tried not to fall off her chair.

Margie added some cream and sugar to her coffee and stirred. "Well, all I can say is, 'All's well that ends well.' "

"What on earth ended well?" said Sophie. She'd just about had it. "Two people are dead. An entire family has been turned upside down by a mother's infidelity and a man's pedophilia. And I was almost killed by a homicidal maniac."

Margie gulped her coffee, then stood. "I'd like to continue this conversation—I really would—but Mick is picking me up in ten minutes and I need to change."

"Where are you headed?" asked Bram.

"House hunting," said Margie. "Mick needs somewhere to live. He's arranged for a real estate agent to show him a couple of places on Summit. He asked me to go with him."

"*Summit?*" repeated Sophie. These were the most expensive houses in St. Paul. He was certainly having a good time with his wife's inheritance.

"Are you two an item?" asked Bram.

"Nah, just friends. But I love looking at houses. A girl can dream, can't she?" She kissed her father, then bounced out of the room.

Sophie rested her chin on her hands. She was exhausted by Margie's exuberance. Dare she use the word *shallow* in front of Bram? She didn't think so.

After Margie had disappeared into her bedroom, Bram said, "Life does go on, sweetheart." He wrapped his warm hand around hers.

"I guess."

"Margie didn't mean to get you in trouble."

"But she sure as hell did."

"I know." He ran his fingers along her arm. "But the two men responsible for those deaths are now behind bars. That's a good outcome. Oh, I forgot to tell you." He pulled his chair up closer to the table. "Al told me something else when I talked to him. Now that the police have both murderers in custody, more of the real story is coming out. Elaine Veelund gave the police a statement last night. She told them that she'd talked to Zander yesterday, and he'd admitted he was a pedophile, that he was the one who'd preyed on Tracy when she was a child. Of course, now that he's got himself a lawyer, he's denying he ever said any of it."

"Figures."

"But here's the thing. Apparently, Tracy was blackmailing Zander. She threatened to tell her grandmother what he'd done to her if he didn't help her."

"Help her with what?" Sophie hadn't talked to Elaine after the phone message she'd left yesterday. Apparently, she'd missed a lot.

"Well, he stole a gun and a rifle from her grandfather's gun collection for her. And then later, she demanded that he go buy a video camera. She was apparently going to use it the night Marchand came to Margie's apartment. I assume Tracy was planning to get him to say something incriminating on tape so she could prove he was the father of her child. I have no idea how she planned to use it, but it was definitely payback time for the way he'd treated her. Marchand discovered the camera and that's why he went off on Tracy. He took the camera with him when he left."

"How come the police know all this?"

"Because they found the camera at his town house. And guess what?"

"What?"

Bram's smile was triumphant. "He never erased it. The entire attack is on tape."

Sophie's mouth dropped open.

"But here's the real kicker. Apparently, Tracy had never used a video camera before. Neither had Zander. She told him that when he bought it, he needed to learn how to use it so he could teach it to her. And what did he take a video of?"

Sophie closed her eyes.

"Girls at a playground. Six-, seven-, eight-year-olds. Except for the beginning few minutes, the whole tape is nothing but little girls."

"Not exactly proof of pedophilia."

"No, but if you add it to everything else, it's one more

nail in his coffin. The police think they've got a great case against Zander for Millie's murder."

"But there was no eyewitness," said Sophie.

"That's true in a lot of cases. Why does it bother you so much?"

"It just does." She couldn't explain it. It was just a feeling she had. She knew Elaine thought the police had been dragging their feet, that they should have arrested someone a lot sooner. But Sophie had the opposite reaction. She felt the police had acted too fast. There were so many people who had strong motives for wanting to see Millie dead. Sure, Zander was one of them, and the case against him was fairly straightforward. He was as good a guess as any. And he *was* a pedophile, someone who belonged in prison. Still.

Bram picked up their coffee cups and motioned for Sophie to follow him into the living room. Once they were settled on the couch, with Ethel and her tennis ball fast asleep on a pillow by the door to the patio, Bram put his arm around Sophie. "I know you're angry with Margie, and you have every right to be, but if she hadn't followed up with that call, Marchand might have gotten away. And if he'd returned to Canada, as he was planning, the camera would have gone with him."

"You're right. I am angry with Margie. I think you better give me some time to work that one out."

"Sophie, if anything ever happened to you, I don't think I'd live through it. But you're okay. You're here and you're safe. After what happened last night, I want to dance a jig, shout from the rooftops that my wife is alive and well. And," he said, wiggling his eyebrows, "Nathan Buckridge is dating Elaine Veelund, tra la, tra la. I hope they sail off into the sunset, preferably to some faraway island without phones or mail service."

Sophie had been thinking about what her mother had said the other day—that in this world you couldn't love two men. Or maybe, more accurately, you could love them, but you couldn't have them both. Sophie had made a vow to love and honor Bram for the rest of her life. And she did love him. So much, sometimes, it hurt. If only Nathan could find happiness. Sophie didn't believe he ever would with Elaine, but it was out of her hands. Sophie had made her choice. Taken a vow. For better or worse. For richer or poorer. But she wanted to add to those promises now. She vowed not to be stupid—or sentimental. She vowed never to take her life with Bram for granted.

Margie picked that exact moment to sail through the room on her way out the door. "Bye, all. I'll be gone a couple hours."

"Bye," called Bram.

"Don't rush back on our account," added Sophie. Thankfully, Margie's apartment would be cleaned up and ready for her to move back in early next week. "You're my guy," Sophie said to Bram, kissing him tenderly.

"I wish we didn't have to be at the police station in less than an hour." He nuzzled her neck.

She drew her head back. "Are you suggesting something indecent?"

"That was the idea."

"Well," she said, flinging her arms out wide. "If we're a little late, what can they do? Arrest us? Toss us in jail and make us wear hideous orange jumpsuits?"

Bram grinned. "Living on the edge does have a certain allure. As long as you're there to keep me company."

"Always," said Sophie. She put her arms around his neck as he lifted her and carried her into the bedroom.

Every now and then, being a shrimp had its advantages.

36

Danny flew back to New York on Friday night. He'd stayed an extra few days to ensure that the new financial relationship with his siblings was agreed upon and put down on paper. He had no wish to change anything substantially. The truth of his parentage notwithstanding, had his mother outlived him, had her bigotry and anti-Semitism been allowed to run its course, his family would have been cut off without a penny. Of that Danny had no doubt. But it was all in the past now.

He took a cab in from La Guardia and arrived home around ten. Manhattan was ablaze with lights as the cab drove down Second. It was a real sea change after the dark nights he'd spent on the Minnesota prairie. From half a block away, he could see Ruth standing on the steps of their brownstone. The expression on her face was both tentative and expectant. He'd seen that expression so many times before that he'd memorized it.

Once the bags were out of the trunk and the cabbie was paid, he held Ruth in his arms. It was finally over.

"You look tired," she said, touching his beard with her fingertips. "And thinner. Have you been eating?"

He squeezed her hand, kissed her fingers. "I'm fine now that I'm home."

They carried his bags inside.

Ruth had prepared a few snacks. Cheese and fruit. His favorite crackers. An unopened bottle of cider rested next to a couple of glasses on the dining room table. But food was the last thing on his mind. He crushed her against him, kissing her hair, her cheeks, her lips. He felt as if they fit together perfectly, like two pieces of a puzzle. "I've missed you so much," he whispered in her ear. "I'll never go away again."

"Promise?"

"Not even to get groceries."

"What about picking up the cleaning?"

"Yeah, I suppose I could do that."

They tumbled onto the couch together, laughing. Ruth always made him laugh. His heart ached, he loved her so much.

"Tell me truthfully," she said as she leaned against him, cradled in his arms. "How are you feeling?"

"Relieved. And sad."

"And Alex?"

"How would you feel if your lover had just been arrested for killing your niece?"

"Pretty rotten."

"That about covers it."

"Elaine?"

He tipped his head back. "She's a survivor. But it will take some time to get her feet back under her."

"She'll never get over Tracy's death."

"No."

"What about Doc Holland?"

Danny sighed. "He was staying at my mother's place after she died, you know."

"I know."

"The day we found out that he was Alex and Elaine's biological father, he went back home. I think he was too ashamed to continue staying at the house. He's so frail now, Ruth. So very frail. Nobody really noticed it until after Mom died. We were all worried about him, so Elaine finally drove over to his place to see how he was doing. The house was a mess. Dirty dishes everywhere. The yard hadn't been mowed in months. Dirty clothes were piled up because the washing machine is in the basement and he can't get down there anymore."

"That's so sad."

"He simply isn't managing very well anymore. So Elaine made him come back to the house with her. She's going to hire new staff. Part of their duties will be to care for Doc."

"I'm glad."

"Yeah, I am, too. He's been so good to us for so many years. He wasn't an innocent bystander, but I can't help but feel that Mom used him just like she used everyone else."

"Is that how you see your mother? A user?"

Danny's eyes filled with tears. "No, not entirely. If I lived to be a thousand, I don't think I'd ever figure her out. She wasn't a bad mother, not all the time, but I think she was a horrible human being. Does that make sense?"

"I suppose," said Ruth. She brought his hand up to her lips. "Did you ever tell your family about—"

"My cancer? That it's come back?"

She nodded.

"No. And I don't plan to. I beat it once, Ruth. I'm going to beat it again."

"But the chemo. You're supposed to start next week. You'll be sick again, and you can't exactly hide it."

"Sure I can. Elaine and Alex have their lives, I have mine. I can talk to them on the phone, or e-mail them. It will be fine." And it would be fine, now that he knew his family would be taken care of after . . . well, in fifty years, after he died at the ripe old age of ninety-four. After he finished his seventeenth novel and had won the Pulitzer for his literary genius.

Danny had always reached decisions by thinking of himself as a character in a book. That's how he'd come to the decision about returning to Minnesota. He never outlined his stories, so he was never absolutely sure what would happen. And that's what his real-life story had been like. He hadn't been certain what he would do until he came face-to-face with it, until his pragmatism—and his fear—had to fight it out with his ethics. He'd never considered himself an evil man. But he was evil, in the same way so many people were. Quietly. Harboring dark thoughts, secret desires, secret hatreds, but gutless, without the courage to become the hero—or the villain—in his own life.

"You seem tired, honey," said Ruth. She stifled a yawn.

"I think you're the one who's tired."

"It was a long day. Two classes and then I had office hours until six."

He got up, pulling her up with him. "You go get ready for bed."

"What will you do?"

"I'm still kind of wired from the flight. I think I might go out for a short walk."

She turned to him, a worried look on her face. "You won't be gone long?"

"No, just a few minutes. I need some fresh air, a little exercise. Otherwise I won't be able to sleep."

While Ruth was taking a shower, Danny removed his shaving kit from his suitcase. He unpacked a few things into the medicine cabinet, then placed a small package in the breast pocket of his jacket. Glancing at Ruth for a moment standing behind the steamed glass, he sent up a silent prayer of thanks. She would be safe now. So would Zoe and Abbie. Even if he died, they would be taken care of. And that's all that mattered.

He left the house and walked along Madison Avenue until he came to a small bistro where he and Ruth often had lunch. Taking the package from his inner pocket, he checked the contents to make sure nothing had been left behind. "One syringe," he said to himself. "Two empty vials of insulin." That was it. The final detail. He tossed the package into the garbage can, then turned, glancing at a familiar neon sign across the street, and walked on.

Chez Sophia's Torta Milano

This is a spectacular cake! It's fun to make and well worth the extra effort.

Serves 12 (or eight pigs).

Sponge Cake

8 eggs, separated
1 cup granulated sugar
2¼ tablespoons orange juice
2 teaspoons orange zest
½ teaspoon salt
1½ cups flour

Cut a piece of parchment paper to fit the bottom of a 13-by-9-inch cake pan. Butter the pan, then place the parchment on top of it. Butter the parchment.

Preheat the oven to 325°F.

After separating eggs, beat egg whites until soft peaks form. Slowly add 1 cup of sugar, beating until thick and shiny stiff peaks form.

In a separate bowl, beat the egg yolks with ¼ cup sugar until they turn pale and the texture becomes ribbonlike. Add the orange juice, zest, and salt and beat well.

Using a rubber spatula, fold the egg yolk mixture into the egg whites. Sift flour over the mixture and fold in.

Pour the batter into the pan. Bake until the top is golden and the cake begins to pull away from the sides, about 30 minutes. Remove the cake and cool, at least 20 minutes. Invert the cake onto the platter. Choose a platter that's a good 2 inches wider than the cake. (A silver platter is recommended, of course.) Cool completely before removing the parchment paper.

Simple Sugar Syrup

½ cup water
½ cup granulated sugar
½ cup light rum
¼ cup orange liqueur (triple sec or Cointreau)

Place water and sugar in saucepan and bring to a boil over medium heat. Stir occasionally to dissolve the sugar. Boil one minute. Remove from heat and cool.

Combine the sugar water, rum, and the orange liqueur.

Pastry Cream

2½ cups milk
½ cup granulated sugar
3 tablespoons cornstarch
pinch of salt
6 egg yolks
1 teaspoon vanilla extract
½ cup finely diced dried apricots
½ cup heavy cream

Heat 1½ cups of the milk in a saucepan over medium heat until bubbles form around the edges of the pan. In a bowl, whisk together the ½ cup sugar, the cornstarch, the salt, and the remaining 1 cup of cold milk until the cornstarch is all dissolved. Pour about half the hot milk into the cold milk, whisking constantly until the sugar is dissolved. Scrape the mixture in the bowl into the pan and heat over medium flame, stirring constantly until the mixture comes to a boil and gets thick, about 2 or 3 minutes.

Whip the egg yolks together in a bowl until mixed well. Slowly add a bit (⅓ to ½ cup) of the milk mixture, beating the yolks constantly. Then add the egg mixture slowly to the milk mixture in the saucepan and return to the heat, stirring constantly until thickened. Remove immediately and stir in vanilla.

At this point, it's a good idea to strain the pastry cream. Then add the diced apricots. Cool to room temperature covered with plastic wrap directly on the surface. This prevents a skin from forming on the top. Chill.

Whipping Cream

2 cups heavy whipping cream
½ cup granulated sugar

Whip the cream and sugar before assembly.

Assembly

With a long, preferably serrated knife, cut the cake horizontally into three even layers. Brush the bottom layer with about a third of the syrup. Spread half the pastry cream over the top. Next, spread about one cup of the sweetened whipped cream. Top with the middle layer of the cake. Repeat—one third of the sugar syrup, one third of the pastry cream, and one cup of whipped cream. The final layer goes on next. Top with the rest of the pastry cream and all but ½ cup of the whipped cream. At this point, the cake needs to be refrigerated for 2 hours, or up to a day.

To serve, pipe the ½ cup reserved whipped cream decoratively around the top. Serve with fresh blueberries, strawberries, apricots, raspberries, or whatever fresh fruit is available. Arrange the fruit decoratively around the sides.

Enjoy!

Don't miss this tasty mystery from
Ellen Hart

DIAL M FOR MEAT LOAF

"This is a hearty, satisfying meal of a mystery,
with chunks of good characters and more than a
dash of wit."
—*Alfred Hitchcock Mystery Magazine*

As Minnesota housewives race to meet the deadline
for the *Times Register*'s meat loaf contest, an unsavory small-towner is blown to smithereens by a
car bomb. Days later, the town's former mayor,
John Washburn, near death from a stroke, confesses to the killing. As his family vehemently denies
it, Sophie Greenway, food maven and friend of the
family, happens upon an old snapshot, a bundle of
letters, and a tattoo of a red-eyed snake, and
begins to wonder about Washburn's innocence.
This murder is seasoned with spicy secrets and a
generous portion of scandal, which Sophie dares
to bring to a roiling boil.

Another culinary delight from
Ellen Hart

Slice and Dice

"The pace quickly bubbles from simmer to boil. . . .
the complexity of Hart's novel is admirable."
—*Publishers Weekly*

If all goes according to plan, Connie Buckridge's culinary empire will soon boast a cooking academy and restaurant in her home town of Minneapolis-St. Paul. But just when the kitchen queen and her entourage embark on a publicity tour, so does a bestselling investigative writer who, primed by an anonymous email informer, is cooking up an exposé of Connie's strategies for success. The one missing ingredient in the unsavory stew is murder, and when food critic Sophie Greenway finds a cooking colleague stabbed with his own kitchen knife, a fire that has been smoldering for forty years suddenly bursts into flame.